Praise for *The*

'Steeped in rich mythology and distinctly Irish in all the best possible ways, *The Silver Road* is **a thrilling tale of bravery, unlikely friendships, and new beginnings.**'
Joseph Elliott, author of *The Good Hawk*

'*The Silver Road* is Sinéad O'Hart's finest piece of work to date . . . A **powerful, intense and dazzling** saga magically bridging the gap between the ancient past and life as we know it today. **Pure gold.**'
Eve McDonnell, author of *The Chestnut Roaster*

'A magical adventure that catapults ancient Irish mythology into the 21st century, with a heroine full of heart and courage . . . O'Hart's writing sings from the pages, like a love song for old Ireland, remixed for a modern generation. **My children's book of the year. Phenomenal.**'
Kieran Fanning, author of *Irish Fairy Tales, Myths and Legends*

'Sinéad O'Hart's best book yet . . . Casting the same sort of magical spell as Susan Cooper's *The Dark Is Rising*, **I expect *The Silver Road* to become one of those classic books that children and adults return to time and time again.**'
Katharine Corr, author of *Daughter of Darkness*

'Wonderful. Hart skilfully mixes Irish mythology and old magic with the new to create **an outstanding tale of courage, bravery and friendship.**'
Julie Sykes, author of Unicorn Academy

THE SILVER ROAD

Thanks to the Arts Council of Ireland,
An Chomhairle Ealaíon, for their
generous support for *The Silver Road*.

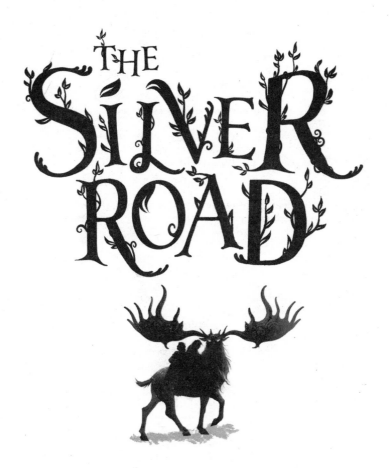

THE SILVER ROAD

SINÉAD O'HART

Illustrated by Manuel Šumberac

Piccadilly
PRESS

This edition published in 2023 by
PICCADILLY PRESS
4th Floor, Victoria House, Bloomsbury Square
London WC1B 4DA
Owned by Bonnier Books
Sveavägen 56, Stockholm, Sweden
bonnierbooks.co.uk/PiccadillyPress

A CIP catalogue record for this book is available from the British Library.

ISBN: 978-1-80078-509-0
Also available as an ebook and in audio

1

Typeset by Envy Design Ltd
Printed and bound in Great Britain by Clays Ltd, Elcograf S.p.A.

Piccadilly Press is an imprint of Bonnier Books UK
www.bonnierbooks.co.uk

Do m'athair agus mo mháthair,
le gach grá, le grá go deo

Dear Reader,

In *The Silver Road*, you'll meet lots of amazing characters – buried gods, an army of spirits, a mighty queen, a wolf-warrior and his pack, and more. Some of these characters are invented by me, but others draw on the rich and age-old mythology of Ireland. I'm not the first person to write about the terrifying fire-eyed giant, Balor, or his wife Cethlenn, or the monstrous Fomorian tribe they both belong to – they're found in the Mythological Cycle, one of the four 'Cycles', or groups, of Irish mythological tales which were written down over a millennium ago, and which had been passed down through generations of fireside stories for many thousands of years before that. Balor has been reinvented time and time again, by artists and writers alike, and several aspects of how he appears in the old stories have made it into my book. My version of Cethlenn is largely made up, though I based aspects of her appearance and her skill with a spear on what we know of her from her legend. I invented the Silver Road, and the Mac Tíre, and the Shaper, and the Cauldron Keeper; I invented Catshee, though I borrowed his name from folklore. I did not invent the majestic Irish elk, or the Hill of Tara, or the Lia Fáil – and while I did invent the character of Rose Darke, her name comes from Róisín Dubh – meaning 'Dark Rosaleen' – which is an old poetic name for Ireland itself.

Whenever a story is retold it takes a new shape, and so it is with this book too; I've put my imagination to work and reshaped some of the characters, making them my own, and connecting them to the modern world. More information about the mythology behind this story, as well as a guide to pronunciation and words taken from the Irish language, can be found on page 321 of this book.

And now . . . the Old Magic is calling for its allies. Will you answer?

Happy reading!

Sinéad

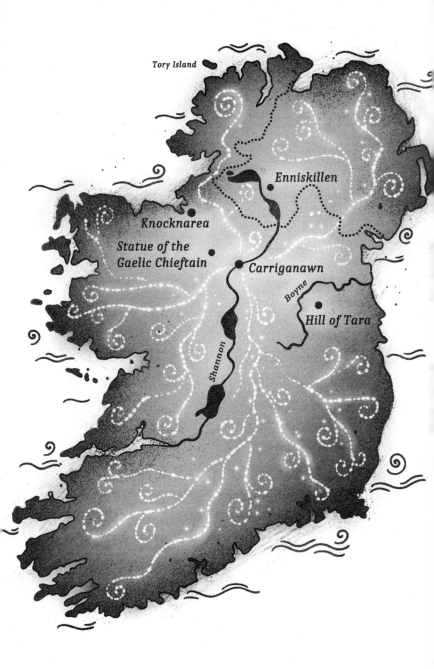

And on a bright day with birdsong trilling and hawthorn in full bloom, the Tuatha Dé Danann cast their net of silver full wide, covering all the land of Ireland with their power and protection. It was Old Magic, true magic, An tSeandraíocht, and if you have a will to listen, I'll tell you more . . .

From Old Irish Myths and Legends

Prologue

Lightning clawed through the coal-black sky, throwing jagged brilliance onto the ruined earth. Cold rain lashed the island like a whip and, far below, the sea writhed endlessly. The land was facing a mighty onslaught, one not seen since the long-ago battle of Moytura three thousand years before.

And if I do not stop this here and now, thought Sioc, as he dragged himself through the mud, *that terror will be unleashed once more.*

'Are you ready to surrender, ice giant?' came the roar of the witch, Cethlenn, her voice more than powerful enough to be heard over the howl of the storm. Fresh needles of hair were already pushing through her bald scalp, growing quickly, almost ready for her to rip out by the handful again. Each one, when thrown, would become a red-hot spear.

'There are none now to relieve you. None to fight for you. None to fight *with* you. It is time for me to take what I need and then end you, just as I destroyed your king and the rest of your clan!'

Sioc lifted his head and peered through the frost-flecked rain, his thoughts heavy with the devastation Cethlenn had brought and the damage she could yet do. The image of Oighir, king of the ice giants, tumbling lifeless into the waves only moments before, was like a spike in his mind, and Cethlenn's shriek of triumph was still echoing cruelly in his ears. He tried to push back the pain and focus on the enemy. Cethlenn stood on a rocky outcrop battered on both sides by the sea. It was all that remained now of Tor Mór, where Balor of the Evil Eye had once lived. Balor had been the most feared creature in all of Ireland until the forces of the Tuatha Dé Danann – including the ice giants – had overcome him at Moytura, and the great god Lugh had finally brought him down. The witch, Balor's wife, had been there that day, too; she and the ice giants had remained enemies through the centuries that followed. And now she was taking her revenge, almost as if the intervening years had been nothing more than a lull in the fighting.

As Sioc tried to gather his strength, his thoughts turned back through the centuries to the last time he'd faced Cethlenn in battle. After Moytura was done, and before anyone could stop her, Cethlenn had used her magic to retrieve a weapon from the carnage of the battlefield – the *tathlum*, the powerful stone that Lugh had wielded in his mighty sling, and which had put out the poisonous light of Balor's evil eye. Cethlenn, in secrecy and darkness, had hidden the stone away ever since, guarding it with her life, biding her time and building her power – until now. She had come back here, back to the island of her husband's birth, and to the ice giants that could only mean one thing – the thing they feared the most. Destroying the clan of the ice giants – the Guardians of Toraigh – hadn't been Cethlenn's aim, Sioc knew; it would have added to her sense of victory but they were not the reason she had come. All she wanted was a handful of the soil of Toraigh – the final step in a plan she must have been waiting thousands of years to bring about, a plan that would have dire consequences . . . unless she could be stopped. Sioc's spirit quailed at the thought. Cethlenn was powerful but she was even more cunning; she'd waited until the ice giants had grown careless and her own strength was high before striking this fatal blow. He tried to gather his strength. If he was the only hope left, he would fight to the end. *She has not won*, Sioc told himself. *Not yet.*

As Sioc struggled to get to his feet, Cethlenn conjured two balls of flaming magic, one in each hand. Their terrible red-and-yellow light burned between her fingers, licking her skin and shining against the teeth that suddenly pushed their way out of her mouth.

'You will not take it from me,' Cethlenn growled. Her teeth grew further, twisting, sharp-edged and dark as obsidian. 'My lord Balor's time has almost come again, and you will not stand in his way.' Cethlenn brought her hands together and her fire spells melded into one gigantic sphere of power. The ice giant could feel its heat, and he trembled with fear.

Then, in the darkness behind the witch, Sioc spotted something unexpected. Further out on Tor Mór, impossibly close to the pounding sea, a white-silver shape appeared, crawling one-armed over the rocks. A pulse of roaring hope burst through Sioc's chest as he recognised the figure. *Oighir!* Cethlenn had sent him tumbling down the rocky cliffs with a lance of red-hot magic, but somehow the king had survived. Sioc looked back at Cethlenn, knowing his task now was to distract her, to keep her busy enough not to notice Oighir's approach. He closed his eyes for a moment and braced himself, then he raised his head even further and got slowly to his feet, his long arms swinging as he stood before the fire witch.

'Still not ready to admit defeat? Pathetic creature,' Cethlenn gurgled, her words almost lost in the noise of her teeth clashing and grinding against one another. 'No matter. Soon you will be something I never have to think about again.' She laughed, the sound thick and phlegmy, and Sioc noticed each strand of her fast-growing hair was now like a blade.

Her laugh stopped, and in the next heartbeat Cethlenn threw her fire spell.

Sioc raised his arms, casting a shield of protection, pouring every shard of his power into it. He knew no shield, no matter how thick, would withstand Cethlenn for long – but he called upon Lugh Lámhfada, the warrior god, as his spell took shape. Lugh had felled Balor once; Sioc needed his spirit now to prevent Cethlenn from raising him once again.

Lugh, hear me! Sioc called inside his mind. *Lugh the Skilled, Lugh the Brave, Lugh the Sure-Shot, Lugh of the Long Arm – aid me!*

With a shriek of rage, Cethlenn's attack cut off and Sioc dropped his shield to see her struggling against a restraint, like a rope made of ice magic. It looped around her chin, pulling her mouth open, preventing her from closing it.

I cannot hold her for long, came Oighir's voice inside Sioc's mind. *Even now her magic overwhelms mine. You must reach in and find the stone – and then flee!*

Sioc did not hesitate. Cethlenn's eyes burned red with hatred, her body jerking as she fought to be free of Oighir's grip, and Sioc plunged his arm down into her throat, hoping with all he had that the stone – the *tathlum* – would make itself known.

Then he felt its warmth against his hand, almost like the stone had leaped into his palm. He pulled it free, hearing Cethlenn's ferocious shrieking. Her eyes tracked the *tathlum*'s path as Sioc wrapped his fingers around it.

GO! Find a guardian for the stone. Oighir's words were urgent. *I must release her before she kills me!*

Sioc looked past the struggling witch. Oighir, his king, was clinging to the rocky promontory.

But, Your Majesty – Sioc began, sending his words to Oighir's mind, as was the way of his kind.

No more! Oighir's command was clear. *Fly! Trust the Seandraíocht to guide you.*

Sioc nodded, turning away, feeling the ripping pain of betrayal at abandoning Oighir. He began to run and then took advantage of a gust of stormy wind to lift himself into the air. Instantly he became a cloud of glittering ice shards, the stone held at its heart.

He didn't dare to look back again, but he knew that Cethlenn was already on his trail.

Seandraíocht! he called as he flew, using the old name for the Old Magic. *Wake, and guide me!*

And, far below, the Old Magic began to stir, its silver tendrils spreading out across the countryside. It urged Sioc on as Cethlenn's fiery fury drew ever closer, and he flew as fast as he could, hoping to find a place of sanctuary before the witch caught up with him – and their last hope was extinguished forever.

1

Rose heaved a silent sigh as Emer McGuire and her scattering of cronies approached. *Oh, great*, she thought. Even finding herself a nook in the quietest corner of the school yard wasn't enough to escape. *I can't believe I've got to put up with her in nearly every class and I can't even get a break at lunchtime.* Out of the corner of her eye, Rose watched as Emer sat on the bench opposite, plonking her school bag down beside her, taking up all the available space. At her feet, her 'fan club' (as Rose liked to call them) settled, trying not to look awkward as they made themselves as comfortable as they could on the chewing-gum-speckled tarmac. Biting back her irritation, Rose refocused on her book, trying to block out everything but the words on the page.

This corner of the yard was where people came to sit when they wanted to read, or listen to music on their phones. It was cold, it smelled a bit odd, the wall-mounted benches were uncomfortable, and it was close to the entrance nearest the staff room, so Rose had been sure Emer wouldn't be caught near it. Yet here she was.

'So yeah, Lanzarote was *so* good,' came Emer's voice a few moments later, buzzing into Rose's thoughts like a persistent, irritating fly. 'It was, like, twenty-*seven* degrees most days? Maybe hotter, even. Dad would've been crispy if he'd been with us. At least Mum and I take care of our skin in the sun, but you know how *he* is.' As Emer spoke, she casually touched her flawless dark cheek with a perfectly manicured finger. 'Dad's paler than paper but just refuses to put on sunblock, even when we visit Mum's family in Lagos.' This was greeted with giggles, and Rose rolled her eyes. She took another bite of her sandwich and flipped over the page of her book.

'He stayed home again, then?' someone asked.

'Too much work, yada yada, the usual,' replied Emer. 'He's too busy making money to spend any of it.'

Or spend any time with his family, Rose thought.

Though I can hardly blame him.

'You are *so* lucky, Emer,' sighed one of the other girls. 'All *we* did for Easter break was go to our holiday chalet in Wexford. I mean, *boring.*'

Rose glanced across at them. Emer held her pink-cased phone in one hand, angling it so that her fan club could check out her holiday photos.

One of the fan club gasped, her eyes bright with jealous admiration. 'OMG, your mum let you wear a *bikini*?'

Emer shrugged. 'Mum lets me do whatever when we're on vaycay.' She raised an eyebrow and flicked to the next photo.

'That's the pool?' someone squeaked. 'It's bigger than my garden!'

Rose sighed, closing her book carefully. It was due back to the library in a few days – she'd been hoping to finish it this lunchtime so that Mam could drop it off tomorrow on her way to work, but she'd try to do it later instead. She put the remains of her sandwich back into her lunchbox and stood up, brushing crumbs off her uniform and zipping up her jacket, before turning to leave.

'Oh, *sorry*,' Emer said, sitting forward. She locked

her phone and put it down. 'Are we disturbing you, Rosie-Roo?' Her mouth was pursed sympathetically, but Rose could see the glint in her dark brown eyes.

Rose gave a tight smile. 'No, not at all. I'm just done.' She put the book beneath her arm and tried to walk past the group, but just as Rose thought she'd managed to get away, Emer stuck her legs out. Rose stumbled, dropping her book and her lunchbox. The book landed face-down, crumpling some of the pages. Rose pressed her lips together and stayed quiet. Speaking back only made Emer worse.

'Oh, whoops!' Emer trilled, as her friends laughed. 'Rachel, pick up Rosie-Roo's little book there, will you?'

A red-headed girl Rose recognised from Maths picked up the book by one corner and tossed it to her. '*A Wizard of Earthsea*?' Rachel scoffed, as Rose caught the book. 'What's that about?'

Rose tried to flatten the damaged pages as she answered. 'It's – there's a wizard, named Ged, who lives in this place called Gont, and –'

A gush of laughter from the others drowned out Rose's words. She looked up, her pale cheeks flushing, to see Emer's eyes shining with cruel amusement.

'Oh my God, she actually thought you *meant* it!'

Rose stared at them. 'Well, you asked,' she said in a small voice.

'Most of us gave up reading books about *wizards* when we were, like, *eight*,' Emer said, her eyes on Rose. 'But I'd hardly expect you to understand, right? I mean, where you come from, things are probably done a bit . . . differently.'

Rose squashed back the words she wanted to say. She was from Carriganawn, the same town as Emer and most of her gang – but that's not what Emer meant and Rose knew it. She lived in a council estate while Emer lived in a fancy house on the far side of town. She'd gone to a small primary school not far from her house while Emer had gone to the posher one a few miles outside Carriganawn. And last year, most of Rose's friends had gone to the community school at the top of Druid's Hill, but Rose had taken the entrance exam for Carriganawn Grammar School. She'd not only passed but gained a full scholarship. Now she was here, and Emer never let her forget that she didn't, and would never, belong.

'Look, lunchtime's nearly over, so . . .' Rose shrugged, hoping Emer would take the hint and move her leg. Emer paused for a painfully long moment, and Rose could feel the weight of her judgemental gaze, before she finally sighed, delicately, and pulled her legs back. She tucked her school skirt neatly beneath herself and shifted to sit up properly.

'It's Irish after lunch, right?' she called, as Rose walked past. 'Save me a seat, Rosie-Roo!'

Rose shuddered as she picked up her lunchbox and strode across the yard. Emer was in most of her classes except, luckily, for Maths (one of her favourites) and Art, but it didn't really matter. If Emer wasn't keeping an eye on Rose in person then one of her gang was doing it instead. Rose felt watched all the time and she hated it. But there was no point in talking to the teachers, who never seemed to take any side that put them in opposition to Emer McGuire or her family, and there was no point in talking to her parents, either. Her dad worked for Mr McGuire, Emer's dad, and Rose was painfully aware of how much would be put at risk if the two men were to fall out.

Rose put the battered copy of *Earthsea* back into her locker and took out the schoolbooks she'd need for the afternoon. Irish, Geography and Science. Her head thudded as she pushed them into her bag. *At least I can call to visit Nellie and Gracie on the way home*, she thought, trying to console herself with the prospect of friendly company, but also, hopefully, of tea and cake. Feeling brighter, she closed her locker and slung her bag onto her shoulder, making her way to her Irish class just as the bell began to ring.

Emer slid in late, as usual, whispering apologies to Ms O'Connor, as usual, but the teacher just raised an eyebrow as Emer took a seat behind Rose.

A few minutes into the class, as Rose was writing out verb conjugations, she felt a jerk as her chair was pushed forward. She stiffened, forcing herself not to look around. *Don't give her the satisfaction*, she told herself, trying not to imagine the smirk on Emer's face. In the next moment there was another sharp kick as her chair was nudged again. Rose put her pen down and squished her hands into fists for a minute, before picking up her pen once more and starting to write – only for her work to be ruined when another push from Emer made her hand jolt, sending a scribble through her carefully laid-out columns of words.

She turned her head, catching Emer's mocking

eye. '*Stop!*' she whispered.

'Rose! Cad é an fadhb?' said the teacher. 'What's going on?'

Rose whipped her head around again, to face Ms O'Connor. 'Tá brón orm,' she apologised.

The teacher raised both eyebrows disapprovingly, and Rose swallowed a mouthful of irritation at herself. She'd given Emer what she wanted: she'd made the teacher angry *and* she'd get marked down for messy work. It was all so unfair! Everything had been going wrong lately, and sometimes – like now – it just seemed to build up, like water behind a dam, until it felt overwhelming. Rose squeezed her eyes tight shut, willing herself to stay calm.

Think about cake. Rose's breathing slowed. *And being out of here.*

Mr Murphy's Geography class passed quietly, mostly because Rose managed to get a seat on the far side of the classroom from Emer, but by the time the bell went for Mrs Mooney's Science class, the last lesson of the day, she was so tired that she could barely keep her eyes open. She wasn't paying enough attention to notice Emer sliding onto her bench, taking the seat beside her, until it was too late.

'Right, everyone,' Mrs Mooney began, clapping her hands for attention. 'I want to talk to you all today about your end-of-year project. We have about six weeks until summer break, okay? And in that time we're going to focus, in pairs, on a topic that I'll assign you at random. The person you're sharing a bench with today will be your partner for this project until the end of term.' Muttering greeted this pronouncement, and Rose turned to Emer with undisguised distaste.

Emer winked. 'Guess you're stuck with me, Rosie-Roo,' she whispered, her words smelling like bubble-gum.

'I'm going to leave a card face-down on your benches as I pass,' Mrs Mooney continued. 'When every pair of students has their card, you may all flip them over and see what your topic is. No peeking!'

Rose ignored her bench-mate, keeping her eyes focused on the small piece of white card that Mrs Mooney had placed in front of them. She didn't care what the topic was – the idea of doing any sort of project with Emer was stomach-turning.

'Now,' Mrs Mooney announced from the back of the class. 'You can all check your topic.' Rose reached for the card, but Emer, whip-fast, grabbed it first.

'Oooh,' Emer said, staring at Rose over the top of the card. '*This* should be good. I'm sure I can leave most of it up to you, since you're practically Greta Thunberg anyway.'

Rose frowned. 'What? Just let me see it, please.' She snatched the card from Emer. *The Climate Crisis* was written on it in Mrs Mooney's neat lettering. Rose's heart sank. Emer was right: Rose knew, right away, that this project wouldn't be a team effort. *Even if it had been on the chemical composition of lip gloss, I would've had to do it all myself*, she thought, bitterly.

'If anyone has any questions, come to me at the end of class,' Mrs Mooney said, striding back to the top of the room. 'Now, if we're all ready? Let's get back to the life-cycle of the sheep fluke, please!'

Rose stuffed the card into her pencil case. Emer was guaranteed a mark for doing nothing, and Rose knew there was nothing to be done about it. She ignored her for the rest of the lesson, despite Emer's best attempts to distract her, and when the bell rang for the end of the day, Rose jumped into the queue of students wishing to speak to Mrs Mooney, in the hope that Emer would get bored waiting for her and leave. She didn't actually have a question for the teacher, but she hoped it would delay her long enough for Emer and her gang to be gone. Out of the corner of her eye she watched Emer slowly pack her bag and shuffle out of the classroom, and Rose heaved a relieved sigh.

But then she made it to the top of the queue, and she still didn't have a question for Mrs Mooney. 'Well, Rosaleen,' the teacher said, using her full name, 'I'm surprised to see you here.'

'Um,' Rose began, desperately trying to think of something that didn't sound stupid. 'I was just . . . wondering, about the project. I mean, can it be a diorama? Or an experiment? Or does it have to be, just, written out, or whatever?'

Mrs Mooney gave her a quizzical look. 'It can take whatever form you and your project partner –' the teacher's expression softened – 'or whatever form *you* want it to.' Mrs Mooney gave a sympathetic grin. 'I know you'll do a great job,' she continued in a whisper.

Rose brightened, settling her bag on her shoulder more comfortably. 'Thanks, Mrs Mooney,' she said.

'Now, go on,' the teacher continued, ushering her

towards the door. 'You'll be late home.'

Rose frowned as she walked out into the corridor. It didn't matter if she was late – her baby brothers were at the childminder's, and her parents were both at work, so there was nobody there to notice what time she got home.

When she got to her locker, Rose checked her phone. She kept it on silent and locked away all day, following school rules, but as she saw, with a sigh, it wouldn't have mattered anyway. There were no messages. Nothing from Sophia or Rory – her closest friends from primary school, who had started ghosting her weeks ago – and nothing, thankfully, from Emer, or anyone in her class. She threw the phone into her school bag along with the books she'd need for homework, and made her way out by the school's small side entrance, which led towards the old heart of the town of Carriganawn. Using this gate usually meant she could avoid Emer and her fan club. Plus, she thought with a grin, it was the quickest way to get to Hargate Street, and on Hargate Street she'd find Nellie and Gracie.

Rose had first come across Nellie and Gracie when, like today, she'd been searching for a way home that took her away from Emer and the others. She'd lost herself in the warren of the old town and eventually found herself on a quiet street with a quaint shoe repair shop (which she'd since learned was called a 'cobbler's') on one side and a sweet-shop opposite, and a pedestrian crossing in the middle. *Gréasaí*, she'd read over the cobbler's shop, and the sound of the word – *Gracie* – had sighed through her head. And then the man himself had appeared, emerging out of his shop and striding across the pedestrian crossing with the air of one who fully expected any traffic to wait until he was good and ready. Rose had been enchanted by his long, knobbly limbs and his tufts of snow-white hair, and when an equally ancient lady with a face full of softness and sunshine had greeted him on the far side, standing in the doorway of her sweet-shop, Rose had smiled. The lady had given her a fond wave before they disappeared inside the sweet-shop, and that had been that. Even though Rose's first visit to the sweet-shop hadn't happened that day, they'd been friends ever since.

Thinking had sped Rose's feet, and soon she found herself at Nellie's. She pushed the sweet-shop door open, hearing the *ting* of its little bell, and she was greeted by the sound of music – or at least singing, of a sort.

'Ah, hello, love,' Nellie said, bustling through from her kitchen into the shop, her arms laden with a tray of freshly made sweets. She nodded towards the sound of the singing. 'Gracie's in good order, as you can hear.'

'Hi, Nellie,' Rose said, slipping her school bag off her shoulder and down to the floor. 'Can I help?'

'Not at all, not at all,' the older lady said, making her way around the back of her counter. It had a large glass-fronted display cabinet, the type that curved at the top to give customers the best view of the delicious treats inside, and every nook and cranny behind the glass was piled high with sweets and chocolates. Hanging on the wall next to the window was a metal scoop for digging out the goodies; on the counter beneath the scoop was a pile of paper bags, ready to be filled. Nellie's skilful hands quickly placed the fresh sweets into an empty compartment, and Rose could see her satisfaction as she gazed at the display. 'There now,' Nellie whispered, putting the tray down and wiping her hands on her apron. 'We're all set.'

'It's yourself!' came Gracie's voice, and Rose

21

turned, already smiling, to see the old man come climbing up the steps from Nellie's kitchen and into her shop. The kitchen door stood open behind him at the end of a short corridor, and Rose could see the small, cosy room, its lace-curtained windows letting in the light. 'Had you a good day, mo chroí?'

'Oh, you know,' Rose replied. 'The usual.'

'Indeed, and I don't know,' Gracie chuckled, shuffling around the back of Nellie's sweet counter. He reached in a gnarled hand to help himself to a lump of fudge, fast enough to avoid being smacked across the fingers by Nellie. He twinkled at Rose as he scurried away. 'It's been so many centuries since I sat in a classroom that I can't remember a thing about it.'

'Well,' Rose said, drawing in a breath, 'it's nothing that can't be fixed with a cup of tea.' She looked at Nellie hopefully. 'And whatever might be in the oven?'

'It's soda bread today,' said Nellie, with a wink. 'But there's plenty of fruit in it. I might see if I have any golden syrup to drizzle over it, if you're feeling fancy.'

Rose gave a wide grin, her tummy already gurgling, and the worries of the day starting to fade. 'That sounds *perfect*.'

An icy whirl swept through the night sky, approaching the sleeping town of Carriganawn. In its midst spun a blood-red stone, worn smooth by time. Sioc couldn't help but check, again and again, that he still had the weapon in his grasp – he could hardly believe he'd been successful in taking it from Cethlenn, and he thought gratefully of Oighir's courage, without which everything would already be lost. But he felt his energy waning, and knew the time was soon coming when he would have nothing left to draw on.

For now he flew on, casting about for somewhere to land, the stone seeming to grow heavier with each passing second. Below, he could see the Silver Road, like a gigantic net spread across the countryside. The web of bright magic shone into the darkness, and Sioc knew that the Seandraíocht had heard his cry for help.

23

It was doing what it could to aid him, but he couldn't help but notice that its sheen was dim – worryingly so. Cethlenn truly had chosen well: it was not only the ice giants of old who were weak but the very magic of the Seandraíocht itself. All the more reason, Sioc knew, to guard this stone with everything he had, until its true protector could be found. Grimly, he tightened his grip on the *tathlum*.

He became aware, somewhere below, of a ripple in the Silver Road – a knot in its net that seemed to shine more brightly than the rest. A junction of particular power, perhaps? Or maybe a human person who knew the old ways of the Seandraíocht? Someone who would know what to do and where to go, someone who would be a worthy keeper of the stone . . . The sparkling threads of power glowed once again, and that was enough. Sioc swirled one last time to take a look behind him. The witch was coming, blacker than black, sucking the light from the stars with every yard she flew. But still there was time.

There *had* to be time.

Sioc thickened himself into hard pellets of ice and began to fall, the stone clutched tightly in his frozen heart, and hoped for the best.

Rose's parents and brothers had gone to bed hours ago. The house was silent and still. Only the noise from the road outside, which never really stopped, was keeping her company – but Rose was used to the hum and whoosh of the passing cars, and the swoop of their headlights as they went by.

Yet somehow, despite nothing being out of the ordinary, Rose was wide awake.

She sighed as she sat up in bed. There was no point lying there staring at the ceiling, after all. Everything was covered in a filmy grey shadow, a little light seeping in through the crack where her curtains didn't hang quite closed. Her mamó, her dad's mam, had made them for her when she was a baby, and they were still covered with the dinosaur pattern Rose had loved when she was little – but the carefully stitched loops had started to come loose and Mamó wasn't here to fix them . . . Rose swallowed hard as she looked away. Mamó had become sick almost a whole year ago, and that had been the beginning of everything going wrong. Rose had started at the Grammar School in September, a few months after Mamó's first big operation, and Emer had been a problem right from day one. Then things got worse:

Mamó had spent Christmas in hospital, and she'd died a few days afterwards, just before the end of the year. Rose missed Mamó so much. Nothing seemed right any more. There was a jagged gap in her heart which just wouldn't close over, no matter how hard she pushed it. And Mamó had left traces of herself all over the place – photos, books, her old knitting needles and wool, things she'd made or fixed or built – so sometimes Rose felt there was nowhere she could look that wouldn't remind her of their huge loss.

She wiped her cheeks, tossing back the duvet and swinging her legs out of bed. Pushing her thoughts about Mamó away, she slid her feet into her furry slippers and straightened her nightdress. As she passed her chair, she grabbed her cardigan from where she'd thrown it earlier. She pulled it on and then crept to her bedroom door. The day had been warm for April, but now the air seemed cool; Rose wrapped the cardigan around her as she peered out of her room. Moonlight pooled in the upstairs hallway. From the next room she heard her dad's rumbling snore and her mother coughing in her sleep. The gentle glow of the nightlight spilled out of Colm and Brian's room, but there was nothing but silence from behind their door. Rose tiptoed towards it and peeped in at the sleeping babies in their side-by-side cots; they were plump-cheeked and rosy, their tiny eyes shut and their arms and legs spreadeagled, like they were playing star-jumps in their dreams. She smiled and crept out again, counting her quiet steps as she made for the stairs.

The soles of her slippers went *swish-swish-swish* on the tiles as she walked towards the kitchen, and Rose pressed her lips together as she went. *This is your house, ninny*, she told herself. *Plus, whoever heard of a Darke afraid of the dark?* Still, she was relieved when she reached the kitchen and was able to switch on the light. The naked bulb hung over the dining table and shone brightly enough for her to see the whole room. Everything, of course, looked entirely normal. *Boringly* normal. Almost ridiculously ordinary. Rose smiled at herself. *If Emer McGuire could see me now* . . . Her smile faded a bit. 'I think about her enough when I'm at school,' she whispered, pushing her hands into her cardigan pockets. 'I *really* don't want to think about her here.' She shuddered, pulling a face as her eyes fell on her school bag.

I could make a start on my Science project, Rose thought. *Or I could try to finish* Earthsea *so Mam can return it.*

It was an easy decision. Rose pulled her library book out of her school bag and curled up in the old fake-leather armchair by the back door, the one Grandad O'Mahony had loved to sit in whenever he visited, and picked up the story from where she'd left off earlier.

Just as she was starting the next chapter, Rose heard something odd. She sat up, senses jangling, and listened hard.

There it was again. A *pop*, like a stone hitting the window – or landing on the glass of the skylight over the kitchen.

Quickly, she shut the book and pushed it back into her school bag. Then, on slippered feet, she stood up and slid forward, step by slow step. Keeping her eyes on the skylight, Rose waited.

Another barrage of popping made her jump. She spun on her heels, surveying the room. The empty kitchen was to her back now, and facing her was the messy dining table, covered in the twins' finger paintings which her mam had left out to dry overnight.

She saw the sagging, dusty bookcase in the corner, the playpen set out in front of it and the bottom shelves still crammed full of Rose's favourite baby books, which her brothers now spent many happy hours chewing to pieces. She let her gaze hop to the back door, its window dark as the night outside.

Pop. Pop. Popopopopop.

Rose gasped, stifling a yell. There was no grumbling or groaning from upstairs, no sound of the floorboards creaking. *How can they not hear it?*

The noise returned with explosive vengeance, and Rose looked straight up. The pane of the skylight above her head was quickly filling with tiny white crystals – hard, round balls of ice. Every time one landed, it made a *pop* against the glass.

'Hail?' Rose whispered, her eyes widening. *But there's so much of it – and it's so loud!* Her skin prickled with unease. Acting on impulse, she reached out and opened the cutlery drawer, pulling out a wooden spoon. Gripping it tightly, she looked to check if the back door key was hanging on its nail beside the fridge. She lifted it down.

Wrapping her cardigan around her, Rose unlocked the door and stepped outside into the small square patch of garden. The moon was bright, and the garden swam in silver light.

The ground was covered in a sea of white.

As she walked her steps crunched, her ankles and legs pimpling into gooseflesh as the cold breeze swept around them. She stared up into the sky. The moon was full and the night was clear.

The hail was coming down hard, yet somehow it didn't hurt. It landed in her hair and on her face, melting almost as quickly as it came, and her breath was like a cloud around her head. She stood and watched it fall, mesmerised by the patterns it made in the air, wondering if this was the universe's way of telling her to get started on her Science project after all. It had been a mild, settled day, with barely a wisp of breeze and no cold forecast – so conditions weren't really right for hail. Yet, here it was.

Then Rose looked at the ground – and her breath caught in her throat. On the grass, right in front of her, the hail was beginning to form into two piles. She raised the wooden spoon like a sword as the hail built itself into two frosty towers.

Something colder than the icy night shivered its way through Rose's body as she stared at the two hailstone heaps, which had taken on the unmistakeable shape of legs. They grew taller and taller until they met to form a torso, which branched out into two huge arms that seemed to bristle with long, sparkling hair, and then, finally, a gigantic head formed – a head with spikes all around it, like the shell of a conker, and two round eyes that looked like the darkness between stars. The hail stopped, its job done, and the night grew quiet once again.

Rose shook from head to toe as she stared at the giant made of ice, which was standing in her garden. It was taller than the kitchen roof, and the longer it stood there the more real it seemed to get.

'Who –' she began, looking back up at the ice giant. 'Wha-what –' The words wouldn't form, and the giant said nothing. In fact, when she looked closer it didn't seem to have a mouth.

After a few moments the giant started suddenly, as though it had heard an unexpected noise. It crouched, lifting its massive head to the sky and then back to look at Rose. The darkness of its eyes seemed to suck at Rose like a black hole. It reached out one gigantic hand, unfolding three long fingers and a thumb which had been curled protectively around something.

It was a stone, reddish and oval-shaped, and the giant held it out for Rose to take.

Her brain swirling with thoughts and questions, Rose looked up at the sky, wondering what the giant had heard. Everything seemed quiet; all she could see were stars, twinkling silently in their usual formations – and then she felt something cool and heavy on her shoulder. It was the giant's other hand. Her attention was pulled away from the sky and back to the face of the ice giant, which was now only inches from her own.

Please, the giant seemed to say, offering her the stone once again. *You must take it.*

Rose blinked away from the ice giant's eyes and reached into its palm. She lifted the red stone free. It was warm somehow, despite the ice giant's touch, and Rose closed her own fingers around it as best she could, just as she'd seen the ice giant doing.

The creature had no mouth to smile, but Rose knew it was pleased.

Then the ice giant straightened up and, with a leap, it was in the air. Rose watched it as it flew through the

darkness, its body white enough to stand out against the night sky – and then it seemed as though some of the blackness of space moved to intercept it. Rose's mouth opened in shock as she watched. Quick as a blink, the gigantic frost creature disappeared, like the night had swallowed it.

The red stone suddenly grew uncomfortably warm, and Rose opened her hand to look at it.

Instantly she knew she shouldn't have, and she closed her fist tightly around it again.

She looked back up at the sky overhead and saw something in it twist about, as though a shape in the darkness had turned to search for her, and Rose's panic bypassed her brain. She whirled around, dropping the wooden spoon in her haste, her slippers skidding a little on the hail, and ran for her house. The back door was still open, spilling the light from the kitchen out into the night, and Rose hurried towards it. Seconds later she barrelled through and pulled the door closed, her fingers numb enough to struggle with the key. Finally, the lock clicked shut. She rested her forehead on the door and tried to catch her breath,

listening to the regular ticking of the kitchen clock as her heart settled back into its normal rhythm. After a minute she realised the coldness creeping through to the soles of her feet was coming from her sodden slippers, so she kicked them off and shoved them into her cardigan pocket.

On bare feet, Rose crept to the corner of the kitchen. Stretching a little over the sink, she reached for the window, pulling apart two slats in the kitchen blind, and looked out into the garden.

The night sky gazed back at her innocently, some clouds scudding across the face of the full moon. Rose glanced at the ground outside the window where – her brain screamed at her – a few moments earlier, a giant made of hail had just been standing.

On the grass Rose could see two gigantic footprints edged in frozen white – footprints made by feet with four huge toes, each footprint easily as long as Rose's arm. Already the hail was melting away to nothing.

Rose clutched the red stone in one hand as she let the slats clack together, closing out the night once again. Slowly, feeling light-headed, she dropped down off her tiptoes. She slid the stone into her cardigan pocket without looking at it again, its unfamiliar weight seeming to pull her askew.

She turned off the kitchen light and padded her way back up the hall, pausing at the bottom of the stairs as she looked up into the darkness. It swallowed everything from the fourth or fifth step, and all beyond it was silent. Her father wasn't snoring. Her mother wasn't coughing or mumbling or talking in her sleep. The babies weren't grizzling or whining at their dreams, as they sometimes did. All that lay at the top of the stairs was emptiness, and Rose squashed her eyes shut at the thought of it coming to life, suddenly reaching out its fingers to snuff her out . . .

Then, like an eye opening, the moon seemed to come out from behind a cloud, and the window over the upstairs landing flooded with silver light once again. The moonlight trickled down the stairs, banishing the darkness, though it seemed reluctant to leave. Rose swallowed her fear and ran up the stairs two steps at a time. She hurried to her bed, clambering into it from the bottom like she used to do as a kid. A moment later there was a muffled thump as she pushed her cardigan, with her still-sodden slippers in one pocket and the mysterious stone in the other, out onto the carpet, and Rose lay there, her head beneath her duvet, thoughts ping-ponging around inside her brain. *None of that was real, it was a dream – it* had *to be a dream . . .*

It only seemed like minutes later when she jerked awake, her eyes popping open at the sound of her mother's voice from downstairs. The room was bright with daylight, and Rose realised she'd slept through the night.

'Who left my good wooden spoon out in the garden?' Mrs Darke shouted. 'Rosa*leen*!'

Rose's head emerged from underneath her duvet. Her face, behind a tangle of hair, was pulled tight into a grimace.

3

'Honest to God, Rosaleen Darke, what possessed you? My only decent wooden spoon, destroyed. By the time I'm finished scrubbing it clean, all I'll have left is a matchstick.'

Rose swallowed a mouthful of porridge. 'You can take the price of a new one out of my pocket money,' she said. 'Or you *could* if I had any.'

'Ho, ho – very funny,' her mam replied, giving an amused huff.

Rose sighed, focusing on her breakfast. To her left, at the far end of the cluttered table, sat her twin brothers. *Not so cute now you're awake*, she found herself thinking, just as Brian (the older twin by six minutes) whacked his identical brother Colm across the head with a plastic beaker.

'And now the two of *them* are at it too,'

Mrs Darke muttered, rushing to haul Colm out of his highchair.

'That's not my fault,' Rose said, her words lost beneath her brother's wailing.

'What were you doing out in the garden anyway?' her mother said, wandering away with Colm perched on her hip.

'I heard a noise,' Rose replied, thinking fast, trying to come up with something her mam might find plausibly scary. 'Screaming, sort of. Like a fox.'

'And I suppose you thought waving a wooden spoon at it would help?' Mrs Darke shook her head, distracted by Colm, who was chewing hard at a crust of toast, red cheeks puffing in and out.

'I don't know, Mam,' Rose sighed, walking past her mother to put her porridge bowl into the sink. 'I was afraid to go out on my own, I suppose.'

'Well, now, there's wooden spoons and there's wooden spoons,' Mrs Darke said, breaking into a smile. Rose grinned back. 'My one was a fancy model, but I couldn't call it a companion I'd love to have with me on a midnight quest. Next time you're afraid as you go out wandering after a banshee, bring the breadknife with you.'

Rose snorted, half-laughing, and her mother gave her a wink. Then she turned back to Colm and pulled a funny face at him as she continued. 'Now. It's time for you to be off to school, and these fellas to be away to Mrs O'Leary's, and me to be in work.'

As her mother prepared the boys' buggy, Rose pulled on her school bag, something nagging at her mind like a loose thread. She took in a deep breath as she realised what it was.

'Ready?' Mrs Darke said, slinging on her jacket.

'Just one minute,' Rose said, running for the stairs.

'Rose! Hurry on, now – I can't be late again,' Mrs Darke called. 'And if you're looking for that mobile phone, you're not supposed to have it in school anyway!'

Rose ignored her as she entered her bedroom. Her cardigan was lying on her bed, and even from the doorway Rose could see the bulge in its pocket. It wasn't her slippers, Rose knew; she'd pulled those out and left them to dry on her radiator first thing that morning. This bulge was something else. She felt drawn towards it, as though she were being forced to come near. She slipped her hand into the pocket and instantly she felt it, the smoothness of the stone.

Rose swallowed hard. She picked it up and stared at it, her gaze lost in its strange whorls. As large as her palm and warm to the touch, the stone was oddly mesmerising to look at. *I found this on the ground. Didn't I? There's no way a giant ice thing actually fell out of the sky and handed it to me . . .*

'Rosaleen Martina Darke!' Her mother's shout made Rose jump. 'You have five seconds, young lady!'

Rose stuffed the stone into the pocket of her school coat and ran for the top of the stairs, clumping down them in a noisy flurry, trying to push all thoughts of ice giants and eyes like universes out of her head.

'I'm *coming*,' she muttered, pushing past her mother in the narrow hallway and picking up her school bag from where she'd left it. She fastened its top flap and slung it onto one shoulder, ready to go. She couldn't help but check quickly that her mobile was in the front pocket, switched to silent. Really, it was her dad's old mobile, too slow for anything besides calls and texts, and often deciding it wasn't in the mood to have its battery charged, but Rose knew it was the only phone she was likely to have for the foreseeable future.

'You've got everything?' Mrs Darke said, keys already jangling in her hand. Rose nodded, and her mother unlocked the door. With a creak, it gave way to a bright morning. Mr Darke's van was already gone, the muddy marks on the path outside their house the only clue that it had ever been parked there. Rose helped her mother manoeuvre the boys' buggy through their cramped porch and finally they were ready to go.

They walked to the end of their road in silence. Rose knew her mam was watching her carefully out of the corner of her eye, but still she found she didn't have the words to tell her about the stone – or anything else.

'Are you all right, love?' Mrs Darke finally asked.

Rose turned to her, too fast, and pulled a tight grin. 'Yep, fine!' she said, looking away. Mrs Darke was about to speak again when, from the buggy, one of the twins let out an excited shriek at the sight of a dog on the far side of the road. The dog's owner waved, and Rose and Mrs Darke waved back. A few more quiet moments passed, and Rose felt the weight of everything that was on her mind settle once again. *School . . . Horrible people . . . Mamó being gone . . . Nobody to walk to school with now that Sophia and Rory take the bus to Druid's Hill . . .* Then Rose's thoughts turned to the creature in the garden and the twisting of the stars right before it vanished. *It was a dream*, she told herself, even as she squeezed the stone inside her pocket. *It was* definitely *a dream.*

She glanced at her mam, trying to find the words to tell her about the giant made of hailstones, and found that they just wouldn't come. Her mouth opened and she drew in a breath, but then – nothing. Mrs Darke gave her a curious look.

'You sure you're all right?'

Rose stared at her mother. She could see the tiredness in her eyes. Rose knew her mam worked hard. She'd taken on extra shifts to pay for Mrs O'Leary, the childminder, after Mamó had grown too sick to care for Rose and the boys, and Rose knew her place at school was expensive, even with the scholarship. Still, Mrs Darke smiled at her daughter and Rose tried to smile back. *Mam has enough on her mind*, Rose told herself.

'Yeah, it's nothing. Sorry, Mam. Just . . . you know. School and things. I'll tell you later.'

'All right, love.' Mrs Darke looked away from

Rose towards the corner just ahead where they'd have to part ways. They stopped to say their goodbyes. Mrs Darke settled Rose's collar, then searched her for anything out of place which could be wiped or licked or brushed until it lay straight.

'God, Mam. Stop, will you?' Rose said, pulling herself out of her mother's reach. It was bad enough she had to walk this far with Mam and the boys, but if anyone saw her being *fussed over* – she'd never live it down. Rose stared at the ground, but sealed up inside her were the things she wished she could say.

Bring me with you, Mam. I'll sit at the back of the butcher's counter, you won't even see me, I promise.

I don't want to go to school. Emer McGuire is going to make my day a misery – again.

Mam, I had the weirdest dream last night. Except I don't think it was a dream. But if it wasn't a dream then I think I might have something loose inside my head . . .

'Right, so,' Mrs Darke sighed, putting both hands back on the buggy. She looked at Rose for a long moment, her eyes clouded with concern. 'I love you, sweetheart.'

Rose nodded, looking at the ground between her

mother's shoes, and then Mrs Darke was gone, towards the supermarket where she worked. Rose watched her mother go around the corner with a soft pang of loss, and then she headed the other way, towards her school – but she didn't take the direct route, the one her mother probably expected her to use.

She walked towards a pedestrian crossing and made straight for the opening of a narrow, shaded alleyway on the far side of the road. The alley looked like a crack in the world between two plain grey-faced buildings, but she could see daylight gleaming through from its far end like moonlight on water – a strange and beautiful silver-blue.

Seconds later, she was out the alley's other end and onto Hargate Street.

She rubbed the stone in her pocket as she walked. Hargate Street was quiet; very few cars went this way, and the shops that opened onto it were so haphazard and with such irregular opening hours that Rose often wondered how any of them were still in business. Sometimes she thought she'd walk this way to school even if Emer McGuire and her gang weren't lying in wait along the shorter route; there was just something *nice* about this street. Something

44

peaceful. Rose looked down at her feet as she walked, her head fizzing and overflowing with thoughts. She wondered if Dad would make it home in time for dinner that day, and if her mam would stop looking so tired some time soon. She worried about her end-of-year project and how it would never look as good in reality as it did inside her imagination, and how Mrs Mooney was going to be disappointed. Her friends' faces – or, her *old* friends, she reminded herself – popped into her mind's eye. *Rory and Sophia.* It had been forever since they'd hung out. Not for the first time, Rose wished her dad had just let her go to the school she'd wanted, but it was too late now. She thought, in a flickering way, about Emer McGuire before forcing the image of her face away.

And she thought about the 'dream' she'd had the night before. The dream that hadn't been a dream. The red stone grew warmer in her hand, deep inside her pocket.

Halfway down the street, Rose could see a figure in a flowered apron standing outside the front of her shop, and she grinned. *Nellie.* The woman saw her approach, and she raised one arm in greeting. In her other hand she held a large purple watering can.

'Morning, little duck,' Nellie said, smiling at Rose as she drew close. 'Come to visit myself and Gracie again, have you?'

'Ah, there she is now!' The call came from the far side of the road, and Rose and Nellie turned. Gracie stood outside his cobbler's shop across the street, waving at Rose. 'If it isn't herself.'

'Hi,' Rose said, feeling her heart begin to lift. Maybe it was because she'd lost Mamó, but she felt there was something special about Gracie and Nellie. They were the one good thing, Rose sometimes thought, about being picked on by Emer. If she hadn't started going to school via Hargate Street, she might never have met them. *And if Mamó was here, you could tell her about the dream,* she told herself. *Mamó would understand. So maybe you can tell Nellie and Gracie instead.*

Nellie lifted the watering can, water sloshing about inside it as she aimed for her hanging baskets. Rose's eyes were drawn to the flowers as Nellie gave them a drink; they looked like nothing she'd seen before. Some of them opened right before her eyes, like a fist unclenching, almost like the plant was aware she was there – and the petals were so bright and silver-white that they were quite dazzling.

'Oh, now,' Nellie muttered, her hands beginning to shake with the effort of holding the watering can. 'I'm not as young as I used to be.'

'Hey, let me,' Rose said. She reached up to help, but before Nellie could hand her the watering can, their attention was caught by a clattering noise at their feet. The red stone had fallen from Rose's pocket and was now skipping over the pavement – right towards a drain at the side of the road. Rose watched it with her heart in her mouth, knowing somehow that if it reached the drain and slipped down into its darkness, it would be lost forever. The eyes of the icy giant burned in her memory, and she felt the urgency with which he'd given her the stone. She had to keep it safe!

'Gracie!' Nellie called – but the old man was already there. He stopped the stone with the toe of his shoe, kicking it quickly back towards Nellie and Rose. It skidded to a stop between them, spinning slowly.

'I have you now, you tricksy thing,' Gracie muttered darkly. Then he looked at Rose, his smile wide and guileless. 'Will you pick it up, like a good girl, and save an old fella's back?'

Rose nodded, her heart thudding. She picked up the stone, feeling its strange heat once more, but before she could put it into her pocket, Nellie reached out to touch her fingers.

'I think maybe we need to have a little chat,' Nellie said. She glanced over at Gracie, who stood nearby whistling through his teeth, looking carefully up and down the street as though checking for witnesses – or spies.

Rose looked between them, from Nellie to Gracie and back again. 'I don't – I mean, I can't stop for a chat,' she told them. 'I have to get to school. If I'm late, the secretary will ring Mam, and she'll get in trouble if she has to step out of the meat counter to take a call at work, and –'

Gracie cleared his throat. Then he lifted his head and stared at the sky. 'Stad,' he declared in a clear voice, and everything seemed to stop for a moment – like the world had taken a breath – but when the moment passed, all was changed. Rose felt fuzzy and disoriented, as though she'd been underwater and had just broken the surface.

'What – What was that?' she said. Things *seemed* normal enough – traffic still moved on the main road way behind her; somewhere not too far away a café was setting up for the day, and the smell of roasting coffee and frying bacon wafted through the air.

But something was different. *Time* seemed different, like everything was on pause.

Rose swung her bag around and pulled her mobile out of the front pocket to check the screen. The clock displayed hours, minutes and seconds, but something was wrong – the display was flickering, like it was stuck. She stared at it, before looking up at Gracie in confusion.

'You'll not miss a minute of your schooling, now,' Gracie said, winking at Rose with his glacier-blue eyes. 'I'm a big fan of the schooling, myself. Here's one I learned, and I only a gasún.' He took a deep breath, held it for a dramatic pause, and began to recite, in a voice that sounded like an ancient violin. '*Mise Raifteirí an file, lán dóchas is grá, le súile gan solais, le ciúnas gan chrá –*'

'Will you put an end to your blethering?' Nellie told him affectionately. 'Sure, that Raftery fella was long after your time.'

Rose felt dizzy, like someone had suddenly swept her off her feet and swung her around before placing her back down again. 'What's going on?' she said, looking at Nellie in confusion.

'Come on inside for a minute, child, and we'll do our best to tell you,' Nellie said.

Rose allowed herself to be ushered into Nellie's shop. It seemed smaller and darker than usual, the long, narrow room filtered with strange shadows. The display cabinet shone, as it always did, polished to perfection, and the door to Nellie's kitchen was firmly closed.

'Now,' Nellie said, bustling behind her counter. She nodded at the stone in Rose's hand. 'Put that thing away, will you, love?' Rose put the stone into her pocket again – carefully this time, checking the bottom of the pocket for holes just in case, as Nellie busied herself choosing treats. 'What'll we be having? I think a few of these laddie-boys will do the trick to start with.' Nellie grabbed the scoop from its hook on the wall and pushed it into a pile of something that looked like jellybeans, expertly pouring them into a paper bag that she'd somehow managed to slip into her other hand without Rose noticing.

She handed the bag to Rose. The beans sat inside it, sparkling like precious stones. 'I don't have any money –' she started to say, and Nellie began to flap her hands like she was shooing flies away.

'Will you go on, out of that!' the old woman said. 'Money, she says. Did you hear that, Gracie?'

Gracie had shuffled past them and was heading down the corridor towards the kitchen door. As he turned the handle to push the door open, greenish light seemed to glow from somewhere beyond it.

'Money!' the old man cackled. Rose couldn't quite see him, but his voice sounded close by. 'It's far from the likes of money we were reared.'

Rose blinked, looking away from the kitchen door. She stared down at the sweets again, her belly tightening into a knot. *Get out of here*, pulsed a voice inside her head – one that was not her own. Her ears felt muffled, and she was somehow aware of the stone in her pocket; its weight and its odd heat seeped through the fabric to her skin.

'You're entirely safe under this roof,' Nellie said. Her voice, solemn and steady, parted the fuzz in Rose's brain like sunlight passing through clouds. The heat of the stone subsided. 'I promise you. On the beard and the belly of the mighty Dagda, I promise you.'

Rose looked at her. The old woman seemed different somehow, as though the hazy light coming in her window was making her blurry. 'I don't know what's happening,' Rose whispered.

'Craythur, I hardly know myself,' Nellie answered.

Rose glanced down at the bag in her hand. 'What *are* these?'

Nellie smiled. 'Drops of courage,' she said. 'I call them croigíní, for the fun. My own recipe, I'll have you know.'

Through the green doorway they could hear Gracie whistling again, a jaunty tune that made Rose feel as though she were breathing in sunlight, as though the golden rays were filling her up, toes to top. She felt the urge to walk through the door, to go into Nellie's kitchen where she'd been so many times before, a place of comfort. But, Rose felt, if she passed through the doorway now, that everything would be different. She thought about the word Gracie had used outside – 'stad', which meant 'stop' in Irish – and about what he'd actually done. Had he stopped time? Made everyone drop into a daydream, so they wouldn't notice? That's how it felt. But how was that even possible? All Rose was sure of was that something in this place, this safe place, had changed, and she didn't understand it yet. She pulled her gaze away from the green light and met Nellie's eyes once more. The old lady looked calm, but there was something ancient and timeless in her gaze – something powerful and patient and wise.

'Have you lived here a long time, Nellie?' Rose asked.

'Yes, child. I've dwelt here many summers now.' Nellie paused, looking steadily at Rose. 'But if you wish, you may leave at any time. There is no compulsion. No geas is laid upon you to set foot into this realm, nor will there ever be. You are free, Rosaleen Darke, to come and go as you please, and so it shall be until the cauldron runs dry.'

Rose blinked, feeling the world snap back into focus around her. 'What cauldron?'

Nellie hung up her scoop. Her mischievous grin was back. 'Do you want a look at it?'

Rose shrugged. 'Is it far?'

Nellie's eyes twinkled. 'Get a handful of cróigíní into you, there, and you'll be well set for the journey.'

Rose pushed her fingers into the sweets inside the bag. They slid and slithered over her skin like smooth, sea-washed pebbles, and she closed her fist around as many of them as she could reach. Then, she dipped her face into her palm, taking three or four of the shining treats into her mouth.

As soon as the cróigíní touched her tongue, Rose felt warmed through, like she'd been caught in a sudden sunbeam. The cróigíní melted down into her tummy and Rose took a deep breath, a sense of joy and confidence and strength trickling through her. *Cróigíní*, she thought, looking down at them. 'Cróga' in Irish was 'courage', and she realised Nellie had meant the name literally. *Actual drops of courage!*

'These really work,' she said.

'Sure, don't I know that?' Nellie replied. She lifted the front of her apron and danced a few steps, her feet flickering back and forth with incredible ease. 'I take two or three every morning, and that's why I'm as nimble as a pig.'

Rose grinned and the old lady smiled back. 'But – how do you make them?' Rose asked.

Nellie tapped the side of her nose. 'Sugar, mostly,' she whispered. 'And a drop of water from that cauldron

I was telling you about. Now. Will we go and have a look at it?'

Rose shoved the remainder of the cróigíní into her pocket, walking towards the green-lit doorway. 'Is it through here?'

'You'll find your own path,' Nellie said, as Rose went past.

Rose stepped through the doorway and stopped for a moment, amazed. She set foot on the top step of a short flight of stairs leading down into a room – but it was not the room that usually lay beyond this door. Instead of Nellie's small, homely kitchen with its lace-curtained window over the sink and shelves filled with copper saucepans, Rose gazed into a large, long, sunken kitchen with windows on all sides. Each window was divided into panels. Some of the panels were fitted with coloured glass, but most were clear. A pair of open double doors led from the far end of the room into a beautiful garden, its greenness rolling away in all directions. Sunlight was pouring through the windows like honey, tall flowers brushed the breeze outside everywhere you looked, and the buzz of bees seeped through the open door, the joyful hum of a world at work, at peace. Beyond the doors was a foot-worn path, leading towards a hillock. Steps, looking as though they'd grown there, rose up the hillock's side. Something was on top of the low mound, but Rose couldn't see what.

The room itself was a wonderful jumble. Right at the centre was a long dining table made from heavy, dark wood, every visible inch of it carved with swirling designs. It was surrounded by chairs, none of which matched, and laden with *things* – bowls of fruit, plates of sandwiches, a shining teapot with steam coming from the spout, a cake with a slice missing, piles of books and drawings and, in the centre, a huge vase of flowers. There was a range in the corner – an old-fashioned one with large cast-iron hob and oven; there was a string suspended above it to which were pinned several bunches of herbs and flowers (and a stray pair of socks), all hung to dry in the heat of the stove. The walls were lined with low bookcases, each of them stuffed with books, and in another corner was a tall grandfather clock. The hands on its face were still, besides the twitching second hand, and Rose took out her phone again. The second display was still flickering, showing two numbers superimposed over one another. She frowned as she noticed that her signal had dropped – it was like the entire phone had frozen. She shook it gently, but nothing changed. With a sigh, she pushed it back into its pocket.

On the floor beneath the table was a large woven rug, and in front of the range, tucked into a comfortable-looking basket, was a cat – or, as Rose squinted at it, an animal which *looked* a bit like a cat, but . . . *wasn't*.

'Now! The tea is wet,' said a voice, and Rose looked away from the creature in the basket and back at the table. Gracie was sitting in one of the chairs, grinning up at her. 'Will you have a cup?'

Rose slowly walked down the steps into the kitchen. She glanced back; Nellie was right behind her. 'You'll find nothing here but safety, little one,' Nellie said, and something in Rose's heart knew it was true.

She turned to face the kitchen. The animal in the basket was now on Gracie's lap, and he was stroking its long, silky back. The creature regarded Rose calmly as she made her way towards the table. It had ears like ferns, which grew incredibly long; as Gracie stroked them, they flattened down along the creature's back before springing up, standing straight for a moment before coiling gently into

58

soft spirals once again. It put a long silver tongue out of its mouth, licking at its whiskers as it observed Rose with curiosity.

'Now, Catshee,' Gracie murmured to it. 'Be welcoming to our guest, won't you.'

Catshee gave Rose an imperious glare before slinking down from Gracie's lap and stalking towards the open door. It gave one last flick of its tail – which looked exactly like a clump of ferny fronds, each furling and unfurling, shining like delicate silver lacework – before disappearing into the garden.

'You never can tell with that lad what sort of mood he'll be in,' Nellie said, taking a seat at the table. The chair creaked welcomingly beneath her weight, and Gracie reached out to pour her a cup of tea. The steam from the spout seemed to billow forth with as much gusto as it had a few moments before. Rose let her school bag slide to the floor and sat on the chair beside Nellie, looking around.

'Everything is so different,' she whispered in amazement.

'And yet somehow it's all exactly the same,' Gracie chuckled. Rose looked at him and felt her fear begin to settle, until it disappeared completely.

Nellie picked up her cup and gave Rose a searching look. 'Now,' she began, as Gracie poured a cup of tea for Rose. The scent of it was delicious enough by itself, and Rose closed her eyes as she breathed it in. When she opened them again, a plate bearing a large slab of cake and a delicate fork had somehow appeared beside her cup. She glanced at Gracie, who gave her a wink. 'Will we get started?' Nellie continued.

'We will, we will,' Gracie said, clearing his throat and pretending to come to attention. Rose grinned at him as she picked up her fork.

'That stone in your pocket,' Nellie said. Rose met her gaze. Nellie's voice was quiet, and her eyes – though still kind – looked slightly clouded over. 'Where did you come across it?'

Rose swallowed her mouthful of cake. 'I was going to tell you both about it anyway, just so you know, okay? But, what happened was someone – or, well, some*thing* – gave it to me. Last night.' Speaking the words sent a shiver through her. She picked up her cup and took a mouthful of tea, hoping it would warm her.

'What sort of a something, now?' Gracie asked. His white-tufted head tilted a little to one side as he gazed at Rose across the table.

Rose searched inside herself for the words, not knowing quite how to continue. 'If I was talking to anyone else, this would sound completely unbelievable,' she finally began. Catshee padded back from the garden as she spoke, looking as ungracious as he had a moment before. He climbed into Nellie's lap and she began to stroke him absent-mindedly. Rose blinked away from the creature's unsettling eyes and looked back at Gracie. 'But here? It sort of makes sense.'

'Everything makes sense in its own way,' Nellie said. 'You'll find things don't always fit together the way you'd expect, but there'll always be someone to help, if you ask.'

Rose nodded. 'Maybe there's no other way for any of this to make sense,' she said, mostly to herself. Then she looked up at Nellie. 'I'm not, like, *dreaming*, am I? Or did I get some sort of head injury and you guys are figments of my imagination or something?'

Gracie hooted with laughter. 'Will you look at that?' he wheezed, pulling out a handkerchief to wipe his eyes. 'This slip of a thing, imagining she could have dreamed up such a character as me.'

Nellie gave Rose a warm smile. 'You're not dreaming,' she said. 'And, thank the Dagda, you're not injured. And while this place is a bit *unexpected*,' she said, glancing around, 'it's not imaginary.'

'But it's magical,' Rose said, realising the truth of it as she spoke. 'Right?'

Nellie's smile grew warmer. 'After a fashion,' she said.

Rose nodded. She stared at a knot in the wood of the table, focusing hard on it for a moment or two. *It wasn't a dream*, she thought, recalling the icy giant's trusting eyes. Something drew her mind back to Mamó, and the feeling of being nestled in her arms, reading stories – until that had grown too boring and Rose had wanted to play with friends instead. But, Rose realised, this was what Mamó's stories had been about: giants and magic and unbelievable things. She couldn't remember the details, but she knew they were all inside her, along with her memories of their teller. *And they're not just stories any more.* They were coming to life, all around her.

She blinked out of her thoughts. Gracie was tucking away his handkerchief and Catshee was sitting on top of the table, curled in a pearlescent heap, his two fernlike ears sticking straight up. Nellie was gazing at her, patiently cradling her warm teacup.

'A giant gave it to me,' Rose finally said.

Nellie's eyes flashed with alarm and Catshee got to his feet and hissed. Gracie reached out and pulled him off the table, and he disappeared back into his basket with an aggrieved yowl.

'Did I say something wrong?' Rose asked, staring at the grown-ups, wide-eyed.

'What sort of a giant?' Gracie asked, his voice clipped. 'How many eyes had he? And had he long hair, or none? Had he a tattoo at all? He didn't give you his name?'

Rose's mouth fell open as she struggled to process all these questions. 'He – or *she*, right, or *they*, I don't know anything about that stuff – didn't have any tattoos. Or any hair. There were, like, spikes all over their head. But there was no speaking. This giant didn't have a mouth.'

Nellie and Gracie glanced at each other, and then they looked back at Rose. 'Was it sealed shut, or –' Nellie began.

'It wasn't *there*,' Rose insisted. 'I heard the hail falling and I went out into the garden, and when I got there the giant . . . *grew*, or whatever, out of the hail and the ice. They just sort of *appeared*, and handed

63

me the stone. And then,' she paused, gulping, 'the sky *ate* them.'

'Sioc,' Nellie whispered, her eyes widening. 'A Guardian of Toraigh. It must have been. He came to you?'

Rose nodded. 'It looked like something was after him. And he wanted me to have the stone.'

Gracie cleared his throat. 'Could I see it, Rose? If it please you.'

Rose put her hand into her pocket. The stone met her touch. It was unpleasant, feverish, as she pulled it out. It clicked against the wood of the tabletop as she set it down, and then she took her hand away.

The red stone sat there, in the midst of everything, rocking slightly. Nellie, Gracie and Rose stared down at it. For the first time, Rose noticed that the strange whorls on the stone's surface looked a little like an eye. She frowned at it, staring harder, wondering if she was imagining things or if it really *was* an eye, and –

The stone's eye opened, staring right back at her.

5

Catshee shrieked, launching himself from the floor onto the table. Nellie got to her feet and grabbed a tea towel, throwing it over the stone.

Gracie, on the far side of the table, was muttering something to himself, his own eyes wide with alarm.

'What – *What?* It *looked* at me!' Rose said, feeling Nellie wrap her up in a hug.

'It won't have seen you,' she told her in a soothing tone. 'Its power won't work here. And I have it covered now. Keeping it in the dark is the best thing. You did well, putting it into your pocket. Its hold over you is lessened if it can't see you.'

'Its *power?* You mean, it's dangerous? So why do *I* have to have it?' She tried to let Nellie's hug keep her calm. 'And – what *is* it?'

Nellie took a deep breath, as though she was

considering her answer. 'It's a weapon,' she finally said.

'A what?' Rose's voice trembled as she spoke.

'It's more of a warning, I'd say,' Gracie said, shooting Nellie a look. 'Nothing to get too worked up over, mo chroí.' He looked at Rose, smiling warmly, but his eyes were still wary. He reached over to put one large, work-worn hand over hers, and gave it a comforting squeeze, but Rose knew he wasn't telling the full truth. Like her dad sometimes did, he was bending the situation a little to try to keep Rose from getting afraid – but all that did was make her *more* afraid.

'What sort of warning? A warning about what?' Rose looked from Nellie to Gracie and back again. 'And you said its *power* wouldn't work here – what power? It's just a rock! Isn't it?'

'The stone has mighty power, which is neither good nor evil in itself, though it has allowed itself to be used by both in times gone past. Perhaps it bends a little more to the bad than to the good, to tell the truth,' Gracie said, gazing vacantly at the tea towel. 'But all it wants is to destroy, and whatever it takes to achieve that end, the stone will do.'

Rose stared at him. 'What?'

'I think we should take another sup of this good stuff,' Nellie said, resuming her seat and lifting the teapot once again.

'I don't want *tea*!' Rose shouted, pushing her chair away from the table. 'I want to know what's happening!'

Nellie put the teapot down and regarded Rose calmly. 'Come on out into the garden for a minute,' she said. 'There's something I want to show you.'

Rose stared at her, incredulous, as the old woman got to her feet. Catshee went out before her, and Gracie met her at the door, graciously offering her his arm as she stepped out into the sunlight. Rose was left alone in the kitchen with the weird, unticking clock. 'Hey!' she shouted. 'Wait for me!'

She got to her feet and ran through the door. The warmth of sunlight bathed her as she went into the garden, and the grass was soft as cotton wool beneath her feet. Overhead, the sky was a perfect blue, dotted with some high-up wisps of cloud. On the horizon, far beyond the expanse of garden, was a mountain range that Rose didn't recognise. She stood for a while just gazing around, wondering where on earth she was. *This isn't anywhere*, she found herself thinking. *There's no way Nellie could have a garden like this, just off Hargate Street. There's supposed to be the community hall car park back here, and beyond that the shopping centre . . .*

She pulled herself out of her thoughts and looked towards the hillock. Gracie, Nellie and Catshee were climbing the steps, and none of them seemed to care if she was following. Rose set her jaw and marched indignantly forward, her feet brushing through soft grass studded here and there with bright white flowers. Down one side of the wide garden, to Rose's right, an ancient-looking hedge ran, gnarled and knotted, threaded through with sweet-smelling woodbine and thick-leaved ivy. It reminded her of a huge arm curled protectively around the house, the garden and everything they contained.

Rose reached the hillock and put her foot on the bottom step. She began to climb, expecting it to be straightforward, but instantly she began to struggle. The steps, which had looked so easy to climb from a distance, were deceptively shallow – and steep. Rose found herself falling forward, struggling to gain a foothold or handhold on the strangely sheer hillside. She glanced up; above her she could see Nellie and

Gracie climbing with ease, their arms interlocked, their steps effortless. She looked back down at her own hands and feet, wondering why it felt like she was trying to haul herself up a mountain.

She took a deep breath and continued, determinedly digging her fingers into the side of the hill as she dragged herself, inch by inch, up its slope. *It's not going to beat me*, she told herself as she climbed.

Eventually, she felt hands clasping her around the wrists and helping to pull her the rest of the way. Rose looked up, her heart thundering with effort and fright, but all she could see were Nellie and Gracie, standing at the top of the strange hillock. Catshee flowed past, stalking something smaller than himself for dinner, no doubt, his ears furled tight and his tail spread in a fan. Rose got to her feet between Nellie and Gracie, before looking behind her. The hillock was barely higher than a grown-up, and the steps looked perfectly smooth, each tread a comfortable height and depth. She struggled to catch her breath, her brain whirling with confusion.

'Here we are now,' Nellie said, and Rose turned.

Set into the top of the hillock was a giant bowl. It was as if the hillock had grown around it somehow.

Parts of the bowl stuck up out of the soil, its ancient metal sides and fittings covered in moss and flowers. A bird fluttered down to land on the lip of the gigantic vessel; it chirped a song for a second or two before flying away.

'What – What is this?' Rose said, licking her lips as she spoke. She realised she was dreadfully thirsty.

'If you'd had that cup of tea you'd be feeling the better for it,' Nellie chided very gently.

Rose took a step closer to the edge of the bowl. It wasn't, as she thought might be the case, endless – she could see the curve of its sides and the sweep of its base. It seemed decorated, like the table in Nellie's kitchen – everywhere Rose looked, she could see carved faces peering back at her, faces with antlered foreheads and wise eyes, animal heads and humanlike ones, side by side. She could see trees and flowers and fruit, bunches of grapes and piles of apples and sheaves of wheat, all made with extraordinary skill. The sides of the bowl gleamed with a jewel-green growth of algae and moss. Between these patches of green it gleamed a vivid, deep bronze. The bottom was covered with a pool of pure water so still that

70

Rose could see her reflection in it, the blue sky right above her.

'This is amazing,' she gasped, and the sound of her voice whispered back up at her from the bottom of the bowl. Nellie appeared beside her in the reflection, and Rose turned to look at her.

'This is the Cauldron of the Dagda, the generous and good,' Nellie said, her voice low and reverent. 'It is one of the four treasures of the Tuatha Dé Danann.'

Rose wrinkled her nose. 'The who?'

'Well, now, that's the best I ever heard,' came Gracie's scratchy-sounding voice. Rose looked to her other side. The old man was gazing at her sadly. 'Who are the Tuatha Dé Danann, indeed. Are they to be forgotten so soon?'

Nellie clucked kindly, stroking Rose's hair behind her ear. 'It's not the child's fault,' she said. 'The Old Magic, and its stories and truths, are no longer sung as they once were, and its power has been failing now for years beyond reckoning.' She paused, her eyes dipping with sorrow. 'Isn't that why we're in this pickle to begin with?' she added in a near-whisper.

Tuatha Dé Danann, Rose thought. Another image of Mamó floated into her head, and a half-formed memory of being snuggled up beside her one rainy day, listening to stories of old Ireland, tales of gods and battles and heroes as bright as the sun . . . Then, the picture faded, and Rose let it go with a twinge of sadness.

She looked back into the cauldron. The water in it was perfectly smooth, like a mirror – not like water at all. There were no drops falling into it, no insects skidding across its surface, no ripples made by wind. It simply *was*, and it looked at her as if it expected her to do something. 'It's a treasure?' she finally whispered.

'One of four,' Nellie said, her voice warm. 'The Spear of Lugh. The Cauldron of the Dagda, the greatest of all the gods of Old Ireland. The Lia Fáil – the Stone of Destiny. And the mighty Claíomh Solais, the Sword of Light. Four treasures were brought by the Tuatha Dé Danann, the great gods and goddesses that once walked this land, and only two remain. This, and the Lia Fáil on the Hill of Tara.'

'What happened to the others?' Rose wrapped her arms around herself as she spoke.

Nellie smiled sadly. 'Millennia have passed. Things get lost. So it is.'

Rose's eyebrows lifted. 'Millennia? Wow.'

'This is the cauldron of plenty,' Gracie said, suddenly enough to make Rose start, and turn towards him. 'It never runs dry. It has the power to satisfy any hunger. None in need ever leave it without being filled. If you ask it, the cauldron will grant you whatever you need, by the power of the Dagda.'

'Brilliant,' Rose muttered, looking back into the water. 'I'll have a million quid, then, please, Mr Dagda.'

The water reared unexpectedly, rising like a tower before collapsing once more, splashing and surging around the bottom of the cauldron until it finally settled into stillness. Rose was so shocked that she flung her hands out to either side. She grabbed a fistful of Nellie's apron and Gracie caught her around the wrist, and together the three of them managed not to topple head-first into the huge metal bowl.

'What was that?' Rose gasped.

'The cauldron grants you what you *need*, not what you want,' Nellie said. Rose glanced up at her. The woman's face was grey and her lips were thin as she stared into the water. 'And it does not take kindly to ridicule.'

'I wasn't –' Rose began, but Nellie turned her

shrewd eyes towards her, and the words dried up in her throat. 'Okay,' she continued. 'Sorry.'

The water remained impassive. 'If you have a need,' Gracie said, 'speak it.'

Rose's head filled with thoughts as she stared into the pool of water. Her mam, her dad, her brothers, her stress about her school project, her sorrow for Mamó – and finally, her jumbled brain settled on one thing. *Emer McGuire*. Rose swallowed hard. Emer McGuire and her pointed words, her cruel eyes, her unkind mockery. *Let her leave me in peace*, she whispered, deep inside herself. The pool rippled gently, as though stirred by the faintest breeze.

'I don't – I don't need anything,' Rose finally said. 'I'm good. Thanks.'

Gracie sucked at his gums. 'The Dagda will decide that,' he muttered.

'Why did you bring me out here?' Rose said, sudden fear bubbling up through her. 'I mean, what time must it be now? I'm *so* late for school, and Mam's going to kill me –'

'Do you still not understand, child?' Nellie said.

On Rose's other side, Gracie chuckled gently. 'You're not going to miss a split-second of your schooling. Didn't I tell you already?'

'But I must have been here for an *hour*! I mean, Mam's probably already phoned the Guards, and they're probably on patrol looking for me, and –'

'I invoked my power to Shape this day to our purposes,' Gracie said in a quiet voice. 'As long as my power holds, time will not pass, and nobody – not even those Guards with their fancy uniforms – will notice. Nobody but us.'

'But that's impossible,' Rose whispered.

Gracie gave an inscrutable smile.

The water in the cauldron rippled again, and Nellie turned towards it. She muttered something under her breath and bowed towards the cauldron; Gracie did the same, their movements respectful and slow. After a moment's indecision, Rose gave the cauldron a quick wave, hoping nobody else saw. She wasn't quite sure yet what was happening, but it seemed clear that the cauldron was important. She didn't want to bow, but she wanted the cauldron – or whatever was inside it – to know she was a friend. A sudden wind blew around inside the cauldron, sighing with the sound of a warm voice, its bronze walls humming like it was singing, and then everything fell still again.

'I have my answer,' Nellie said as she straightened up.

'What was the question?' Rose asked her.

'I'll tell you over tea,' she said, placing an arm around Rose as they turned away from the cauldron. The return journey down the steps was much easier than the climb up, and a moment later Rose found her shoes sinking into the moss-soft grass. They made their way back to the house, passing beneath the hawthorn tree that grew over the back door like an arch. Catshee led them, and very soon they were stepping into the shade of the kitchen again.

The clock was still ticking without moving. The range was still warm. The teapot was still steaming, the trail of white from its spout making dancing clouds in the air, and the towel was still covering the stone. Rose found her gaze being drawn towards the lump beneath the blue-and-white checked pattern on the cloth.

Nellie settled into her chair, groaning a little as she sat. She poured Rose's cup first, then her own, and finally Gracie's, setting the teapot down once she was done. Rose watched the steam from its spout, mesmerised by its movement.

'The Dagda knows our need,' Nellie said, her voice low in the stillness of the kitchen. Through the windows, the unchanging golden light poured in. 'He knows that the ice giant, Sioc, has visited you and given you the *tathlum*, Rose, which is the old name for the stone with the red eye, the stone that was taken from an ancient battlefield and kept in secrecy for three thousand years by the foulest of witches. I would have given it to the cauldron, if the Dagda had willed it, but he has said the *tathlum* has already been given, and that it has been received, and that everything is as it should be.' The clock tick-ticked. 'He has asked that you keep it, Rose, and watch over it, and let none separate you from it, and said that its purpose will be revealed in due course.'

Rose stared at the old woman, feeling like pressure was building behind her eyes, growing worse with every heartbeat. Nellie returned the gaze, her eyes calm and steady.

'But . . . why?' Rose said. 'Why is it *me* who has to do all this? Why not someone like you, who knows what's going on?'

Nellie's gaze grew kind. 'The Seandraíocht – the Old Magic – does not make bad choices, nor does it make choices lightly. Whatever the reason, you have been chosen by one whose power goes far beyond mine.'

'Might it be the Silver Road?' Gracie's voice was soft, and he spoke to Nellie.

'It might,' the old woman assented, glancing at him. She looked back at Rose. 'You walk the Silver Road every day, Rose. So perhaps its power is in you too.'

Rose frowned. 'What? What's the Silver Road?'

'Hargate Street,' Nellie said. 'Its proper name is Bóthar na hAirgead. The Silver Road.'

'It's part of an ancient Way of great power,' Gracie added. 'And it's our task, Nellie's and mine, to guard it and protect it from all harm.'

Rose stared at him, but he didn't crack a grin. She glanced at Nellie, who was equally steady and unsmiling. 'But . . . this can't be right,' Rose whispered, staring at the table. 'I don't want any of this. I have *enough* on my plate without all this stuff too.' She looked back at Nellie and Gracie. 'Listen, I really – I really like you both? And coming here, knowing you, is basically the best part of my day, right? You know that. But I can't deal with . . . whatever this is. I've got to go.' She pushed herself out of her chair. 'Why don't I just give you the stone? It's safer here, isn't it? I don't even want it.' She leaned down to pick up her school bag, only to find Catshee sitting on top of it, staring at her with his unblinking gaze. His two long ears stuck up from his head, fanning out like the crest of an exotic bird. Rose reached for the bag anyway, shooing away the strange cat, but he hissed so menacingly that she drew back her hand.

'Hey, what's up with Catshee?' she said, turning back to Nellie and Gracie – but Nellie and Gracie were no longer there. Instead there were two people wearing robes and shrouded in white light, their faces at once looking ancient and ageless, standing on either side of the table and gazing down at Rose. She blinked and looked again. They *were* Nellie and Gracie – just changed.

'I am Nellie Sweeney, the Cauldron Keeper,' said Nellie.

'And I am Gracie Kinch, the Shaper,' Gracie added.

'And I am officially bugging out,' Rose muttered, staring at them.

'The Dagda has decreed it, and it must be so,' Nellie said, light shining from her body like a halo.

'The stone must be guarded for it will be needed, as it was once before, to fell an ancient enemy. You, Rose, have been chosen as its guardian. The Seandraíocht has chosen you, and it does not choose wrongly.'

'What – ancient enemy?' Rose whispered.

'Balor of the Fomorians,' Gracie said. 'Balor of the Evil Eye. A creature of chaos and destruction.'

Rose felt her panic rise as she scrambled around on the floor for her bag, ignoring the scratch of Catshee's claws. Gracie and Nellie's gazes remained calm and impassive as Rose grabbed up her school bag and ran out of the kitchen. She didn't stop until her feet hit the pavement outside Nellie's sweet-shop. The flowers in the hanging basket still peered at her, their silver-white petals seeming to turn in her direction.

Her fingers fumbled her mobile out of its pocket, and she looked at the clock face. The minute hand ticked forward, finally, as Gracie's spell, or whatever he'd done, winked out like a bubble popping. Rose glanced back at the empty sweet-shop, then shouldered her bag as she set off down the road.

All the way to school, Rose didn't dare put her hand into her pocket. Somehow she knew – despite the fact that the stone had remained on the table, and nobody had touched it since Nellie had thrown the towel over it – that if Rose reached in to look for it, the stone would be waiting there, pulsing with its strange heat, its weird red eye open wide.

6

'Are you all right, Rosaleen?'

Rose looked up to see Mr Hartigan, the History teacher, standing at the front of the classroom with a textbook in his hand, looking at her expectantly.

'Sorry, sir,' Rose said, snapping herself out of whatever daydream she'd been in. The room around her seemed to click back into focus with a *whumpf*.

'Tell me three facts about Iron Age Ireland, so.'

'Um. Well. It was – BCE? Third century BCE. And they used iron to make things.'

Mr Hartigan cleared his throat. 'I think you can do better than that.'

A ripple of laughter washed around the room. Rose looked away from her teacher and her gaze fell on Emer McGuire, who'd turned right round to stare at her. She was smirking and chewing gum –

which Mr Hartigan clearly hadn't noticed her doing. As soon as Rose's eyes met hers, Emer winked. Rose looked away, feeling her cheeks begin to burn with embarrassment, and when she glanced back Emer was shaking with silent laughter, leaning against the girl next to her.

'And there were . . . the bog bodies,' Rose muttered.

'Pardon?' Mr Hartigan said.

Rose looked up at him. 'They buried people in the bog,' she repeated in a louder voice.

The rest of the class exploded in a peal of laughter. 'Quiet!' Mr Hartigan shouted, and the noise gradually fell away. 'For *that*, now, you can all write a page on the treasures of Iron Age Ireland, to be delivered to me here tomorrow. Right? And no wasting space by writing in big letters either. Now,' Mr Hartigan continued, over the mumbles of discontent, 'I want you all to read page forty-seven and forty-eight of your textbook – in *silence* – while I get the whiteboard ready. Understood?'

'Yes, sir,' Rose muttered along with everyone else. She flipped to the pages in her History book, but before she could start reading, someone at the next desk jabbed a ruler into her ribs. She jerked, taken by surprise, and looked over. Matthew, the boy who'd jabbed her, held up his mobile phone, and Rose looked at the screen before common sense kicked in.

She saw a photo of herself, her nose buried in her library book. Emer must have taken it in the yard without her knowing. There was a filter over the image making Rose look as though she'd just swum through a river of muck. She was filthy and animated flies buzzed around her head. Letters in bright neon colours appeared across the bottom of the screen, spelling out *POOR LITTLE ROSIE-ROO!!!* Beside this was a cartoon face holding its nose.

Rose looked away, her insides roiling with shame, noticing at least half the class pulling their phones out of pockets or pencil cases, looking at their screens, nudging one another and giggling. Several people turned to look at her, but she kept her eyes on the board. The classroom filled with mocking whispers but Rose forced herself not to listen.

'Right!' All the phones magically vanished back into their hiding places as Mr Hartigan turned around, and the class settled as he stared at them. The whiteboard was displaying images of beautiful metal objects, covered with patterns similar to the ones Rose had seen at Nellie's house. For a moment her head swam, and she felt like she was standing on the edge of the hillock, staring down into the Dagda's cauldron.

Was that just this morning? she thought, feeling dizzy. *How was that just this morning?*

'The Broighter Collar!' Mr Hartigan said. 'Where was it found? Malachy Sheehy, do you know the answer?' Rose watched as the teacher pointed at one of the kids closest to him, who stammered a bit as he tried to think. 'You didn't read your book, so!' Mr Hartigan said. 'Now, who else? Hassan Abaza.'

'Er, Northern Ireland, sir?' Hassan answered.

'Good work, Abaza,' Mr Hartigan said.

Rose stared at the image on the whiteboard. The patterns on the Broighter Collar looked just like the inside of the cauldron. Only, where the cauldron was huge and sang with some strange power, the collar seemed tiny and flat by comparison – and where the collar was bright gold, the cauldron had been darker, and *older*, its bronze even more ancient than the Broighter treasures. Rose's eyes began to hurt and her head ached, its throb in time with her pulse.

She put up her hand.

'Darke!' Mr Hartigan barked. 'Have you got something to contribute?'

'Sir, I – I need a toilet pass,' Rose said, gritting her teeth against the sniggering that this would bring her way. 'Please.'

Mr Hartigan reached into a drawer in his desk and pulled out a plastic card. He held it up, and Rose gratefully got to her feet. Her legs felt wobbly and weak as she walked up through the classroom.

'Five minutes,' Mr Hartigan said, pressing the card into Rose's hand. 'Right?'

'Yes, sir,' Rose replied. 'Thank you, sir.'

Rose wondered if she *would* actually be sick before she reached the toilet. She stumbled her way into a cubicle and sat down on the closed toilet lid. She tried to take a few deep breaths, even though the stink of bleach was enough to make her gag, but after a while she could hardly smell it any more. Eventually, she felt herself calming, just a little.

A minute or two later, the door to the bathroom opened. Rose knew who it was from the moment she heard the footsteps on the tiles – and her suspicions were confirmed as Emer McGuire started humming. Rose imagined her looking at her reflection in the mirror, maybe applying the lip gloss that they weren't allowed to have at school – yet, somehow, no teacher ever confiscated from her. Emer was the only girl who seemed to have it all her own way, all the time.

Rose felt a surge of anger at the *unfairness* of it powering her legs as she stood up and flushed the toilet. She unlocked the cubicle door and strode towards the sinks, determined not to look in Emer McGuire's direction.

'Oh, *there* you are!' Emer crooned. 'I asked Mr Hartigan if I could come after you, just to check you were all right. Wouldn't want anything happening to you, would we?'

Rose ignored her and focused on washing her hands.

'Must be such a novelty for you, coming to school,' Emer said with a sigh. 'Where we've got running water and flushing toilets, and all that stuff? I know it must be hard not to have them at home.' Rose turned to look at Emer, overcome with quiet rage. Emer was pouting with mock sincerity. 'I was going to start a petition, y'know, that we could send to the council, to put indoor plumbing into your house. It might *help*. With some of your little issues.' She wrinkled her nose, as if she'd smelled something bad.

'Leave me alone, Emer,' Rose said, her voice quivering.

'What?' Emer raised her hands in the air. 'I'm not doing anything. Here I am, trying to help you, and here *you* are, being rude.' She tsked, turning back to her reflection. 'It must run in the family.'

Rose's head whipped around to face Emer. 'What?'

'Daddy says your father's the same at work,' Emer said lightly. 'Doesn't know his place.' She primped at her reflection, touching up her sugar-pink lip gloss. 'Which is *weird*, right, because without my dad you wouldn't even be here, would you? You're not exactly Grammar School material, Rosie-Roo.' Emer turned to Rose, her brown eyes glittering cruelly. 'Doesn't my dad, like, pay your fees?'

Rose pressed her lips tightly closed to avoid letting anything out through them. *I got a scholarship!* she shouted inside her head. It was true that the wealthier parents, like Emer's, contributed to a fund each year for scholarship students. The knowledge burned inside her.

Don't say anything, don't say anything, don't say anything! She pushed hard against everything she wanted to spew out, because she knew . . . *Whatever I do or say will get back to Emer's dad, and if her dad hears about it, my dad will suffer at work.* Rose knew her family couldn't afford that.

But she also heard her dad's calm voice inside her. *Never let anybody put you down, sweetheart.*

She stood for five heartbeats staring at Emer, who was still preening at her reflection. Back and forth, back and forth went the wand of lip gloss, and as Rose watched, the urge to bite back built up inside her, growing and growing and . . . 'I think you've got enough,' she couldn't help saying finally. 'Any more and you might stick your mouth shut, and what a tragedy *that* would be.'

She spun on the spot, trying to suppress a smile at the sound of Emer's surprised gasp from behind her, but as she strode away a noise stopped her in her tracks. It was the clattering sound of something skittering across the tiled bathroom floor – something hard, like the blood-red stone.

The stone that was supposed to be hiding in Rose's coat pocket, back in the classroom. The stone that had, inexplicably, ended up in the pocket of her school trousers instead, among the balled-up tissues and pen lids and paperclips. *Not again!* Rose thought desperately.

'What's this?' Emer said.

Rose turned to face her. At her feet, as if it had been deliberately placed there, sat the red stone. Its eye was closed, like it was trying to look innocent.

'That's *mine*!' Rose shouted, lunging for it – and realising at the same moment that this was exactly the wrong thing to do. Emer dropped to a crouch and had the stone in her hand before Rose had made it halfway across the bathroom.

'Hey, now! Finders keepers,' Emer said, jumping to her feet again and holding the stone high. She was taller than Rose, who stared hopelessly up at the lump of red rock held in Emer's careless fingers. 'So, is it a treasure? A *toy*? I could use it as a fidget to get me through Maths.' Emer laughed. 'I should probably hand it in to Mrs Etchingham, right?'

Mrs Etchingham was the school principal, a fair and kind lady who had always been very nice to Rose – but once a confiscated object was in her office it was never seen again. Rose almost felt like throwing up at the thought of the stone ending up in one of her desk drawers. If it found its way in there, she'd never get it back.

'Please,' she choked out, trying to sound calmer than she felt. 'Emer, come on. It's nothing – it's only a stone! Don't be weird.'

Emer gave Rose an amused look. 'It's not *nothing*. I can see that.' She closed her fingers around the stone and shoved it deep into her skirt pocket, keeping her hand clamped around it. 'Now. We'd better get back to class or Mr Hartigan will be sending a search party in after us.'

She pushed past, bumping her shoulder against Rose's as she went, and disappeared out through the bathroom door. Rose stared at herself in the mirror for a moment, looking into her own face with horror, before following Emer McGuire back to class.

'So there you are!' Mr Hartigan announced to the whole room, as she and Emer made their way back through the door. 'Did ye fall into the toilet, girls?'

Quiet laughter washed over the room, and Emer fixed the teacher with her most winning smile. 'Sorry, sir!' she chirped. 'Rosie felt a bit sick so I was helping her. But she's grand now. Aren't you, Rosie?'

Emer nudged Rose in the side, making Rose almost lose her footing.

'Yes,' she whispered. She cleared her throat and tried again. 'Yes, sir. I'm okay.'

Mr Hartigan frowned at Rose, looking concerned. 'Do you want to go to the office and have the secretary ring one of your parents?'

Rose shook her head, and Mr Hartigan ushered them both back to their seats. Rose sat, her legs feeling even wobblier than they had earlier.

For the rest of the lesson, she fought to keep her eyes away from Emer McGuire, who spent the remainder of the class working diligently on her History – with the blood-red stone sitting right on top of her desk, winking malevolently whenever Rose glanced in its direction.

The Seandraíocht does not choose wrongly, went Nellie's voice, spinning around and around inside Rose's head, until it was the only thing she could hear.

7

Rose squinted as she stepped out the side door of Carriganawn Grammar School, just after the home-time bell had rung. The sun was *bright*, like it had somehow zoomed several million miles closer to Earth over the course of the day, and as Rose began to walk, she could feel prickles of sweat beginning to gather at her back. She swung her bag down to the ground, took off her jacket and school jumper, and did her best to stuff them both inside. Eventually she had to tie her jacket round her waist instead, rolling up her shirt sleeves as she walked.

'Woohoo!' came a shout from behind, and Rose turned to see a group of fourth-years come thundering past. She jumped into the hedgerow out of their way, but they paid her no attention. The air was filled with shouts of delight from all directions as the students were freed into the unexpectedly hot afternoon.

I wonder if this how it feels to be a slice of bread inside a toaster, she thought, shading her eyes with her hand as she looked up at the sky. It was solid blue, no wisps of cloud anywhere, and the sun was a relentless burning eye staring down at everything below. She reached around to grab her water bottle from its pocket on the side of her bag, hoping there was enough left to quench her sudden thirst. She stepped out into Rookery Way, one of the small streets that eventually led to Hargate Street, only to be greeted by a friendly *bip* – it was the horn of her dad's work van.

With a grin, she looked up to see him parked not too far away. The van was emblazoned with the words *Michael McGuire Plant Hire and Construction* and covered with mud and dirt. Rose saw her dad in the driver's seat, giving her a happy thumbs up. She checked for traffic before jogging across to pull open the passenger door and hop inside.

'How did you know I was here?' she asked as her dad reached over to give her a hug.

'Call it an old fella's intuition,' her dad replied

with a grin. 'I never liked going with the crowd either. So I took a guess you might be the same.'

Rose smiled at him as she pulled on her seatbelt. 'You guessed right.'

'So, milady,' Mr Darke said in his grandest voice as he set the van in motion, 'where to? Straight home or shall we take the scenic route?'

'Scenic route, for sure,' Rose replied, squashing back a guilty feeling. *I can go and visit Gracie and Nellie tomorrow*, she told herself. Her dad didn't often get a chance to collect her from school – this was a special treat.

But you need to tell them about the stone! shouted her inner voice.

Rose ignored it.

'Yes, ma'am.' Mr Darke pushed some buttons on the dashboard and cold air began to gush out of the vents. Rose sighed with relief. Her dad glanced over at her, his eyebrows raised. 'Some weather, isn't it?' he remarked, as they turned at the end of the road. He flipped his sun-visor down as he drove. 'The forecast didn't mention anything like this earlier.'

'It's *weird* weather,' Rose muttered, looking out at the world. Everything seemed bathed in yellow, like a strange filter had been placed in the sky.

'So, what sort of a day had you?' Mr Darke asked. When Rose didn't answer right away, Mr Darke glanced over again. 'Is everything all right?'

'Oh, you know,' Rose mumbled. 'Just the usual stuff.'

Mr Darke was silent for a moment. 'Is Emer McGuire bothering you?' he asked in a quiet voice.

'Dad, it's nothing,' Rose began. 'Really, I promise.'

'Is she why you go so far out of your way to get to school in the morning, love? And why you come home the long way too? Is it to avoid running into her at the main gate?' Her dad's voice was gentle.

Rose pressed her lips tight. '*No,*' she said, staring out the side window. *Why do parents have to* know *everything?* She'd thought her long way to school had been a secret.

Mr Darke grumbled a bit as he checked his mirrors to make another turn. 'I'll have a word with her father,' he said.

Rose turned to him, eyes wide. '*Please*, Dad, don't. It's fine, honestly. I'll – I'll sort it out with her myself tomorrow.'

Mr Darke darted a look at his daughter. 'All right.

But if you have any more trouble, love, you come to me. Right? You're not to put up with nonsense. Not from anyone.'

Rose swallowed hard. 'I know.'

'And *especially* not from a McGuire. You're not to take it, just because you're afraid it'll cause trouble for me.' Her dad met her eye again. 'I'll deal with Michael McGuire. I'm dealing with him for fifteen years at this stage.'

Just then there was the sound of a phone ringing. Mr Darke gave Rose an apologetic look as he tapped the hands-free headset in his ear.

'Johnny,' he said, greeting the person at the other end of the phone. 'Right. Yes. Right . . . I'll make my way back. No, – that's grand. Listen, can you give me an hour or so? I've to drop my daughter home first and then I'll be straight there. Right? Okay . . . Okay, Johnny. Thanks, now. Bye.' He tapped his ear again, muttering under his breath. 'Sorry, love,' he said, looking at Rose.

'Work?' Rose asked, gazing at him sympathetically.

'What else?' Her dad sighed. 'Let's get you home. I'll say hello to your mother, and then I have to head back to the site. Hopefully I won't be too late.'

'There's nothing wrong, is there?'

'Ah, no – nothing wrong, as such. Just busy. We've started a new job, the biggest one we've had – a massive excavation up Enniskillen direction. It's all hands on deck now for a while to get the work done.'

Rose nodded, not wanting to know any more. Her dad's job was something she didn't like to think about too much. All his company seemed to do was destroy things – uproot trees, divert waterways, wreck the land, and tear up the countryside so it could be replaced with houses, shopping centres and factories. She knew her dad needed the work, but she hated the price being paid for it. Her thoughts turned to her Science project, and Rose wondered if she could somehow tie it in to her dad's job. A small grin lifted the side of her mouth as she thought about Emer's face the day they handed in 'their' project – a critique of Michael McGuire and Co., and its lack of environmental protection policies . . .

Before too long, they were pulling into their road. Mr Darke glanced at the clock. 'Tell you what,' he said, looking at Rose. 'I'll just head straight on. Okay? Will you tell Mammy where I am?'

Rose nodded. 'Take care, Dad,' she said, leaning over to kiss him on the cheek.

'I'll see you before bedtime, sweetheart, with any luck. Right?'

Rose slipped out of her seat and closed the van door, and, just like that, her dad was gone. She watched the van disappear around a corner before she turned back towards the house.

'Was that your dad?' came her mother's voice from the kitchen as Rose opened the front door. Mrs Darke stood in the kitchen doorway, a tea towel in her hands. From somewhere behind her, Colm and Brian were screeching for their dinner. 'Is he all right?'

'He has to go back to the site for something,' Rose said, sliding her school bag off her back and down to the floor. 'He'll be home for bedtime.'

'Right.' Her mother sighed wearily, ducking back into the kitchen. 'Have I two *ogres* in here or is it my own two *baby boys*?' she called, as she walked towards the twins' highchairs. 'What's all the squawking about?'

The twins stayed crotchety all evening long – 'It's the heat,' Rose's mother said, sponging them down with a cool cloth as they sat in the bath – and Rose did her best to help. As her mother put the boys to bed, she tidied off the kitchen table and wiped it clean, and she'd almost finished putting away the twins' toys when her mother came downstairs, looking red-faced and exhausted.

'You're a pet,' Mrs Darke said, smiling at her daughter. 'Thank you, sweetheart.'

'I boiled the kettle too,' Rose said, straightening the raggedy old board books on the twins' bookshelf. 'If you want tea.'

Mrs Darke hummed as she busied herself in the kitchen, and Rose pulled out her school bag. She sat at the table and flipped through her books, wondering what to do first, before settling on her Science book and flicking to the section on climate. She pushed aside her half-joking thoughts about her dad's job from earlier, and tried to settle on a topic. Research for her project would need time at the library, or maybe using the internet on her mother's phone, but it couldn't hurt to start with her textbook. She read through the chapter, thinking about the day's weird weather, and, as she read, she realised what the strange, almost vicious heat earlier had reminded her of.

The stone. Rose lifted her eyes from the book,

her heart suddenly picking up pace. The stone – the *tathlum* – had that same sickening, feverish warmth. *And it was so sudden*, Rose thought, *almost like something that's just been set free . . .*

She looked back at her textbook, trying to take in a diagram explaining the carbon cycle, but after a few minutes' staring at it, she realised it wasn't going in.

Finally, she shook her head and slapped the book shut. Time to tackle History instead.

'Do you know anything about the Iron Age, Mam?' Rose asked Mrs Darke. Her mother was sitting in the easy chair by the back door, quietly knitting.

'Not a thing, love,' Mrs Darke said cheerily. 'I never had a head for dates or anything like that in school.'

'I've to write a page on the treasures of Iron Age Ireland for History,' Rose sighed. She began to flick through the pages of her book, hoping it would inspire her.

Mrs Darke counted her stitches before replying. 'Read out the pages from your book there, and I'll ask you questions afterwards. Maybe that'll help you find a way to start.'

Rose cleared her throat and did as her mother asked. 'The Broighter Hoard,' she began. 'The finest trove of Irish Iron Age art ever found, consists of a model boat made entirely of gold, several necklaces and torcs of different types, the most impressive of which is the Broighter Collar, and a bowl or model cauldron –' Rose's voice faltered, and she fell silent.

'Go on,' Mrs Darke said, her needles click-clacking. 'I was getting interested in that.'

Rose licked her lips. 'A bowl or model cauldron, which may have had ritualistic significance.' She blinked, looking over at her mother. 'What does that mean?'

'It means the cauldron was something they would have used in a ceremony,' her mother answered, frowning at her knitting. 'Something important, not because the actual object itself was important, but because it represented something else. Something bigger.' She looked up at her daughter. 'Maybe it had some connection to the cauldrons you'd hear about in myths, like the one belonging to the Dagda.'

Rose's jaw dropped. 'The *what*?'

Mrs Darke shrugged and kept knitting. 'We had a book of Irish myths and legends at home when I was a kid – your mamó bought it for me and Uncle Ger when we were little. It might be here in the house somewhere. Ger's favourite story was the one about the Mac Tíre – the mighty wolf-warrior who's buried under the Hill of Tara. But I always liked the Dagda. In the book, he was drawn to look a bit like Santa. Big and round and always laughing.' Mrs Darke smiled at the memory.

'And his treasure was the cauldron,' Rose said, suddenly feeling dizzy as all the strange spheres of her life began to overlap, right here in her own kitchen.

'I can't remember now what the others were,' Mrs Darke said, pulling on her knitting to check its tension. She frowned as she thought. 'But I know there were four.'

'The spear,' Rose whispered. 'The stone. And the Sword of Light.'

Mrs Darke's eyes opened wide. 'Exactly!' she said, looking delighted. 'Did you do them in school?'

Rose gave her mother a weak smile. 'Yes,' she said. 'That's it.'

'Well, now, there you are,' Mrs Darke said, getting to her feet. 'I'm just going to check on the lads.

But you could write your page about the treasures in your book, and then mention the treasures from the legends too. Like a comparison or something. Would that be good?' Rose nodded, and Mrs Darke opened the kitchen door. 'I'll have a read of what you've done when I get back. Right, love?' She vanished into the hallway, closing the door behind her.

Rose couldn't move. Eventually, she picked up her pen but it felt like her fingers were too stiff to hold it. Finally, she began to write.

She'd just finished the page when her mother came back downstairs holding a slender hard-covered book, which she gently placed in front of Rose. *Old Irish Myths and Legends*, read the title. Rose picked up the book and began to leaf through it. The dust jacket was torn and faded, but the pages inside were still clear and easy to read. The illustrations leaped from the pages. *To Gerard and Marcella, with love forever from Mammy*, Rose read – her mamó's handwriting on the title page. Her eyes filled with tears, which she quickly squished back before her mother saw them.

'Here you go,' Mrs Darke said, stroking Rose's

head. 'Sorry I was so long upstairs. I went rooting around for this.'

'Can I read it?' Rose asked, looking up at her mother.

'It's yours now, sweetheart,' Mrs Darke said, bending to kiss Rose on the forehead. 'You can do whatever you like with it. But you'll probably know all the stories anyway. Your mamó loved the old tales, and she used to tell them to you when you were younger – same as she did for Uncle Gerard and me.' Mrs Darke gave a sad smile, her gaze far away. 'Until we all got too big and cool and grown-up to listen to her, of course.'

'I miss her so much,' Rose said, blinking hard.

'I do too, darling girl,' said Mrs Darke, her eyes shining. She stroked Rose's cheek very gently. 'But we have her stories, and that's the way she'd like us to remember her, I think.'

Just as Rose carefully closed the book, she heard the sound of her dad unlocking the front door. She stood in the kitchen doorway, looking down the hall at him as he balanced on one foot and then the other, taking off his heavy work boots. He was covered in grime and concrete dust, his eyes like two holes in the dirt.

'The swamp monster's home,' he gurgled, waving his arms like tentacles, and Rose gave him a fond grin. Her dad returned it. 'Just let me go and get this washed off, pet.' He vanished up the stairs, and Rose heard the floorboards creak as he peeked in at the twins before making his way to the bathroom.

Mrs Darke set the oven to warm, and she and Rose retreated to the sitting room. Rose had the book of myths in her hand, almost like she was afraid to let it go. She settled herself in the corner of the sofa as her mam switched the television on.

Mrs Darke sat in her armchair and, a few minutes later, just as the jingle for the news was beginning to play, Mr Darke came in too, smelling like soap. Rose leaned her head against his shoulder as he sat beside her on the sofa. He had his plate of dinner in one hand, and he balanced it on his knee as he ate.

'Tonight's headlines,' the newsreader began, as the screen showed a woman wearing large sunglasses and a fancy scarf that not only covered her entire head, but was also pulled up over her mouth, being led out of the High Court in Dublin. A man wearing a very smart suit extended his arm to help her into a waiting car. It looked sleek and expensive, as did the woman herself. 'Major court victory for prominent developer in land ownership case,' the newsreader continued, as the car drove away.

Mrs Darke looked at her husband. 'Is that the thing you were telling me about?'

'What thing?' Rose asked.

Mr Darke swallowed a mouthful of dinner. 'That's it,' he confirmed, pointing at the television with his fork. Mrs Darke turned the volume down as he continued. 'Kathleen Ennis. Madame Moneybags herself. My new boss,' he said, looking at Rose. 'Remember that huge job I told you we'd started? Well –' he waved a fork at the screen again, even though the news had moved on to the next headline – 'it's her job. She's planning a new town, I believe, and she's faced down massive opposition. Archaeologists, specialists, you name it. They all had it in for her. But it seems she's won.' Mr Darke shrugged, shovelling in another mouthful of food.

'So it's good news for us?' Mrs Darke said.

'At least a two-year contract, love,' Mr Darke said to his wife, jabbing a potato with his fork.

'Well, hallelujah for that,' Mrs Darke said. 'A bit of good luck, at last.'

Mr Darke turned up the volume again as the newsreader began to talk about the Kathleen Ennis case. Rose couldn't stop staring at the woman on the television screen.

And somewhere deep inside her, very faintly, a tiny alarm bell started to ring.

8

Nellie's sweet-shop looked deserted. Rose had hurried down Hargate Street as fast as she could, hoping she'd have a chance before school to tell her and Gracie everything that had happened since the day before – but now it looked like Nellie wasn't even here.

Rose stopped to catch her breath. Even though it was early, the day was already building up to be hot. She took off her school jumper and tied it around her waist.

Nellie's hanging baskets swung in the warm breeze and one of them bumped lightly off Rose's arm as she stood peering into Nellie's shop window. The plants in the basket looked a little dried up; the once-silver petals were dull and shrivelled. Rose stuck a finger into the soil. It was dry and dusty.

'You guys need a drink, don't you?' she whispered,

reaching around for her water bottle. 'I wonder why Nellie hasn't had a chance to look after you today.' She swallowed back a sense of unease as she unscrewed the lid of the bottle and began to pour some water into the hanging basket.

Instantly the flowers inside the basket revived, their petals becoming plump and sleek again, filling with silver and unfurling slowly. Several of them turned in Rose's direction, as though they were looking at her, and she stared at them in fascination. 'Hi,' she whispered.

She used the last of her water on the flowers in the next basket, and soon there was a profusion of blooms around Nellie's doorway. Rose gave a satisfied nod as she put the cap back on her bottle before turning her attention to the shop once again. She knocked on the door, gently at first and then more loudly. 'Hello?' she called, trying the handle. The door was firmly locked and didn't budge. Then, to her surprise, she felt something rubbing itself against her shins. With a gasp, she looked down to see Catshee, twining himself between her feet. She stumbled slightly, her hand still on the door, as Catshee batted his paw against the lower pane. Silently, the door opened, just wide enough, and Catshee slipped through. He stopped in the middle of the floor, turning back to look at Rose expectantly.

'O-kay,' Rose murmured.

She entered the sweet-shop and carefully closed the door behind her, barely noticing that the bell didn't give its usual *ting*. There was still no sign of Nellie, but Catshee went straight for the kitchen door, nudging it with his head until it opened a crack. Rose tiptoed towards him, but just as she was about to push the door open fully, she realised there were voices coming from the room beyond. Not knowing what else to do, she froze in place, her bottle still awkwardly clutched in her fist. Catshee curled himself into a warm, thrumming heap on top of her foot.

'Are you sure of it?' a woman's voice was saying. Rose didn't recognise the speaker.

'There'd be no reason for her to be on Toraigh otherwise,' Nellie replied.

Rose leaned forward silently, peering into the kitchen through the cracked-open door. A man and a woman, both of them robed and surrounded by light, as was Nellie herself, sat at the table. Between them the teapot steamed, tracing its messages in the air. Rose held her breath. Whoever these people were, they were magical – like Nellie and Gracie. She frowned as she thought about Gracie – there was no sign of him, and Rose couldn't help but wonder where he was.

'Cethlenn's a crafty one and no mistake,' said the man.

'It's an ancient magic, and terrible,' Nellie said, sighing heavily. 'And for it she needs the clay of his birthplace – the soil of Toraigh.'

'The island where Balor was born,' murmured the woman. 'So, it's really true, then? What we've long feared?'

'The Seandraíocht is low,' the man said mournfully. 'Not gone, thank the Dagda, but not strong. It might be that it's just weak enough for Cethlenn to see her chance.'

'And if she has his resting place, and the soil of his birth . . .' Nellie let her words trail off.

'It's only a matter of time before he rises,' the other woman said, her gentle eyes troubled and sad.

'We should have been better prepared,' the man said. 'The ice giants have guarded Toraigh valiantly, but Cethlenn has grown in strength. In silence and darkness, she has turned into a foe of terrible power. They were unprepared.'

'And, considering that, they fought with mighty courage,' the woman said, placing a hand on the man's arm. 'I mourn their loss, Aengus.'

'As do I, Brigid,' the man said. 'As do I.'

Rose felt Catshee's weight lift off her foot, and she looked down to see the not-cat swishing his way across the sweet-shop floor, heading for the outer door once more. He paused halfway across, fixing Rose with his steady, unblinking gaze, his magnificent ears uncurling.

'What is it?' she whispered, creeping towards him. She kneeled, Catshee's eyes filling her mind. The not-cat rubbed himself against Rose's arm, and before she knew it she had picked him up.

The next thing Rose was aware of was the feeling of being bashed on the arm again by one of Nellie's hanging baskets. She jerked, fully alert, to realise she was back outside the shop. Catshee was at her feet, preening himself, completely unconcerned with her confusion. She looked down at the empty water bottle in her hand, and then at the plump silver petals of the flowers in the basket beside her, wondering if the heat had somehow made her dehydrated and –

'Rose, mo chroí, what a lovely surprise,' came

Nellie's voice, pulling her out of her thoughts. The old lady stood in the sweet-shop doorway, holding it open to welcome her in. Rose met her eye. Nellie's face was warm and kind as usual, but she looked tired and care-worn, her eyes watery around the rims, and Rose's heart lurched. She glanced down at Catshee, who was still staring up at her, his eyes cautious. Rose understood. *Whatever just happened*, she thought, *I can't let Nellie know I overheard her conversation.*

She looked back at her friend, who was examining her hanging baskets. 'Nellie, I have to tell you something. Is Gracie here?'

Nellie's expression crumpled very slightly. 'He isn't, love. He's away on business of his own. Whatever you have to tell, you can tell me alone. But first –' she reached out to usher Rose through the door – 'we'd better fill that bottle of yours up again. I can't have someone minding my plants and me not minding them in return.' Nellie shuffled through her shop and down into the sunken kitchen. There was no sign of the man and woman who had been here moments before; all that remained was the ever-present golden sunlight streaming through the panelled windows,

114

and at the end of the garden, sheltered by the hedge, sat the hillock and its cauldron. Nellie placed Rose's bottle beneath an ancient-looking black spout that stuck out over her sink. She pulled a handle and water began to flow, crystal-clear. In a blink, the bottle was full again, and Nellie handed it back.

'It's from my own well,' Nellie said. 'You'll not taste better. So. What do you need to tell me, little one?' The old lady resumed her seat at the table and Rose settled into a chair. She hauled her school bag onto her lap, pushing her bottle back into its pocket. The teapot was on its stand, steam curling from its spout like it was freshly filled; it smelled like Nellie had something wonderful baking in the range. If Rose had the choice, she would have stayed exactly where she was for the rest of the day, but she knew she couldn't.

She drew in a deep breath and began.

'It's the stone,' Rose said. Her heart began to stutter, feeling like it was missing beats, and she wondered if she had the courage to continue. 'Nellie, – I've lost it. I'm sorry.'

For a moment, Nellie didn't react. She stared at Rose, not saying anything. 'Gone?' she finally whispered, her watery eyes filling.

Rose shook her head. 'No,' she said. 'I know where it is. Or, I know who has it. But I don't know if I can get it back.'

Nellie shuddered, placing her elbows on the table and resting her head in her hands as she gathered herself. 'Well. That's something. Can you try, do you think?'

Rose nodded. She sucked hard on her lower lip, feeling it sting. 'I can try,' she said.

'Good girl,' Nellie said. She reached forward and took Rose's hands in her own, squeezing them gently as she spoke. 'The stone's important, Rose. It's *vital*. And while I know the Dagda has his eye on all that goes on, and he's doing his best to help, he can't do everything himself.' Nellie met Rose's eye. Her gaze was piercing. 'He needs our help. He needs *your* help. You were chosen to this task, so I know you can do it.'

Rose blinked hard. 'Okay,' she whispered.

Nellie glanced at the clock. 'Gracie's not here to do his trick with the time,' she said. 'And I'm afraid my own talents lie in a different realm to his. So, today, you're going to have to mind you're not late for school.' Nellie tried to smile, but Rose could see the dark cloud in her eyes. 'I don't want your teachers turning up at my door and accusing me of being a bad influence.'

Rose returned Nellie's smile, even though the feelings that brewed in her chest were anything but happy, and as they got to their feet Nellie pulled Rose into a hug. Rose wrapped her arms around Nellie's stout frame. 'I'm sorry about the last time I was here,' she said into Nellie's shoulder. 'I shouldn't have run away.'

Nellie released her from the embrace enough to look her in the eye. 'Gracie and I shouldn't have given you so much to deal with all at once,' she said. 'The fault is ours, stóirín, not yours.' She stroked Rose's cheek. 'You're a great girl, Rosaleen Darke. I think the Seandraíocht chose well when it chose you. It can always tell when a person has the touch of the Silver Road in them.'

Rose felt her stomach swoop inside her, a mix of nerves and fear. 'Can you tell me more about the Silver Road, Nellie? Is there time?'

Nellie glanced at the clock again. 'We can do our best. Let's go into the shop while we talk.'

Rose picked up her bag and followed the shuffle

117

of Nellie's slippers as the old woman made her way around the back of her sweet counter. She put some cróigíní into a paper wrapper before twirling it around by the corners, sealing it shut. As she placed it into Rose's hand, Nellie nodded towards the front of her shop. 'Outside that window there runs one of the branches of the Silver Road. But as to what it *is* . . . well, it's like a gigantic net, you could say, placed over the entire island of Ireland. Not one you can see or touch, but one made of old, well-woven magic.' Nellie paused, looking urgently at Rose, as if willing her to believe what she was saying. 'You might remember me telling you about Hargate Street's true name – Bóthar na hAirgead, the Silver Road. Very few now are left who remember the reason why it had that name.' As Nellie continued, she began to smile. 'If you could see Ireland from above – like you were an eagle, Rose, if you can imagine that – the Silver Road would look like a million shining rivers, old Ways of magic, all connected, all across the country. And it's there to protect us all, and the land, from anything . . . well, anything *nasty*. Anything unpleasant.'

'Anything . . . bad?' Rose said, sliding the bag of sweets into her trouser pocket. Her mind turned to the conversation she'd overheard between Nellie, Aengus and Brigid.

Nellie nodded, her smile fading. 'Anything bad. It's an ancient enchantment put there by the Tuatha Dé Danann many centuries before you were born – nearly four thousand years ago, all told. Though I remember it, a little.' Nellie twinkled at her. 'A great day it was, and a bright day. I still dream about it.'

Rose swallowed hard, choosing not to think too deeply about what Nellie had just said. 'And some of that magic is in *me*?'

Nellie shrugged, wiping down the counter with a cloth. 'There's a bit of it in all of us,' she said. 'Though there's more of it in some. You're one of the lucky ones, maybe.'

Rose snorted. *Lucky.* 'Right.'

'It used to be unbreakable and unbroken,' Nellie continued. Her eyes looked past Rose now, over Rose's shoulder and into the landscape of her own thoughts. 'Once, the Silver Road would have protected us from all harm. But then there came the death of the old stories, the lack of faith in the old beliefs, and the Seandraíocht began to falter. And next came machines and roads and cities and *noise*, and the old Ways were broken and dug up, the rivers re-routed, the forests felled. Finally, the Silver Road began to suffer. It began to weaken. Holes were torn in its ancient net, and through those holes dark and dangerous things crept – things that would have been better off staying where they were put.' Nellie's voice dropped to a murmur. Rose wondered if she'd forgotten she was even there. 'And now the time has come when the worst of those buried things is rising close to the surface again, his malignancy already seeping back into the world. If he comes, he will bring destruction and terror, famine and war, and his breath will be like fire and death over the land.'

Rose shivered at these words. 'Nellie? Are you okay?'

Nellie shook herself. 'What's that saying?' the old lady said, her voice bright once more. 'Someone walked over my grave? That must be what happened.' Nellie tried to laugh, starting to wipe her counter again.

'This bad thing, rising up. Is it – is that Balor?'

Nellie's mouth was a grim, tight line. 'I'm only rambling, stóirín. Don't pay any heed of me.'

'But you said – things being dug up, and things

being built, sort of *tore* the Old Magic? Is that what you meant?'

Nellie's eyes met Rose's again, and they were dark with sadness. 'If that's what I said, then that's what I meant,' she replied.

Rose thought about Kathleen Ennis, the strange woman from last night's news. *She's building something huge, isn't she?* 'Would someone digging up enough land to build a new town be a problem? For the Silver Road, I mean? It's just . . . my dad. His job, or – well, his *boss*. They've started a new project and it's going to mean huge excavations. Not far from here.'

Nellie blinked wearily at Rose. 'I'll tell Gracie about that and see what he thinks,' the old lady said. 'It wouldn't be good news, now, I'll be honest.'

'That's not what my mam thinks,' Rose said, her heart heavy with guilt. *Dad's work does so much damage*, she thought, not for the first time. *All that destruction – for what?*

'It depends on where you're standing, I suppose,' Nellie replied. From the kitchen, the sound of the grandfather clock chiming the quarter-hour could be heard, and Nellie met Rose's eye. 'You'd better get on, young lady,' Nellie said. 'But come back soon, won't you?' A cloud of worry crossed her face, but not quickly enough for Rose to miss it. 'And do your best to get the stone back, if you can. We must try to keep ahead of things, and the stone's our best chance at that.' Nellie tried to smile, keeping her words light; Rose knew the old lady was trying not to show her own fear, or make Rose afraid. She swallowed back her nerves as she held Nellie's gaze. 'But come again soon to visit old Gracie and me.'

Rose briefly returned her smile. 'I will. Thank you for the water. And the sweets.'

'May they come in handy,' Nellie said. 'They might even help you get the stone back. You never know.'

'Yeah,' Rose said, shouldering her bag. Emer McGuire's smug face flashed across her mind and she shoved it firmly out. 'Maybe.' She pushed open the door to Nellie's shop and stepped out into the street, waving goodbye.

'She's only a girl, Rosaleen, with sorrows of her own,' Nellie's voice seemed to say, as the door closed behind Rose. 'She's no better than you, and nor will she ever be.'

'What?' Rose pushed the door open again, but the shop was deserted. The cloth sat on the counter, but there was no sign of the old lady. 'Nellie?' Rose called, but there was no reply.

Rose pulled her head back out through the door and let it close one more time. Then, she took off for school at a run, hoping she'd make it without a late note going into her record.

She skidded through school reception at two minutes to nine, ignoring the shouts of the secretary to stop running on school property, and pelted down the corridor to her first class. Eventually she found herself at the door. It was closed, which meant the teacher had already arrived. *Fantastic*, Rose thought, leaning her head on the wood for a moment. Finally, she took a breath, and pushed it open.

Emer's smirk was all Rose could see as she entered the room. She tried to ignore it. 'Sorry,' she said, glancing at her teacher as she hurried towards her seat.

'You're lucky I haven't taken attendance yet,' came the teacher's reply. 'Hurry up, now.' Gratefully, Rose slid into her chair and pushed her school bag to the floor.

When lunchtime came, Rose found she was ravenous. All her usual haunts were crowded with other students taking refuge from the heat – every scrap of shade was full, but she finally managed to find a bit of grass to perch on. She tore through her sandwiches, savouring every drop of the still-cold water from Nellie's well and, as she was putting her lunchbox away, a shriek of familiar laughter rose, drawing her attention. She looked up to see Emer and her gang on the shaded side of the yard.

Nellie's worried face, and the feel of her soft, work-worn hands, filled Rose's mind. She'd tried to downplay things, Rose knew – but Rose also knew that Nellie was afraid. And not only Nellie, but her friends too. She closed her eyes, breathing hard, wishing she could just forget about all this stuff – but she knew she couldn't. The only person who could get the stone back was her. She remembered the water in the Dagda's cauldron, the sight of Nellie and Gracie in their true forms as they stood in Nellie's kitchen, and the disdainful Catshee with his incredible ears. All of it would be for nothing if she failed. *The Seandraíocht chose me*, Rose told herself. *I've got to do this*. She opened her eyes again and stared at Emer for a few long moments, watching her snap selfies on the phone she wasn't supposed to have, and share jokes with the fawning members of her fan club.

Finally, she was ready to get to her feet.

As she brushed grass off her school trousers, Rose remembered: she had cróigíní in her pocket. With a smile, she slid her fingers into the packet Nellie had given her earlier, and placed a couple of courage-drops on her tongue. They settled into her like the warmth of a gentle hug as she made her way across the yard.

'Emer,' she said, once she reached the outskirts of the fan club. 'Can I speak to you?'

Emer ignored her just long enough for Rose to begin gathering courage to speak again. 'I don't know,' she finally said. '*Can* you?'

Rose frowned in irritation. 'I need to talk to you about yesterday,' she said. 'About – the thing you took from me.'

'What thing?' Emer snapped. Her eyes were harder than usual. She sat forward, uncrossing her long legs as she stood up.

'You know what I mean,' Rose continued, fighting hard not to lose her nerve as Emer walked towards her. The courage-drops surged in her blood, and she drew on their strength, refusing to take a step back. 'The – the stone that fell out of my pocket.'

'Finders keepers, Rosie-Roo,' Emer sang. 'Looks to me like that stone *wanted* to be found. It sure didn't want to stay in your pocket, anyway.'

Rose cocked an eyebrow. 'It's a *stone*,' she said. 'It doesn't *want* stuff.'

Emer's eyes gleamed. 'I wouldn't be so sure.'

Rose shook her head. 'Look, this is stupid. I've got to have it back, okay? I need it.'

Emer snorted. 'You want it back? Fine. How about we see who deserves to have it? After school today, right? You and me, four o'clock, down by the well. Do we have a deal?'

Rose flicked her gaze around the fan club, who were sitting still and quiet at Emer's back. None of them spoke and all of them were looking at her. Finally, she pulled herself back to Emer's face. 'Four o'clock,' she repeated.

Emer gave one last smirk before turning away. 'Don't be late, shrimp-face,' she said. 'I'll be waiting.'

9

Rose's head ached as she left school – by the front gate this time, as today it didn't matter about trying to avoid Emer and her gang. She wasn't sure if her headache was from the heat, or because she was worried about what was facing her, or a combination of the two. She hadn't been to the well in more years than she could count – it was a place, not far from the school, where the river that meandered through Carriganawn slowed and gathered into a reedy pool underneath a tall, grassy bank. The last time she'd been there she'd been a tiny kid, sitting on her dad's shoulders as they looked for water monsters and green-toothed witches. She had no idea why Emer wanted to bring her there, or what she planned to do, but Rose knew she had no choice but to show up. The sun beat mercilessly on her head as she walked, and she hurried her steps, hoping there'd be shade or at least coolness down by the water.

There was shade, but there was also Emer, who was waiting for her.

'So, you're here,' she said, as Rose stepped off the path and down across the grassy riverbank.

'I'm here,' Rose replied. She pushed her hands into her trouser pockets, making sure there were a couple of courage-drops left. She hoped she wouldn't need them.

'All right. Tell me why I should give you back this stone, weirdo,' Emer said, leaning her weight on one leg and slowly folding her arms. She stared down at Rose, her brown eyes narrowed, her shiny black box braids pulled over one shoulder, cascading down her front.

'I told you. It's important,' Rose said. 'Someone special gave it to me.'

'Who?' Emer sneered. 'Your *granny*? Or whatever stupid name you used for her?'

Rose blinked hard. 'It wasn't from my mamó. Someone else.'

'Is it worth money?'

Rose gave her an incredulous look. 'No? It's literally a *stone*.'

Emer shrugged as she looked away past Rose and back towards the road. 'I don't want to give it to you, right? I like having it around. It . . . makes me feel good.' She faced Rose once more, her eyes hard and pitiless. 'It makes me feel strong. Or, like, *important*. I don't know how to say it.'

'That's – That's because it has a power,' Rose began, trying to find the words to make Emer understand without giving away too much. 'It's not always a good power.' She tried to recall what Gracie had said about it back in Nellie's kitchen.

The stone is neither good nor evil in itself, though it has allowed itself to be used by both in times gone past. Perhaps it bends a little more to the bad than to the good . . . All it wants is to destroy.

'It's dangerous, Emer, and it might hurt you if you keep it. That's all.'

Emer snorted quietly. 'It might hurt me,' she repeated. 'And why do you care?'

Rose blinked at her, genuinely confused. 'I don't want anyone to be hurt,' she said. 'Of course I care.'

Emer tilted her head. 'You *don't* care,' she said

quietly. Rose saw her eyes lose their focus for a second. 'How could you care? Nobody cares about me. Not really.'

'What? Come on, Emer. Your parents –'

Emer's gaze hardened again. 'You're such a *creep*,' she said, moving closer to Rose. 'No wonder the stone didn't want to stay with you. Soft-hearted do-gooder weirdo.'

Rose tried not to move, even though every instinct told her to get away. 'I was given the stone to take care of it,' she said. 'Please, Emer, I really do need it back.'

'You were supposed to take care of it? Well, you didn't do a great job of it, did you?' Emer said, her tone bright, just as Rose heard a shuffling in the undergrowth behind her. She whirled to see three of Emer's fan club standing there, each of them looking like they were trying not to laugh. One of them – the red-haired girl, Rachel – had a mobile phone held out at arm's length, which she was using to film everything that was going on. Rose's heart began to pound.

'I can't believe you're actually *here*,' one of them said.

'Right, I'm tired of all this,' Emer said, tossing her braids back over her shoulder. 'Chuck her in. Go on.'

Rose turned to her, eyes wide with fear. 'What?'

The other girls looked at Emer, too. 'Yeah,' one said. '*What?*'

'You heard me!' Emer snapped, staring at her friends. 'I said chuck – her – in. Throw this idiot into the well. Let her explain her wet clothes to her *mammy and daddy.*' She sneered the last three words, twisting up her face as she spoke, but Rose could see a deep hurt in her eyes too – a hurt that spoke of loneliness and jealousy.

Emer's friends looked at one another. 'I don't think we should, though,' Rachel said. She glanced at Rose briefly before flicking her gaze back to Emer.

'Yeah, me neither, Emer,' said the third girl. Rose thought her name was Mairéad. 'I thought we were just going to have a bit of fun. I don't want to hurt anyone.'

Emer stared at her gang. 'You're *all* idiots,' she said. Her voice was hard, and something about it sounded different, like Emer was pretending to be someone else. Her friends took a step back from her, their mouths falling open in shock and anger, looking at one another in disbelief.

Rose took a step closer to Emer. 'Why are you

doing this?' she said. 'Why are you picking on me, and why won't you give me back my stuff?'

'I told you,' Emer replied, looming over Rose. 'I found it, so it's *my* stuff now. You don't even need it but I do. *I* do. Right? So you're not having it back.'

'Emer, you don't understand! If you don't give it back to me, something *terrible* is going to happen.'

'Oh, give it a rest!' Emer laughed, but there was no humour in it. 'You're not that *important*, Rosie-Roo. Believe me. And you're not having anything from me. And if you're not getting chucked in the well –' she pulled her mobile phone out of her skirt pocket – 'then we've got to find a different punishment for you. Don't we?'

Rose looked at her. 'What are you talking about?'

Emer unlocked her phone and pressed it to her ear. She scrunched up her face and started to sob – it was frighteningly realistic. 'Mum?' she said, after a minute, into the phone. Her breath caught as she fought not to cry. 'Mummy? Are you there?'

Rose looked at the fan club. They glanced guiltily at her, and then back to Emer again. Rachel seemed shifty and uncomfortable but she kept her phone in her hand, filming what was happening, just like Emer must've told her to. Rose glared at her, incredulous. Even now, when Emer was acting this weirdly, her fan club *still* couldn't step in and stand up to her?

'Mum, I'm down at the well. Will you come and pick me up? I'm – Mum, I'm all wet.' Emer sobbed. 'It was Rose Darke, Mum. She threw me in.'

'What?' Rose shouted.

Emer covered the mouthpiece, muffling it. 'Will you tell Dad? Tell Daddy, please. I want him to come home,' Emer said, her voice strained. 'Hurry up, Mum, won't you?'

She cut the call and stared at Rose, a triumphant look on her face. 'You'd better not be here when my mum arrives, Rosie-Roo,' Emer said, taking a step backwards, and then another, getting closer to the edge of the well. She kept her phone held high, away from the water. 'And your dad had better find a good excuse if he wants to keep his job.'

Rose watched in horror as Emer took one last step, dropping down the bank and into the well. The water only came up to her knees, making her school skirt billow around her legs, but Rose felt sick with fear. With one last look at the fan club – who seemed as confused as she was – and the sound of Emer's laughter in her ears, Rose turned and ran up the bank towards the road, her legs trembling. She hurried up the hill, sweating uncomfortably in her school uniform, feeling like the entire world was too loud, too hot, too bright, scanning the cars that passed in case one of them was being driven by Mrs McGuire – or, worse, Mr McGuire. She was already really late for the childminder, and if she didn't hurry Rose knew Mrs O'Leary would ring her mother at work, and then there really *would* be trouble.

By the time she reached Mrs O'Leary's, Rose felt like she'd crossed the Sahara Desert while wearing a hat made of tinfoil. 'Come in here! Oh my God, will you look at the state of you?' the childminder fussed, sponging down Rose's face with a cold cloth. 'Your mother will be *raging* if she sees you like this. What were you thinking?'

When Mrs Darke came to collect them, Mrs O'Leary explained that Rose had gone for a walk after school and that she'd been late, and Rose knew she'd have questions to answer later – but by the time she got home, she had a headache so intense that she could barely see.

'Up to bed with you, now,' said her mother.

'And keep this ice pack on your head. I'll be up to you as soon as I've sorted out the boys. Honestly, Rose! What sort of an idea was that, going walking in weather like this? I don't know what I'm going to do with you.'

Rose muttered her apologies as she crawled up the stairs. Her head was thumping, and the cold compress didn't help much. She lay back on her pillow and tried to think, but no matter what she came up with, there were no answers to any of her problems. She tried to think about them one at a time in the hope they'd seem less daunting, but it didn't do much. First things first: the stone. She knew now she'd never get it back by asking – it seemed to be exerting some sort of power over Emer, making her even more insufferable than usual. But she knew she needed to try again, and again and again if need be, and that was before she even considered how she was going to save her father's job . . . Eventually all these half-baked thoughts turned into a swirling mass of colours and sounds that began to drain away, like water down a plughole.

She sat up, consumed with the feeling that she had to go and talk to Nellie and Gracie – but pain spiked through her head as she moved, and Rose flopped back down onto her bed, her head thumping so hard it made her feel like throwing up. She closed her eyes, replaced the cold compress and tried to relax.

After that, all she knew was darkness.

When she woke, Rose recognised the shapes of her own bedroom – but there was a person sitting in the chair in the corner.

Rose sat up, her head instantly throbbing – but the pain wasn't as bad as before.

The person in the chair started into consciousness, and Rose saw that it was her mother. 'You're awake,' her mother whispered, sitting forward to take Rose's hands. 'I was so worried, Rosaleen.' Mrs Darke's head sank forward onto their joined hands.

Rose glanced at the clock. It read quarter to six. 'Is it morning?'

'I've taken the day off work,' Mrs Darke said, lifting her head to gaze at her daughter. 'I was supposed to be in at seven, but I've got someone to cover me.'

'I'm sorry, Mam,' Rose whispered. 'I'm okay. Honestly.'

Mrs Darke felt Rose's forehead. 'You do feel much

better than you did last night,' she admitted. 'But it's all arranged now. Dad has to go into work today anyway, so it's better if I'm here.'

Rose felt a jolt of something that seemed to be a mixture of surprise and relief. *He hasn't been fired – not yet.* 'I thought this was his weekend off?'

Mrs Darke shrugged. 'This Kathleen Ennis woman has them all driven round the bend, it seems,' she said. 'She's pushing them for progress at any cost, and they really are working around the clock to get her what she wants.' She paused to sigh. 'Money truly does talk, I suppose.'

'I wonder what the rush is,' Rose said. She tried to put things together but her brain felt sticky and mushy still. She felt like there were parts of this mystery that she didn't understand yet. *Things Nellie and Gracie aren't telling me*, she realised. *But, thanks to Catshee, I know more than I'm supposed to.*

She settled herself back down on her pillow as her mam clambered in to lie beside her. They arranged the bedspread around themselves and Mrs Darke quickly fell into a doze, but Rose was wide awake. Gently, so as not to wake her mother, Rose sat up once more.

She looked at her bedside locker and the first thing

to catch her eye was the book her mam had given her – the one with her mamó's handwriting on the title page. Rose glanced at the photo of Mamó on her bedside locker, breathing hard against the ache in her heart, and then she looked back at the book. *Old Irish Myths and Legends* read the title, and beneath it was a beautiful illustration of a young man with flowing red-gold hair, wearing something like a leather cord tied around his head, holding a hurl. A huge long-haired dog with an intelligent face stood beside him – probably a wolfhound. Rose stroked the cover of the book and flipped it open.

She scanned the contents page, her eyes skipping over the stories. *From Setanta to Cúchulainn*, said one; *Queen Maeve and Ailill Come to Blows over a Bull*, said another.

Now, she heard, inside her head. Her Mamó's voice. *Come here till I tell you a story . . .*

Rose blinked hard, but two tears escaped anyway, rolling down to pool beneath her chin. 'I'm coming, Mamó,' she whispered, wiping the tears away with her fingers. 'I'm listening.'

Finally her questing eyes found what they'd been looking for. She read the words that seemed to catch on a hook deep inside herself, like a fish being reeled in and landed, and her mamó's voice, rich and soft, gentle and slow, filled her mind.

The Tale of Balor of the Evil Eye.

All these stories, Rose knew, were part of *her* story already, part of the story she'd shared with Mamó, even if she couldn't remember all their details, and some of the answers she needed were in here – they had to be.

If there was a way to defeat Balor, even without the stone, then maybe it was here, waiting to be found.

Rose drew a deep breath. She glanced at her mother, but Mrs Darke was sleeping deeply now. Rose knew she didn't have long before the boys were awake, clamouring for food and attention.

So she opened the book and started to read.

In a pit not far from Enniskillen, under the stars, stood a witch. Soil trickled through the witch's fingers, staining her skin like oil, and she smiled to see it – though her teeth were jagged like blades and her eyes were lit with a terrible gleam.

'Ar ais, arís,' she whispered, taking another handful

of earth – the dirt of Toraigh, which had nourished and grown the god beneath the ground, the one she had loved so dearly in life, and even more so in death. 'Tar ar ais orm,' she said, as the earth sprinkled down, mingling with the soil of his burial place, his resting place, which would not hold him much longer.

Not if she had anything to do with it.

She focused her energy on the ground under her feet, her toes digging into the softness of it, feeling their way between the scattered rocks and roots and bones. Her claw-like fingers spread wide, her fingernails growing monstrously long, and she plunged them into the soil with vicious strength, pulling the ground apart. Again and again she raked at the dirt, burrowing down, disturbing the earth and all who slept in it, magic crackling from her like electricity. She braced herself, concentrating, pushing her power into the ground as hard as she could, until the effort of it made her gasp with exhaustion – but moments later she relaxed, her expression satisfied. Deep underground she felt the power of her spell gathering like a pool; it crept through the cracks as water does, searching for a root to nourish. She closed her eyes and, through her magic, saw the slumbering forms of the creatures who lay here – the unimaginably huge shapes of the one-eyed god and his servants, themselves giants, who had been buried with him. The witch smiled wider, her fang-like teeth creaking as they grew, until finally she ripped them free and flung them into the darkness beneath her feet. Instantly the soil sucked the teeth down, pulling them like daggers through the long-undisturbed earth, until they neared their target. When they reached him, the witch knew, they would pierce him – not to harm but instead to pump her power into him, to reanimate flesh long left to grow cold, muscles and limbs too long unused, and a heart that had not beaten in more human lifetimes than she could count.

Cethlenn smiled again, her empty gums bleeding, the tips of new teeth already beginning to push through. She spat, mingling her blood with the earth.

'Come forth!' she cried. 'My lord, my beloved. The mighty, the fearsome one. The bearer of the power of the sun. The destroyer. The avenger. The slayer of all!' She paused to spit again. 'Revenge for Moytura will be ours, my lord. The time draws near!'

And, deep beneath her, in the heart of the darkness, Balor began to stir.

10

Rose was sitting in the coolest part of the house – the middle of the kitchen floor – rolling a toy truck back and forth to her brothers. Her mother stood at the countertop, humming as she prepared lunch. Colm seemed happy enough to play, but Brian was grizzling, chewing hard on his fist and looking around with huge, damp, worried eyes. The radio was burbling on low volume but Rose could still hear the presenter interviewing a climate scientist from the university in Galway, who was talking about the extreme weather being felt in Ireland's north-west corner and how there didn't appear to be an explanation – or an end in sight.

She sighed heavily, catching the truck and rolling it back to Colm. At least minding her brothers didn't take up much brain-space. Rose's head was already packed full. It had been just over a week since she and Emer had had their run-in at the well, and Emer had been absent from school ever since. All Rose had been able to think about was the look on Emer's face and the strangeness of her words as she'd talked about how much she liked having the stone around. Rose was worried that there was a connection between the stone and Emer's absence. And the weather had grown hotter and more uncomfortable with every passing day, increasing at the same rate as Rose's anxiety. She knew she needed to get the stone back – but if Emer wasn't at school, what was she supposed to do?

She hadn't spoken to Nellie or Gracie either. On Wednesday after school she'd ventured to Hargate Street, hoping she'd find the courage to explain what had happened, but there had been no sign of either of them. Their shops had been locked and dark, and there had been no Catshee there to clear the way. Even if her friends had been where they were supposed to be, Rose had no idea what she would have said. How could she explain? As far as Nellie and Gracie knew, Rose was working on retrieving their only weapon – but instead, it was no closer to being back in their possession, and if the building heat was anything to go by, their time was running out. She sighed again, the weight of everything she was carrying beginning to press her into the ground.

She hadn't even told her parents what had happened at the well; she couldn't find the words. But, luckily – or, Rose thought with a guilty pang, luckily for *her* – whatever was keeping Emer out of school must also have kept her from telling her father to sack Rose's dad, as he was still going to work every day without a word. From the outside, everything seemed completely normal, but inside Rose's head *nothing* was right. Her sleep was disturbed by the heat and her dreams pulsed with darkness and danger, and all she wanted to do was get up and out – to find Emer and beg her to listen, or to go to Gracie and Nellie . . . but instead she was stuck here looking after the twins.

As usual.

'Here's an idea,' Mrs Darke said unexpectedly. 'You could go and call for Sophia after lunch, couldn't you? Or Rory? And you could go and find a shady corner of the park to sit in. Have a chat or do whatever the cool almost-thirteen-year-olds are doing these days.'

Rose looked up at her mother. 'Really?'

'Well, I can't listen to that sighing all weekend long,' Mrs Darke said, as she turned to put the plates on the table, though there was a warm smile on her face as she looked at Rose. 'You could drop into the shop for me too, and pick up a few bits on your way home. Would you mind?'

Rose shook her head. 'No problem.'

She wolfed down her lunch – cold ham, cold boiled eggs, cold potato salad and a big glass of cold water – and after they'd eaten, Rose stacked the dishes in the sink as Mrs Darke took the boys out of their high chairs. 'Now,' she said, 'I'll put these two down for their nap, and so off you go. Okay? Stay out of that sun, and make sure you bring plenty of water, and –'

'Yes, Mam,' Rose said, suppressing the urge to roll her eyes. 'I won't almost die of heatstroke again. I promise.'

Mrs Darke hefted the boys, one on each hip, as she made for the stairs. 'I'm glad to see at least one lesson has been learned from last week,' she said, glancing over her shoulder at Rose. 'And say hello to Aleksina for me, if you see her,' she added as she disappeared from view. Aleksina was Sophia's mother. Rose and

Sophia had been friends since playschool, mostly because they lived in the same estate. Rose didn't really know how to tell her mother that she and Sophia hadn't hung out properly in ages – but maybe today was the day all that would change.

Rose smiled to herself, feeling her heart lift with something like relief. She could explain what had been happening to Rory and Sophia, see if they had any suggestions, maybe try to figure it all out together . . . Maybe this was exactly what she needed.

Feeling hopeful, Rose texted Sophia. *Want to meet up? See you in the park. R xx.* Her finger hovered over the 'send' icon as she glanced at the last four messages she'd sent, all without any reply. She chewed on her lip, picturing Sophia's face as she told her the truth about what had been happening over the past few weeks and imagining Sophia's disbelieving expression . . . Her hope gradually draining away, Rose deleted the message.

Putting her feelings aside, she shoved her stuff into her backpack – her water bottle, some sunblock, an orange and her book on Irish legends – and finally she pulled on her sunhat and shades. She slid her mother's shopping list and a purse with some money carefully folded inside it into her shorts pocket. 'See you later,' she said, as her mother walked back downstairs to meet her at the front door.

'Don't talk to strangers. And, Rose – don't go far. Okay?'

'I won't,' she said, mentally crossing her fingers, just in case she decided to take the very long way home via Hargate Street. 'I promise, Mam.'

Mrs Darke relaxed. 'That's a good girl,' she said. 'I know I can trust you.'

Rose plastered a smile on over her guilt and waved her mother goodbye as she pulled the sliding porch door closed. Then off she went, down the narrow path that ran along the front gardens of the houses on her street. The houses were all joined together like building bricks, and some people had painted their homes in bright colours to distinguish them from their neighbours'. Rose loved this road; everyone who lived on it felt like her family.

But nobody was out today. Mrs Sheridan wasn't sitting on her front step doing the crossword with her cat, Noodle, at her feet; Mr Okongwu wasn't leaning on his garden wall singing at anyone who passed by. The heat was keeping them all indoors.

Rose noticed the weeds in the cracks of the path, all dried up and brown, and for the first time she heard how *quiet* the air was; there were no birds singing and no insects busily zipping about, doing whatever insects did.

As she walked, she thought about the tale of Balor. She didn't even need to look at the book to call it to mind; it was all there, sitting just beneath the surface of her memory. She'd read it a hundred times at least over the past week, but she also knew that Mamó had told her the tale before. Somehow, even as she'd read it for the first time, she'd known it already, deep inside herself. The story of the one-eyed giant, whose eye – if it could be opened – would unleash fire and death. Balor, the god of destruction and war. The leader of the Fomorians – enemies of the Tuatha Dé Danann . . .

Despite the heat of the day, Rose shivered. She remembered Gracie mentioning the name of Balor too, and telling her that the stone – *the one I* allowed *Emer McGuire to take from me*, Rose told herself, gritting her teeth with frustration – had once been used to destroy him, or at least to stop him for a while. And Balor's powers were connected with fire and the sun . . . There *had* to be a link between him and the weird weather, which seemed focused, like a laser beam, on this corner of the country. Hadn't there? Nellie had said Balor's power was already being felt in the world again. Could this be it? Her thoughts flicked to her as-yet-unstarted Science project for school. Some of this might be down to the climate crisis, but she felt there was something else going on too. The sudden heat was so quick and unexpected and *malevolent*. Rose swallowed back her nervousness. *Which means I've got to find a way to stop it.*

Rose reached the end of her road and stood, the yellow-dry grass verge beside her, looking down the road that led to Sophia's house. Rory lived down there too, on the far side. She took in a deep, thoughtful breath and held it for a moment, trying to let her thoughts settle. *Would Rory believe me?* She wasn't sure, but she knew she had to give it a try. Facing all this alone was just too much. Before she could talk herself out of it, Rose fired off a text. *Going to the park. Want to come?*

Almost straight away she saw the three dots that indicated Rory was texting her back – but then the message came and her heart sank. *Can't, sorry, going to Gran's.*

Rose sighed as she tapped out her reply. *Cool. Give her my <3. Miss you. R xx.*

She waited for a few minutes, but Rory didn't respond.

Rose put her phone away and kept walking. The air tasted like the inside of an oven, and her skin was slick with sweat by the time she reached the park. One side of the green playing area had a high wall built for kicking balls against, and in its shade Rose found a cool place to sit. She stretched out, her legs glad of the touch of grass that wasn't burned to a crisp. The park was almost fully deserted – some older kids were taking shelter beneath the shadow cast by the slide, and a red-faced mother was walking with her baby in a well-shaded buggy on the path around the playground – but none of the toys were being played with. Everything sat untouched, unmoving, the paint blistering in the heat.

Rose leaned her head back against the wall, enjoying its coolness, but just as her eyes began to slide closed, the memory of her fire-filled dreams yanked her back to consciousness. She blinked, feeling the clench of fear in her chest, and looked down at her bag. She reached in and pulled out the book, finding the page she wanted without having to check.

Balor the Smiter was a crafty, cunning god. He took to wife the powerful Cethlenn Crooked-Tooth – a mage-woman wise in the ways of prophecy. It was she who warned him of his fate on the battlefield of Moytura – that the mighty Lugh Lámhfada, Balor's own grandson, would slay him there with stone and sling, casting out his eye with one powerful shot. It was she who wounded the mighty Dagda with a spear-blow like lightning from the heavens, and she whose own fate is unknown. Some say she swam to an island and died there; more say this was not the end of the mighty witch-woman.

'Cethlenn Crooked-Tooth,' Rose whispered, thinking of the conversation she'd overheard in Nellie's kitchen. She fished around in her bag for her water bottle and took a drink. It tasted warm and unpleasant but it was better than nothing. *Cethlenn definitely didn't just swim up to some island and die. She's up to no good, isn't she? Destroying Sioc and his people, doing some sort of terrible magic, searching for the stone –* my *stone . . .*

She stared at the picture in the book as thoughts crashed through her mind. Balor was drawn tall as a giant redwood, his massive eye open, unleashing a scythe of fiery light on the land below. She felt sick as she imagined how that would feel, if it ever happened again.

Rose scanned the pages, just in case she'd missed something, but deep inside she already knew: the story mentioned nothing about another weapon, or any other way to kill – or at least get rid of – Balor. She'd been hoping the words in Mamó's book would have some secret hidden in plain sight, waiting to be uncovered, but there were no useful hints that she could see. Her thoughts spun as she tried to think about what to do.

The stories say Balor was killed by the stone thousands of years ago. But can you really kill an all-powerful destructo-god? She paused to put the bottle back in her bag, then picked up the book from where she'd left it lying face-down on the grass. *And would Cethlenn want to take revenge on the people who killed – or wanted to kill – her husband?* Rose blinked at the words in the book. *It was she who wounded the mighty Dagda . . .*

'Cethlenn's still around. For definite,' Rose whispered. 'I heard Nellie talking about her. And she does *not* sound like she's messing about. So if Cethlenn's doing . . . *whatever* to bring Balor back from the dead, and Nellie and Gracie and me are trying to stop her . . .' Rose gulped, suddenly nervous. *I'm in the middle of a lot of unfinished business.*

'Thanks, Sioc,' she muttered, remembering the desperate look on the ice giant's face as he'd offered her the stone.

A twist of some strange pain that felt like anger mixed with grief flared inside her at the memory of the night everything had changed, the night that powerful, ancient magic had come calling. She flicked to the book's title page and read her mamó's words again, running her fingers over the handwriting, thinking about how her life had become unrecognisable after her mamó had grown ill. Nothing since then had seemed to go right. Her dad's work had been extra busy, her mam had been stressed at work too, Rory and Sophia had disappeared and she'd gained Emer

McGuire and her gang of bullies instead – and then, right before everything in her world had been turned completely upside-down, Mamó had died. She'd *died*, just when Rose needed her most.

'I wish you were here, Mamó,' Rose whispered. 'You always knew what to do.'

As she spoke the words, Rose saw a flicker of silver-white, somewhere among the trees on the far side of the park. Something like a glimmer of sunlight on glass, something that anyone else would have dismissed as a quirk of the light or their eyes playing tricks.

But Rose scrambled to her feet. She kept her eyes on the glint of light as she put her book into her backpack, then she took off at a run. She zipped the backpack closed as she went, slinging it up on one shoulder as she crashed into the undergrowth. Around her feet, dried-up weeds and plants straggled forlornly out of the soil.

'Where are you?' Rose whispered. 'Come back. Please!'

From the corner of her eye, Rose saw it again – the strange flicker of light. This time she was sure she saw the fernlike tail and the curling ears . . .

'Catshee!' Rose called. 'Wait for me!'

But Catshee was gone, into the darkness of the deep forest. Rose ran after him as fast as she could, her feet tangling in the weeds that grew like a network between the trees. *I didn't think the trees went back as far as this*, she thought, gasping for breath. The sunlight piercing the canopy overhead was bright but not as destructively hot as it had been outside. She looked all around; everywhere, all she could see were trees – thick and old and ivy-covered, tall and imposing and ancient.

This isn't the park, she thought, suddenly feeling afraid. She pulled out her phone. *No signal.*

Something touched her ankle. Rose jumped back – but when she looked down all she could see was Catshee, calmly sitting at her feet, preening himself.

'Oh my *God*,' Rose said, slumping against the nearest tree. Slowly her heartrate began to go back to normal. 'Catshee! You could've *killed* me.'

Catshee got to his feet and plodded away, brushing Rose with his long, delicate tail. She watched his ears furling and unfurling, his silvery body flashing in the shadows as he walked. After a few feet Catshee turned, staring at Rose with what she could have sworn was a single raised eyebrow.

'All right,' Rose grumbled. 'I'm coming.' She tried to walk carefully as she followed the creature, but her clumsy human steps were no match for Catshee's. The animal passed through the undergrowth with barely a hint that he'd been there – the leaves hardly moved. Rose clumped after him, apologising to the bluebells and whatever else she could see. Some of the flowers, she was pretty sure, looked like nothing she'd seen growing anywhere else – besides in Nellie's garden.

Eventually, Catshee led her out through a clearing in the trees. He shook himself free of the trailing grasses and seed pods that had clung to his fur, pausing for a moment to lick himself clean, before continuing across a wide green field where the grass grew thick and soft underfoot. Rose followed, bracing herself to step out into the light – but almost as soon as she did, she knew something was different. The sun shone here, but it was a gentle sun. She pulled off her sunhat and blinked up at the sky, brushing her sweaty hair back off her face.

'Where are we, Catshee?' Rose whispered, following the not-cat across the grass. She looked around – there was nothing as far as she could see, no houses or roads or pylons or *anything*, either to the left or right, except distant round-topped mountains, ancient and blue. It didn't look anything like anywhere she recognised, and it was as if all her internal compasses and directions had been set spinning, leaving her with a sickening sense of disorientation. The only thing she had to follow was Catshee, so she hurried after him. Quickly, they approached a bush bursting with yellow flowers, which Rose recognised as a whin-bush, or gorse. She ran to follow Catshee, hoping something would start to make sense soon – but instead all she found was a hollow in the earth beneath the gorse bush, into which Catshee was vanishing.

'No! Catshee!' Rose called, dropping to her knees to peer into the hole. 'Come on – I can't follow you in there!' Rose felt crushed by sudden fear. *I promised Mam I wouldn't go far*, she reminded herself. *I don't even know where I am!*

A moment later, her panic was replaced with relief. Catshee emerged, his ears tightly furled and his mouth full of – something. Rose found herself squinting at it as she tried to work out what it was, then Catshee opened his jaws a little wider and Rose finally saw the squiggly tail and the wriggling body of a tiny animal. In two more gulps, the prey had vanished into Catshee's gullet, and he plopped himself on the ground and began to preen.

'Oh, yuck,' Rose muttered, pushing herself back on to her haunches so hard that she fell on her bottom. Catshee gave her a look of cool disapproval, licking his chops with his strangely silver tongue. 'Sorry,' she whispered, feeling a bit silly as she got to her feet again.

Catshee unfurled himself from the earth with his usual grace, his whole body tensed and ready to fly. He gave Rose one last look and then he was off.

11

'Hey! Catshee! *Wait!*' Rose quickly stopped trying to shout as she needed all her breath for the journey. The ground undulated beneath her feet, dips and hollows and hillocks taking her by surprise. She was spending more time picking herself up off her hands and knees than actually chasing the not-cat. He dashed across the open ground, his silver fur winking in the sun. As they ran, Rose's eye was caught by things moving in the long grass. Tiny creatures leaped out of her way, chittering their disapproval. She did her best to place her feet carefully, hoping she wasn't treading on anything – or anyone. As they passed a rocky outcrop, Rose paused to catch her breath. She put her hand beside what she thought was a clump of white leaves, only to cry out in shock a second later when the 'leaves' turned out to be a flock of feathery butterflies who brushed against her face as they took flight. Her mouth dropped open in amazement as she spotted the patterns in the rock where the butterflies had been roosting – beautiful swirling decorations, carved by skilled hands, entrancing enough to trap the eye . . .

Catshee yowled and Rose pulled her attention away from the never-ending spirals on the stone. She blinked, focusing on the not-cat, and when he darted off, she followed.

She paused for breath again at the top of a rise in the land, her heart hammering, trying to spot Catshee. The creature was now sitting on a slightly larger hillock, not too far away. He appeared to be waiting for her. Rose took off once more, hopping from tuft to tuft, until finally she landed in a sweaty, inelegant heap beside him.

The not-cat licked his front paws with regal grace before turning once more and padding down the other side of the hillock – straight into Nellie's back garden. Rose could hardly believe her eyes. There was the long, ancient hedge with its woodbine and ivy guarding the mound with the Dagda's cauldron sitting in it; there was the beautiful old hawthorn tree overlooking the back of Nellie's house; there was the foot-worn path in the grass leading to her open back doors – and there was Nellie herself, standing in the kitchen, watching them approach.

'Nellie!' Rose gasped as she clattered through the doors and into the room. Nellie reached out for her and Rose fell into her arms.

Rose looked up at the old lady, expecting to see joy in her eyes, – but instead all she could see was sorrow. Nellie was trying to smile but her eyes ached with grief.

'Nellie,' Rose said, standing back a little. 'What is it?'

'Cara mo chroí,' she whispered. 'The friend of my heart, my Gracie. He's fighting hard, but it's almost too late.'

Rose blinked hard. 'Almost – too late? What do you mean?'

Nellie looked at Rose with watery eyes. 'Gracie is the Shaper, Rosaleen. That means part of his task – part of the sacred task handed to him by the Dagda himself – is the shaping of the Silver Road, the keeping of it, the repairing of its protective network. Whenever people, in their greed or in their ignorance, dug too deep or cut too sharply into the earth, disturbing and tearing the power of the Road, Gracie's task was to Shape it back into place again. Once upon a time, Gracie was more than enough to do that job on his own, but now . . .' Nellie's voice faltered. 'Now the task is all but beyond him.'

'Is that the reason you've both been gone? Where were you? I came to see you but I couldn't find you. Either of you.'

Nellie's exhausted eyes were steady. 'We were doing our duty,' she said softly. 'It took longer than we thought but none of it mattered in the end. The magic is failing faster than we can mend it.'

Rose stared at Nellie. 'So what can we do? There's got to be something we can do!' Rose glanced at Catshee, who was staring at her intently. 'Catshee came to get me,' she said, realising it was true as she said it. She looked back at Nellie. 'Catshee came to get me – so there's got to be a reason. What can I do?'

'I have asked the Dagda,' Nellie whispered. 'There has been no reply.'

'But now you've got me, right?' Rose searched Nellie's face for any sign of positivity. 'You told me the magic chose me, didn't you? The Old Magic –

the Seandraíocht. And I'm *here*. I want to help. I want to fix things.' She paused for breath. 'That's got to be good. Isn't it?'

'You're a great girl, Rosaleen Darke,' Nellie said. 'I'm sorry for what has to come.'

Rose faltered. 'For – for what? Nellie, for what?'

Nellie's face darkened and she seemed to shrink, her body looking like it was crumbling from the inside. 'Balor is rising,' she said in a strange, quiet voice. 'Cethlenn's foul work is calling him and his power grows. The burning will come, and the fire in the fields, and the baleful lightning, and the merciless blade. All will fall, and the Fomorians will once more rule the Upper World. It shall be, and all shall die. It has already begun. Even the seeds beneath the earth shall perish.'

Rose took a step back. 'Nellie! *No!*' Her tears were coming so hard she could barely see. 'We can't let that happen.'

Nellie shuddered, reaching out a hand to steady herself. Rose helped her to the nearest chair, then turned to find the teapot to pour Nellie something to drink – but she recoiled when she saw the teapot's spout. Nothing was coming from it, not even the barest wisp of steam. 'The Silver Road is being ripped apart,' Nellie whispered. Rose turned to look at her. 'Torn beyond any fixing. Its magic is dying. And Gracie and I, who have stood as its defenders for lifetime upon lifetime, have finally failed too.'

Rose dropped to her knees in front of Nellie. 'You haven't failed,' she said. 'You *haven't*, Nellie. I won't let you say that! It's not too late.' Catshee rubbed against Rose just like a real cat would, and she took comfort from the gesture. 'My little brothers are too important,' Rose continued, their chubby, sticky faces filling her mind. 'And my parents. And my friends, and my teachers – even *Emer McGuire*! We're all too important to be allowed to – to *die*, if Balor wakes up!'

Nellie looked at Rose. Her eyes, sunken now beneath folds of soft wrinkles, were kind and filled with love. 'You have done well, sweet child of the morning,' Nellie said, her voice barely more than a whisper. She reached out a hand to stroke Rose's cheek. 'I am proud.' Her eyes closed and her hand dropped to her lap. 'But the Dagda has abandoned us. The cauldron is still. The answers are not given. The Shaper's power is almost exhausted and the

Silver Road is about to fall.' She opened her eyes again and stared at Rose in confusion and pain. 'I don't know what to do.'

Rose's own eyes were hot. 'This is all my fault,' she said, blinking away tears. *Come on*, she told herself. *The only one who can do anything about this is you. You've got to try!* She looked back at Nellie, rubbing at her cheeks. 'The stone was given to me and I lost it. But there has to be something we can do. There *has* to be!'

She pushed herself up off the floor and ran out the front door of Nellie's shop, Catshee at her heels. Quickly Rose checked for traffic – though Hargate Street was never usually busy with cars – and dashed across to Gracie's shop. His front door was unlocked. The tiny cobbler's shop was dusty, unused; the rolls of leather looked cracked and unwaxed, and the tools lay in disarray on his workbench. On the back wall was a hand-painted sign, a copy of the one above his door, done on wood in the Old Irish script. *Gréasaí*, it said. Shoemaker. One who makes. A shaper.

'Gracie!' Rose called. 'Gracie, are you here?'

She hurried through the narrow door at the back of Gracie's workshop – a door she'd never passed through before. It led to a comfortable sitting room. A fire burned in the grate – a blue-flamed fire which gave no heat. Tools hung around it – hammers and pliers and pincers, a sharp-pointed metal puncher for making holes in leather, scrapers and thick needles and more things Rose couldn't imagine the use for – and beside it, curled up on a chair like a sleeping child, was the Shaper himself.

Rose ran to him, dropping to the floor in front of his chair. Catshee stood back, his tail rigid, his eyes wide.

'Gracie,' Rose whispered. 'Oh, Gracie, please wake up!'

The ancient man stirred and blinked, looking at her. When he saw that it was Rose, his eyes twinkled with fondness. 'I wondered what was keeping you,' he croaked, before gasping out something that sounded like a chuckle.

Rose couldn't help but smile back, though she knew tears were dripping off the end of her chin. 'You're okay,' she said.

'I am not,' Gracie said, looking into the strange blue fire. 'Not a bit of it. But I'm all the better for seeing you, sweet Rosaleen.' The old man's eyes filled as he met Rose's gaze. 'I'm sorry I couldn't do more,' he said, his voice weakening. 'I did my best.'

'I know you did, Gracie,' Rose said, reaching out to hold his hand. The skin was leathery and warm, the bones fragile as a bird's. 'I know. And now I'm here to help.'

Gracie smiled. 'Sure, now. Isn't that marvellous.' He pursed his mouth and shook his head slightly. 'But what a crying shame it's too late.'

Rose got to her feet, stepping back. 'It is *not* too late!' she said. 'I'm not letting my family die, Gracie. I'm *not*!'

The fire beside Gracie suddenly roared, licking out of the fireplace like a beast trying to break through the bars of its cage. Its blue flames, crackling silver at the edges, were bright enough to make Rose shade her eyes. She stepped back from it, suddenly afraid, and stumbled over something on the floor – then she felt a strong hand around her wrist. She looked down. Gracie had reached out for her, his wizened fingers still with enough power to stop her from falling over.

'The Silver Road must rally,' Gracie said, his eyes burning with almost as much intensity as the fire. 'It must have a reason to gather its strength. Tell it, child! Tell it that there are people yet who believe in it – who know the old stories, who *believe* them. Tell the magic to fight!'

Rose stared into the fireplace. The flames looked a little like a face, she thought, their blue and silver and white and green tongues fitting together in such a way as to show a pair of angry eyes, a mouth with its lip curled, and hair spilling forth like a mighty river. She steadied herself, unafraid, and faced the magic down. 'I'm here!' she shouted. 'You called me, and I'm here, and I'm *ready*. Come on! You've got to help me. I know I lost the stone – but there's got to be something else we can do. Balor was defeated before, and he can be defeated again. We can find another weapon, if we have to. I'll do whatever it takes!' She paused, willing the creature in the fire to hear her, and then the flames rearranged themselves into her mamó's face, proud and glowing. Words came from Mamó's lips, words which linked together like a chain – a chain of light, which fastened on Rose's heart, connecting her to the ancient magic of the stories she and Mamó had shared.

'Mamó,' Rose breathed, blinking away tears. She smiled, and the face in the hearth smiled back –

and then the flames rearranged themselves again. Mamó's face was gone, but Rose stared into the heart of the fire anyway, her own heart surging with courage and the knowledge that she was *right*, and that the time to fight had come. 'We *can't* give up now!'

Then the flames vanished, so suddenly that it felt as though someone had sucked all the air out of the room. Rose fell to her knees before the fireplace, gasping for breath. Catshee appeared beside her, his warmth reassuring, but Rose's heart was racing as she stared into the empty fireplace, wishing her mamó would reappear, even if only for a second ... And then she felt Gracie's hand still tight around her arm. She looked up at him, afraid to see the hope fade from his eyes, terrified that she'd done the wrong thing, that the fire, and the magic, had finally gone out – but instead the old man was smiling. He shone with pride.

'That was well done, my cailín, well done indeed,' he said.

Rose tried to steady herself. 'So now what?' she croaked. She felt exhausted suddenly, as though someone had flicked her power switch off. She glanced back at the empty fireplace. Something bright was catching her eye. One of Gracie's tools – the largest of his hammers, a beautifully made thing, smooth-handled and carved with intricate designs around the head – was glowing blue.

Without a moment's hesitation Gracie leaned forward, pushing off his blanket, and took the hammer from its peg. The blue glow was still there but it was fading slightly. 'The Shaper's hammer,' he said, his voice low with awe. 'Head of iron, shaft of oak.' He looked up at Rose and she met his eye. 'You called upon the Seandraíocht for help, and help has been given. This is to be yours now. So you'd better mind it, and wield it well and wisely. This is a powerful thing, Rosaleen Darke.'

I didn't do a great job of minding the last powerful thing I had, Rose thought, as Gracie placed the hammer in her hands. It was heavy but balanced perfectly. Rose wrapped her fingers around the handle. It felt comfortable, like something she'd held every day of her life. 'What do I do with it?' she asked, her courage wavering.

'When the time comes,' Gracie said, 'you'll know.'

'That's just fantastic,' Rose muttered. 'How very helpful.'

Gracie grinned at her, more gum than teeth, and

Rose's heart lifted. He looked like the old Gracie once again, full of mischief and laughter.

'Come on, till we see if Nellie has a sweet at all that she'd like to donate to an old, sick man,' Gracie said, pushing himself up out of his chair onto spindly legs. He leaned on Rose as he found his balance. 'You never know but we might find her in a good mood. Miracles do happen. Isn't that what they say?'

Rose gave Gracie her arm as they made their way out of the room and through his shop, with Catshee leading the way. The shop looked a little brighter now, the dust somehow not as thick nor the cobwebs as numerous. The old man paused to lift his flat cap from the hat stand beside the front door, fitting it on with care and examining his reflection in a tiny mirror before turning to Rose for approval. 'Well?' he asked. 'Will I do?'

Rose pushed the handle of the hammer into her shorts, pulling her T-shirt down over the head to hide it from view. 'You'll do,' she said with a grin.

'Onward, so,' said Gracie, stepping out onto the path. Nellie was standing in the doorway of her sweet-shop, her hands clutched to her face as she watched Gracie come striding across the road with Rose on his arm.

'The last star has not yet fallen, Nellie Sweeney,' Gracie said, pulling his shoulders back and enunciating his words with the gravity of a stage actor.

'You're still at the blethering, I see, Gracie Kinch,' Nellie replied, her face alight with joy.

'So what do we do now?' Rose asked, as they walked through the sweet-shop and out into the kitchen. Catshee was already there, sitting in the middle of the table with his feather-like tail unfurled, the tips of its lacy fronds held over his head like a crown. Nellie settled into her chair and Gracie settled into his, whistling a tune that made Rose think of the sparkle of raindrops on a sunny day. 'We're not just going to sit around and wait, are we?'

A sudden *puff* from the teapot drew all their gazes towards it. From the spout, Rose was amazed to see a column of steam beginning to rise, which soon began to twist and dance in the air. Nellie gave a wide grin as she reached for the teacups.

'I suppose,' she said, 'that we'll start by having a cup of tea, and we'll see what the rest of the day brings.'

12

Rose was almost home, her belly full of tea and cake and her heart full of hope, when she realised she'd forgotten to go to the shop. Her good mood felt like it had been punctured as she realised that even if she turned around and ran all the way there, and all the way back, it would be a forty-minute trip at least – and Mam probably needed the shopping right now. Her head was still buzzing from the feeling of being in Nellie's kitchen with the teapot steaming merrily. They'd become so wrapped up in talking about what might happen next, and what they could do to help the Seandraíocht, that everything else had simply fallen out of Rose's mind.

'Oh *no*,' she groaned, pushing her hand into her pocket. The purse was still there, with her mother's folded ten-euro note, and the shopping list. *Bread.*

Milk. Margarine. Pound of mince. 'Mam needs this stuff to make dinner,' Rose muttered to herself, her fingers tightly gripping the piece of paper – part of a torn-off envelope.

You could pretend to lose it, said a quiet voice inside her head. *Just pretend it fell out of your pocket and you didn't know what else to do but come home . . .*

Rose felt her grip on the paper loosening, but then – almost like it had shifted position – she became aware of the weight of the hammer she wore thrust through her waistband. She swallowed hard and folded the shopping list back up, shoving it into her pocket again. She took a deep breath, squared her shoulders and kept walking.

She pulled open the sliding porch door and was immediately hit by a wave of wailing. Her brothers were hot, bothered and probably hungry.

'Rose?' came her mother's voice from the kitchen. 'Is that you?'

'Yes, Mam,' Rose said, her heart skittering a bit at the thought of what was going to happen next. She walked slowly up the hall, stopping in the kitchen doorway. Her mam was working at the hob.

'Did you get that mince, love? Dad said he'd be home by six and it'd be nice to have everything ready for him.'

'Mam, I forgot,' Rose said.

Her mother turned to her, the smile dropping away from her face. 'What?' Mrs Darke looked down at Rose's hands, as if expecting to see full bags hanging from them. 'Did you not get *any* of the shopping?'

Rose bit her lip. 'I'm so sorry, Mam. I just – I forgot about the shop. I was busy with Sophia and I –'

'Rosaleen Darke!' Her mother's irritation had turned to a full-on rage. 'I can forgive you forgetting the shopping. I can forgive almost *anything*. But what I cannot forgive is lying!' She pulled the frying pan away from the heat and turned the ring off, all while keeping her eyes on Rose. 'I brought the boys for a quick walk while you were gone and I ran into Sophia and Aleksina at the bus stop. They were going into town to get Sophia a new pair of football boots. So, you're *not* to tell me you were busy with Sophia. I know you weren't.'

'Mam, I –'

Mrs Darke threw her hands up in the air, dismissing her daughter. 'Look, I have enough to do now,'

175

she said, her voice tight with disappointment. 'Your father will be home shortly, exhausted and looking for his dinner, and I have to pull something together for him. So you can just get out of my hair, young lady, and go up to your room until I call you for your meal. Is that understood?'

Rose opened her mouth to apologise but the thunderous look on her mother's face was enough to dry up her words before they emerged. She just nodded and turned away, pausing long enough to pull the purse out of her pocket and leave it on the kitchen worktop.

She dragged her feet all the way to her bedroom and sat on the floor, her knees up to her chest, her arms wrapped around her shins. All the good mood she'd been in as she left Gracie and Nellie drained away, leaving her feeling nothing but exhausted – and scared.

She released her legs and pulled the hammer out of her shorts. It seemed a lot less impressive now; the magic that had made it glow back at Gracie's wasn't flowing through it any more and it just looked *ordinary*, a lump of dark metal attached to an old wooden handle. She tried to remember how powerful it had appeared when it had first started to glow, and how Nellie and Gracie's spirits had lifted as they'd talked about what the Old Magic had been like once, and what it might be again . . . but it seemed much easier to believe in magic when you were sitting in Nellie's kitchen. Not knowing what else to do with it, Rose pushed the hammer beneath her mattress, hoping it would be safe there, and flopped onto her bed.

She reached over to her bedside locker where her photograph of Mamó sat. It had been taken many years before, when Mamó had been her old, happy self, and her illness hadn't yet started to nibble away at her. Rose was in the picture too, her six-year-old gap-toothed grin making her think fondly of Gracie. She touched the photo.

'I miss you,' she said, blinking at the image. Her lip trembled as she fought back the tears she didn't want to cry – Mamó had asked them not to cry for her, but sometimes it couldn't be helped. She clutched the photograph to her heart. When Mamó had died, Rose had felt as though someone had broken her into pieces. The cracks were still there inside her, trying to heal – but somehow they never quite could. 'But things can always be mended,' Rose whispered, remembering something her mamó had often said. No matter what got broken in Mamó's house, she always had a way to fix it – the fingers that could knit and crochet and spin, the patience to glue broken vases and cracked toys back together, the skill to thread a needle and make something look like new again. Rose looked at the photo, smiling at her mamó's happy face. She wiped her cheeks. 'This can all be mended too. I'll find the way to do it, Mamó. I know I can do it.' She kissed the photo and wiped it clean with her thumb, before placing it back on her locker with care.

She heard the familiar growl of an engine. Her dad's van. She hurried to the window and, wincing at the bright sharpness of the light outside, she saw her father getting out of his van, slamming the door shut and leaning heavily on the side of his vehicle.

He looked exhausted. Thin and worn out. He paused to rub his forehead with one grimy hand, seeming to gather his strength before going inside.

Rose dropped back to the floor of her bedroom. Downstairs, she could hear the muffled sounds of grown-up voices talking – an angry conversation.

About me, Rose thought, sucking hard on her top lip until it stung.

'Dinner!' came her mother's voice. Rose pushed herself off the bedroom floor and made her way downstairs.

The twins were already in their highchairs at the far end of the kitchen table. Her dad was sitting at the near end, his back to Rose. He had his head in his hands, his fingers threaded through his hair. Rose threw her mother a look of concern, but Mrs Darke just shook her head, as if to say, *Don't mention it*.

'Hi, Daddy,' Rose said, taking her seat to his left. Mr Darke looked up. His eyes were bleary with exhaustion, but he did his best to smile.

'Hi, love,' he said. 'Good day?'

Rose and her mother exchanged a look. 'Not bad,' she said.

'I heard you forgot to do the messages for your mam,' Mr Darke continued, raising his eyebrows as he lifted his water glass to his mouth.

Rose felt her cheeks roar with heat. 'I didn't *mean* to, and I said I was sorry, and –'

'I just wonder where you were, Rose. And why you told a lie.'

'I was . . . I went to –' Rose began. How could she even begin to tell them? *I woke up an ancient magic and got given a hammer by someone who's over four thousand years old?*

'Yes, indeed,' Mrs Darke said, coming over to the table with her husband's plate. Rose realised that her mother must have raided the freezer to put together their dinner, but it didn't make her feel any better. 'I'd love to know where you disappeared to, that was so important you forgot to do the one job I asked you.'

'I looked after the boys all morning!' Rose retorted. 'That was a job too!'

'Rosaleen!' Mr Darke barked.

Colm jumped at the sound of his father's voice and began to fret. Brian contented himself with banging his spoon against the tray of his highchair.

'I was visiting Mr Kinch and Mrs Sweeney, okay? Gracie and Nellie. I go there a lot. They're – they're my friends.'

'The old cobbler and the lady who owns the sweet-shop on Hargate Street?' Mrs Darke said, dishing food onto a plate as she spoke. 'I haven't thought about them in years.'

Rose blinked. 'Do you know them?'

Mrs Darke shrugged. 'Not really. They've just always been there. It's funny, now that I think about it. I never remember them looking any different – they haven't changed since I was a child myself.' She glanced at her husband. 'How about you, Fergus?'

Mr Darke took a forkful of chicken as he considered this. 'I suppose,' he said. 'I used to drop into the sweet-shop once in a while, when I was going to school.'

'Well,' Rose said, brightening. 'That's where I was. Visiting them both.'

'And you were there all day?' Mr Darke said, his words muffled by chewing.

'Dad, that's yuck. Don't talk with your mouth full,' Rose said, wrinkling her nose.

'Answer the question,' Mr Darke said more clearly. He fixed his daughter with a stare as he stabbed his fork into another lump of chicken. Mrs Darke served Rose and put a plate of food in her own place while she began to feed the twins. Her mother's plate was mostly potatoes, and Rose felt a jolt of guilt. *Mam didn't have enough to feed us all, because I messed up.* 'Rosaleen,' Mr Darke reminded her, and Rose looked back at him.

'Yes, Dad,' she muttered. 'All day.'

'Haven't you any other friends to hang around with? What were Sophia and Rory doing? Did you even try to get in touch with them?' Something about her dad's tone made Rose bristle.

'Yes!' she retorted, unable to control the heat of her sudden temper. 'They don't want to know me any more, all right? Not since – . . . not since I started at the Grammar.'

'I was only talking to Rory's dad the other day,' Mr Darke replied, his eyebrows rising in disbelief. 'He was asking after you, wondering how you were doing, asking me to pass on Rory's love to you. So don't try that one with me.'

'I'm not *lying*,' Rose said, anger and frustration making her eyes fill with tears.

'There's no need for us to get so upset about it,' Mrs Darke said, stirring a pot of food for the babies. 'Okay? You were helping Mr Kinch and Mrs Sweeney – and you're very good to do it, Rose. I'm sure those old people love having you around.' She paused in her stirring, struck by a sudden thought. 'They must be a mighty age now.'

Rose nodded. *If only you knew*, she thought,

helping herself to chicken. It was delicious, and she swallowed it guiltily.

'Anyway,' Mr Darke said, leaning his elbows on the table and looking at Rose. 'There's something else I want to talk to you about, young lady.'

Rose looked at her dad. She forked in another mouthful of chicken, sure she knew exactly what was going to come next.

'Michael McGuire took me into his office earlier today,' said Mr Darke. 'And he told me something I think you might be able to shed some light on.'

Rose swallowed her food too quickly, making herself cough. She reached for her glass and downed a mouthful of water. 'What?' she croaked.

'He told me that, last Friday, he'd received a very irate phone call from his wife,' Mr Darke continued. He set down his cutlery, even though his meal wasn't finished. 'And he said that Mrs McGuire had to pick up Emer after school that day, soaking wet, saying you'd thrown her into the well. She's been sick all week, apparently – nightmares and the like.' Mr Darke sucked a breath through his front teeth. 'So I suppose I want to know why on earth Emer would be telling stories like that to her parents.'

Mrs Darke's mouth dropped open. 'Rosaleen Martina,' she said quietly. 'You'd better not have done anything *like* throwing someone into the well.'

'Of course I didn't,' Rose said, looking from one parent to the other. 'I wouldn't. She – she walked into the well on her own!'

Mr Darke's eyebrows raised. 'So you *were* at the well, then.'

'I was there because she has something of mine and she won't give it back,' Rose replied. 'And she told her mam that I threw her in so that *you'd* get in trouble with her dad.'

Mr Darke huffed out a breath. 'That sounds a lot like Emer, to be fair,' he muttered.

'Fergus!' Mrs Darke said, shooting him a look from the other end of the table as she placed a spoonful of dinner in Colm's waiting mouth.

'Well . . . All right, this is how it's going to be.' Mr Darke rubbed his face. 'Michael McGuire wants a letter of apology to Emer, written and signed by you, by first thing Monday morning.'

Rose gaped at him. 'What?'

Mr Darke fixed her with a stare. 'I think you heard me, Rosaleen.'

'But, Dad – I didn't do anything!'

Mr Darke sighed. 'And I believe you. But unfortunately sometimes it's people like us who have to take it on the chin, while people like *them* –' he jerked his thumb over his shoulder as he spoke – 'get to do what they like and make all the rules. And it's not right but that's what happens.'

'Emer said she'd tell her dad to sack you,' Rose said.

Mr Darke shrugged. 'He can't just let me go like that. But he can make life unpleasant enough that I might jump ship all on my own.'

'Well, maybe you should!' Rose said. 'Maybe you *should* go and find a job that doesn't – destroy the earth and pollute the place, and –'

'Rose!' Mrs Darke snapped. 'Your dad's job keeps a roof over your head and food in your belly. That's enough out of you.'

A tremor of desperation flared through Rose's chest. 'Dad! I swear – I didn't do anything wrong!' Tears of frustration filled her eyes. 'And you're always telling me not to take it – not to let anyone make me feel less than them. So why would you make me write a stupid *letter* apologising for something I didn't do? Emer's horrible to me! All the time. She bullies me every single day. It's all her fault. If she'd just left me alone, I'd never even have *met* Nellie and Gracie. That's why I'm involved in all this mess to begin with!' Rose pressed the heels of her hands into her eyes. She felt hot all over and ready to burst.

'That's a bit dramatic, love,' Mrs Darke said, scraping mushy peas off Brian's chin with the spoon and depositing it in his mouth. 'There's no "mess". Dad and I will talk to Emer's parents. We'll chat to the school. It'll all be sorted out.'

'That's *not* what I'm talking about,' Rose said, lowering her hands again. 'There's – there's something else happening too. Something big, and I don't know how to deal with it.'

Mr and Mrs Darke exchanged a worried look. 'Rose,' her dad said, putting his hand over hers. 'There's nothing you can't tell your mam and me. We'll help in whatever way we can.'

'It's . . . Balor,' Rose said, blinking her stinging eyes as she looked between her parents. 'He's coming. It's his fault the weather's like this, and we have to stop him. *I* have to stop him. And I don't know how.'

Mrs Darke got to her feet and hurried around the

table, almost dropping the bowl of mushed-up baby food as she went. Colm howled his displeasure, but nobody paid him any attention. Mrs Darke crouched beside Rose's chair and pressed one hand against her daughter's forehead, frantically scanning her face.

'Do you have a headache, love?' Mrs Darke asked. 'Any sickness in your tummy?'

'No!' Rose sobbed. 'Mam, I'm not sick. And I'm not making this up. Honestly.'

Mr Darke got up. 'I've got my work mobile in the van,' he said. 'I'll ring the doctor.'

'I don't *need* the doctor!' Rose shouted.

Mrs Darke gathered her daughter into a hug, shushing her gently as she rocked her to and fro. Mr Darke paused in the hallway, hovering there, unsure what to do.

Mrs Darke crooned soothingly into Rose's ear. 'It's all right. How about an early night? That might be the best thing. Okay?' She released Rose from the embrace and sat back, looking at her face. 'You look worn out, love. Go on. Up to bed and get a good rest, and everything will seem different in the morning. Mark my words.'

Rose looked from one parent to the other. Her

father was worried, exhausted, confused. Her mother looked frantic and afraid. *I'm never going to get them to understand*, Rose thought. *They don't believe me – just like Rory and Sophia wouldn't have believed me either. I'm on my own.*

'Okay,' Rose whispered, nodding, as she got to her feet. Slowly, shading her eyes against the light still beaming through the front door, she made her way down the hall and up the stairs to her darkened bedroom. She tried not to focus on her parents, white-faced with fear, watching her from the bottom of the stairs.

13

Rose woke in the middle of the night, her heart clattering around behind her ribs. She pressed a hand to her chest, trying to calm down. She'd kicked off her light bedsheets some time earlier as the night was so clammy and uncomfortable, but at least the darkness was soothing. Her eyes and head throbbed, not painfully exactly, but more like they were bleached out from staring at the brightness of the world all day long.

That's the sign of his power returning, Nellie had said earlier that day as they'd sat around the steaming teapot. *The heat and the short tempers and the dryness and the dust. All that is Balor beginning to seep back. We've got to be watchful.*

Rose took a deep breath as she lay there, her eyes closed. She'd gone to sleep fairly quickly after her mam had sent her to bed, and it did seem to have done her some good. The longer she stayed awake, however, the more her mind cartwheeled, and she felt as if she were gearing up, her sleepiness trickling away. She checked the time on her alarm clock. Ten past two in the morning. *Just like the night with Sioc*, Rose thought.

She sat up, watching the moon through the crack in her curtains, and thought about the ice giant. She remembered how the sky had seemed to swallow him the one and only time they'd met, and she hoped he was okay. *But you're not, are you?* she thought. *Cethlenn came for you, and if I keep poking around in her business she'll come after me too.*

With a sigh, Rose clicked on her bedside light. Right at the top of the pile of books on her locker was *Old Irish Myths and Legends*. Her gaze fell on it and wouldn't budge. *Earthsea* had finally gone back to the library, and there was nothing else in the pile that caught Rose's attention.

She settled back into her bed and picked up the book. Idly she began leafing through the pages, not looking for anything in particular. She skipped past the story of Balor this time and went further back, looking at the illustrations more than the words.

A few pages from the end, her eye was caught by something that seemed familiar. She'd flicked on a little before her brain registered it and so she quickly turned back, page after page, until she found it again.

'There you are,' she whispered. The page was covered with a full-colour painting of a mighty warrior wearing what looked like a wolf-skin, with a low hill behind him. On the hill there was a standing stone. Beneath it, the author had written an explanation of what the image was about. *'The Mac Tíre leaves his slumber beneath the Lia Fáil,'* Rose read. *The Lia Fáil.* Nellie had mentioned that once, she was sure. 'The Stone of Destiny. It's one of the treasures of the Tuatha Dé Danann. Nellie said it's on the Hill of Tara.' And Rose thought about what her mam had said, the evening she'd given her this book – how Uncle Ger had always loved the story of the Mac Tíre when he was a boy. *The mighty wolf-warrior.*

At the front of the book, the artist had drawn a map of Ireland. Rose used her thumb to keep her page as she flipped back to look at it. Gently she tapped the spot where Carriganawn would be, if it were marked on this map, and ran her finger across the country to the county of Meath, where the artist had drawn the Hill of Tara. *Seat of the ancient kingship of Ireland*, it read in tiny letters. A river curled around not far from it, and Rose read its name. 'The Boyne,' she whispered.

Rose opened the illustrated page again. '*The Mac Tíre*,' she read, staring at the image. The sky behind the wolf-warrior looked like it was on fire. 'I hope you're on our side,' she whispered. Whoever, or whatever, this Mac Tíre was, he looked ferocious – and unstoppable.

Out of the blue, Rose yawned widely. There was nothing more to be gained by lying here, wide awake, and she knew she had to try to get some rest. She closed the book and slid it back onto her bedside locker, before turning out the light. As she lay down again, she closed her eyes and wondered whether the Shaper's hammer was safe in its hiding place beneath her mattress, and how she was going to know what to do with it, and *why* on earth the Old Magic kept insisting on *giving* her things, and –

'This is *stupid*,' she whispered. No matter what way she tossed and turned, her brain was awake and humming, and Rose knew sleep was out of the question. Her body might be tired but her mind was not.

She sighed in frustration, opening her eyes – and then she opened them wider still.

Silver-blue light rippled on her ceiling, like it was being reflected off the surface of a shimmering pool. Rose stared up at it, her mouth dropping open in surprise, and then she pushed herself up on one elbow to look down at the floor of her bedroom.

Tiny pops of silver were blooming out of her carpet, rising on stalks that somehow extended out of the floor, their petals unfurling in a way that suddenly looked so familiar. Rose tumbled out of bed and dropped to her knees, reaching out to touch one – and her fingers met exactly what they expected to. Nellie's flowers – the silver flowers that grew in her hanging baskets and in her garden, the flowers that seemed to watch over Rose every time she went near them.

She looked up, her eyes dancing with the sparkle of the shining petals, and then down again as she watched the flowers begin to thicken, growing in a straight line across the floor before blossoming up and over the sheets and mattress of Rose's bed and down the other side – a line of silver flowers as wide as her torso and as straight as a ruler. Rose walked around the end of her bed, watching as they somehow continued blooming through the carpet – and then they spread up the wall and out over the windowsill.

Rose followed the flowers. She parted the curtains and looked outside. The line of silver blossoms continued down the front wall of her house, out around the end of her dad's van, and then – growing as she watched – the flowers spread out into the road, filling it almost instantly with a wave of shining light that led off into the distance. Off towards Hargate Street.

'Nellie and Gracie,' Rose gasped. Instantly she turned from the window and began to pull on whatever clothes were close enough to grab. She was wearing an old T-shirt of her dad's as a nightshirt, one that had the name of a long-ago band on it, so she stepped back into her sweaty shorts and yanked them up, letting the T-shirt hang loose over them. She reached beneath her mattress to pull out the hammer – through the top of her shorts it went, tucked close against her skin. Next she pulled her old cardigan off the chair and shoved her arms into the sleeves, leaving the front unbuttoned. A twist of paper from Nellie's shop, filled with a handful of cróigíní, sat on her chest of drawers and she slid the sweets into her pocket. Her socks were lying in a heap beside the chair; she picked them up and sniffed them, recoiling at the smell, but it was quicker to put them back on than to look for another pair. She snatched up her phone and checked it – but, as she'd half-suspected, it had absolutely no signal. The screen wavered a bit, and Rose couldn't help but grin, very slightly. *Phones and magic don't mix*, she told herself, putting it down.

Rose glanced back up at the shimmering light on her bedroom ceiling. Despite everything – the smelly socks, the uncomfortable shorts, the ancient T-shirt, the weight of the hammer at her waist – she felt her chest puff out with hope and wonder and *excitement*. These flowers were from Nellie. That meant they could be trusted.

As quickly as she could, Rose hurried down the stairs. She grabbed her runners from the pile of shoes in the corner and pulled them on as she rootled through the top drawer of the hall table for the spare front-door key. She unlocked the door as quietly as possible, carefully sliding open the porch door and stepping out into the night. The flowers were still there, their heads bobbing slightly in the night breeze, their glow bluish-white.

Rose locked the door behind her and slipped the key into the pocket of her shorts. She pulled the sliding door closed, hoping it wouldn't bang, and then – finally – she was free. She looked up and down the road. Nobody was stirring. There was no noise – no cars, no barking dogs, no anything. It felt like she was the only person awake, or alive, in the whole universe. *Gracie*, she thought. *He's stopped the world again.*

So she took a lungful of air and began to run, following the line of silver flowers wherever they led.

They streaked through the town like a lightning bolt, heading straight for Hargate Street. Rose was out of breath by the time she arrived, her heart thumping. She paused to rest at the top of the street, watching the silver flowers pool on the road between Nellie and Gracie's shops, their shape reminding her of a slowly spinning galaxy.

She began to walk, the flowers brushing against her ankles and shins. They whispered as she passed, but Rose couldn't make out whether there were any words in the susurration – all she could hear was gentle whishing, like a distant sea. The closer she got to the point on the road between Nellie and Gracie's shops, the brighter the flowers' glow became, until finally, as she drew level with the shops, the whole road exploded in a silent supernova, the glow brighter than day, the ground humming with power beneath Rose's feet. She looked down. The flowers had thickened into millions, the blooms so numerous that nobody could have counted them, their stems and leaves interlocked like soldiers marching arm-in-arm to war. The bright light they gave off stretched away into the distance.

'The Silver Road,' Rose breathed, the beauty of it making tears spring to her eyes.

'Tá sí ina dúiseacht,' came a scratchy, familiar voice to Rose's left. She turned to see Gracie there – or rather the Shaper, the figure who looked like Gracie but who was so much more. He smiled at her. 'She is awake,' he translated. 'At last, the Silver Road is roused. The Seandraíocht is calling for its allies.'

'It's calling you, Rosaleen Darke,' came Nellie's voice. Rose turned to see her, the Cauldron Keeper, shrouded in her own power. Nellie and Gracie walked out into the Silver Road, the flowers brushing gently around them as they moved. 'Are you willing to answer?'

Rose looked down at herself. Her legs were bruised and filthy, a plaster on one knee. The logo on her dad's T-shirt, a sketched heart shape with the letters *SP* inside it, glowed strangely in the light of the flowers. Her hair hadn't been brushed in at least two days.

'I'm not much,' she finally said. 'But I'm here.'

Gracie cackled beside her. 'Not much? Not much, she says. And look at her. Girded for battle. Armed to the teeth. Ferocious as a she-wolf. Not much, mar dhea. You're more than enough, Rosaleen Darke.'

Rose smiled at him, and Gracie grinned back.

The glow from the Silver Road was steady and strong, expectant and ready, but as Rose stood in the midst of its power, she felt her skin touched by a gentle breeze. It was warm, unpleasantly so, like the close breath of some foul creature. She shuddered, spinning on the spot, but there was nothing behind her. All she could see was the Silver Road, stretching away back towards her home. The way she'd come, and the way that led back to her sleeping family. She swallowed her sudden fear and tried to steady her wobbly legs.

'He was felled before,' Nellie said in a quiet voice. Rose looked at her.

'By a literal god,' Rose reminded her. 'And Lugh was *destined* to do it, right? Like, there was a prophecy.'

Nellie met Rose's eye. 'And sure who's to say there's no prophecy about you? There *might* be,' the old lady sniffed. 'And there might not. Either way, you're here, and that's what's important.'

Rose swallowed hard. 'But I'm only me,' she said. 'And I don't have the *tathlum*.'

'You have the power of the Seandraíocht,' came Gracie's voice. Rose turned fully, until she was standing between them once again. 'And you have yourself.' The old man's eyes were kind. 'There are no guarantees, Rosaleen Darke. There never are. But you carry with you more power than has been seen in a thousand years. Don't forget that.'

A faint roar, like the sound of a distant jet engine, sounded overhead. Rose looked up to see a ripple of orange-red flicker across the sky, like the darkness was on fire, before it faded.

'Does this mean . . . Is Balor here?' Rose asked, glancing from Gracie to Nellie and back. 'I mean, is he awake?'

Nellie's twinkle grew dull for a heartbeat's space. 'Not yet,' she said. 'But I fear we don't have long.'

'So there's still hope,' Rose said, staring down the length of the Silver Road, stretching away into the darkness.

'Where there's courage, there's always hope,' Nellie said, reaching into a pocket and pulling out a neatly wrapped packet. 'Take these with you, a stór.' The old lady pressed a bag of cróigíní into Rose's hand. 'I wish I could give you more. But they come from the Cauldron of the Dagda himself, and I hope they will remind you of your courage when you need it.'

Rose blinked as she took it. 'Am I . . . Do I have to go on my own, then?' she said, her gaze flicking between Nellie and Gracie. 'Aren't you coming?'

Nellie and Gracie exchanged a glance filled with sorrow before looking back at Rose. 'This is our station, Rose,' Gracie said. 'And our duty is here. But it's not idle we are: I am Shaping the country, holding it in stasis, trying to preserve the power of the Silver Road as long as I can – so that it may preserve you.' Gracie gave a sad smile.

'And I may not leave the cauldron,' Nellie said. Rose turned to her. 'I swore, Rose, in time out of memory, to guard it with my life. I cannot and will not break that bond.'

Rose nodded, trying to ignore the thudding of her heart. 'It's all right,' she said, squeezing the packet of cróigíní before sliding it into her cardigan pocket. 'I'll be okay.' She sucked her lips against her teeth and raised her eyebrows inquisitively. 'But does anyone know what I actually need to do? I mean, a few instructions would be good.'

Beneath Rose's T-shirt, the hammer began to glow. Through the thin fabric, the bright blue-white of the metal was clearly visible.

'I think that might be your first clue,' said Gracie, nodding at it.

Rose pulled the hammer free. She stared at it, boggling at the light that poured out from the whorls of its design, so like the designs carved on the rock in the magical land beyond the end of Nellie's garden, or like the unfurling frond of a fern. And then, as if the very thought of ferns had brought him,

Catshee appeared, stalking through the flowers. He sat at Rose's feet, preening himself unconcernedly, before looking up with cool impatience.

'Looks like that fella beyond is ready and waiting to go,' Gracie said, nodding down at the not-cat. Then, he turned to Rose. 'Give him a tap,' the old man said. 'Gently, now. Not enough to knock his block off, much as you might be tempted.' He chuckled, wheezing at his own joke, as Rose steadied her grip on the hammer's handle.

'Is – this okay?' she whispered to Catshee.

The not-cat stretched up his head, as if expecting the hammer's touch. Rose gave Nellie a worried look.

'Catshee is older than any of us,' the old lady reassured her. 'He knows what he's doing.'

Rose licked her lips and gave a determined nod. Then, as gently as she could, she stretched out her arm and tapped the Shaper's hammer against Catshee's sleek white forehead.

For a moment, nothing happened. Catshee looked up at Rose with a satisfied expression before bowing his head – and then Catshee *grew*. He changed shape before their eyes, making them all take a few steps back, Nellie's hand on Rose's arm to steady her. Rose shaded her face with her hands, dazzled by the overwhelming glow of Catshee's transformation.

Finally, the glow faded enough for them to see.

'Ah, there he is, now,' Gracie said, reaching out to pat the animal Catshee had become. His hand barely reached the top of its flank. 'I'll say that's a bit of a relief, hah?'

The huge beast regarded Gracie with fond awareness, before looking back at Rose with eyes that were steady and fathomless. Something about them reminded her of the eternity in Sioc's gaze.

Nellie released Rose's arm and gently pushed her forward. 'Go on,' she whispered. 'He won't hurt you.'

Rose stared in shock. Towering over her was the largest animal she'd ever seen – like a moose but bigger in every way. Its antlers were almost as wide as Hargate Street, their upper tines easily reaching the level of the upstairs windows behind which people were sleeping, held in Gracie's magic until this quest – whatever it was – had reached an end. The animal was mostly silvery-white, though a thick line of bluish black ran down its back and around the base of its throat like a necklace. It pawed the ground with hooves that looked as though they were made of iron and its breath hovered around its head like a cloud. As Rose watched, it twitched its ears once, then twice, as though shooing away a fly.

'I've seen pictures,' Rose whispered, reaching out one trembling hand towards the giant animal. 'In books and things. And I saw the skeleton in the museum, on our school tour last year. But I had no idea – I had *no* idea.' She patted its leg, shivering with awe as she felt its heat beneath her fingers, and turned to Nellie, who was beside her, staring up at the magnificent beast. 'It's an Irish elk,' Rose breathed. 'Isn't it? Even though they've been extinct for thousands of years. But it's here. An actual *elk*.'

'And wherever you need to go,' Nellie said, nodding at the elk, 'he'll bring you.'

14

The elk – Rose couldn't think of him as Catshee, not any more – tilted its gigantic head to one side, dipping one massive antler low enough for Rose to climb up onto it. Then, with surprising gentleness, the elk lifted its antler slowly so that Rose could get her bearings, and within a moment or two she was sitting astride its mighty back. Its neck was close enough for Rose to sink her face into the fragrant fur, if she wanted to, and it was solid as a tree trunk in front of her. The elk's antlers stretched out on either side of its head, reaching into the night, and Rose pushed her fingers into the animal's coat, hoping she'd be able to hold on.

'Don't be afraid,' Nellie called. Rose looked down – she seemed so far away. 'You carry with you the power of the Silver Road and the protection of the Dagda.'

'And if that fellow gives you any guff, just hit him a good kick!' Gracie chortled.

The elk snorted, pawing the ground again, and Gracie hopped out of antler-range, still chuckling.

'Where should we go?' Rose whispered to the elk. She looked up to see it turn its head back towards her, rolling its eye towards the Silver Road. 'We should follow the Road? Okay. Good plan.' She clicked her tongue, pulling at the elk's fur as though trying to turn the animal round, and it let out a chuff of hot, irritated breath. 'O-kay,' Rose said, flattening herself against its neck and letting it make its own way. 'Good point.'

The elk gave a loud, clear bellow, powerful enough to rattle windows up and down the length of Hargate Street. The sound echoed into the sky, making even the stars dance overhead, and the Silver Road shone all the brighter beneath them. Then the magnificent animal reared up, lifting its front legs high, and turned with one graceful movement, its hooves hitting the ground with a heavy thump. Rose squeaked, pressing her eyes tight shut and squishing herself as close as she could to the elk's neck, desperately hoping she wouldn't fall off.

And with that, the elk began to gallop.

Rose turned as much as she could, trying to look over her shoulder. She caught a glimpse of Nellie and Gracie – Nellie with her hand to her mouth, Gracie reaching out for Nellie to wrap her in a hug – and then they were gone. Rose blinked hard, trying to clear her vision, and then she turned away. She pressed her face against the elk's body, letting her tears – her sorrow at parting and her fear of what was to come – trickle into its pelt.

The elk's hooves pounded the earth, the rhythm almost like a giant heartbeat. Rose saw the Silver Road passing beneath them, the flowers growing as thickly and as brightly here as they had back on Hargate Street. Buildings and streets swept by on either side, so quickly that Rose felt sick as she tried to figure out where they were. She closed her eyes again, hoping her stomach would settle. Then, suddenly, the elk skidded to a halt. It snorted, shaking its incredible head, its antlers swooping from side to side, and Rose's eyes popped open again in shock as she fought to stay anchored on its back.

'Whoa!' Rose shouted, because it seemed the right thing to say. 'What is it?' She leaned around the elk's neck to look for whatever might have caused it to

stop, fearing the worst, expecting to see something that had crawled out from the pages of her mother's book – a terrifying giant or a man with a spear and a roaring face . . .

'*R-Rose?*' came a quivering voice.

Rose stared. In the centre of the Silver Road, dressed in pyjamas, a fluffy purple dressing gown and rabbit slippers, stood Emer McGuire. She stared up at the gigantic elk with wide eyes, her teeth chattering with terror.

'*Emer?* What on *earth* are you doing here?'

'This is a dream,' Emer said, still not blinking. 'It's a dream, it's a dream, it's got to be a dream, there's no way there's a literal *dinosaur* in the middle of the road –'

'It's not a dinosaur,' Rose said, confused. 'It's an Irish elk.'

Emer flicked her gaze away from the elk and stared at Rose, frowning slightly. 'And again with the weirdness.'

Rose pressed her lips tight, anger making her muscles quiver. 'Are you ever going to just give me a break?'

Emer blinked, her face shifting into something that looked a little like embarrassment, but Rose

told herself she was imagining it. In the next blink, Emer's sneer was back in place. 'You make it too easy,' she muttered.

Rose shook Emer's barbed words away. 'Why are you even awake?' Thoughts zipped through her head, panicked and hot. *Gracie's spell might be weakening. He's supposed to be keeping the whole country still and steady, but if Emer's here, and she can see me . . .*

Emer pulled her gaze away from the elk to look at Rose again. 'I was awake anyway. I haven't been sleeping much the past few days. I've been sick all week – didn't your daddy tell you?' She wrinkled her nose in what looked like distaste. 'Ever since I got soaked, down at the well. And we all know whose fault that is.'

Rose let out a strangled, exasperated breath. 'You walked in by yourself,' she said in a level voice.

Emer raised an eyebrow. 'And who'll believe that, do you think?'

'I don't particularly care,' Rose replied. 'Pretty soon it won't even matter, anyway. Not if . . .' She paused, swallowing nervously. 'Not if things go wrong tonight.'

Emer blinked, looking confused. She seemed to shrink a bit as she stared back at the elk. 'I've seen

all this,' she whispered, her forehead creasing in a frown. The light of the Silver Road sparkled in her dark eyes. 'This giant deer-thing, the shining path, all of it. I've *dreamed* it. Except . . . it ended in fire. And lots of screaming.'

'You've dreamed about the Silver Road?' Rose felt a shiver run over her skin.

'And then tonight, I saw the flowers,' Emer continued, as if Rose wasn't there. 'Just like in my dream.'

'You saw the flowers?'

Emer nodded, finally looking back at Rose. 'Did you?'

Rose rolled her eyes. 'Well. Obviously.'

Emer pulled her dressing gown tighter around her neck. She glanced to the left and right, seeming afraid. 'Are we, like, the only people awake? I set the house alarm off by mistake when I was leaving, and it took me ages to remember the code to reset it. But Mum didn't wake, nor did Dad, and nor did George.' She looked up at Rose. 'He's the groundskeeper,' she told her needlessly.

'It's . . . hard to explain,' Rose said. 'But, yes. Basically. It's just us.' Relief flooded her at the thought that Gracie's magic wasn't weakening, but she couldn't help but wonder why Emer would be the only other person left unaffected by it. And then, an even more worrying thought: was it Gracie's magic or the power of the *tathlum* that had kept Emer from falling asleep, and placed her in the elk's path?

'So, what *is* going on here?' Emer said, clutching her neckline tighter.

'Emer, listen,' Rose began. 'Do you have it? The stone? Did you bring it with you?'

Emer's expression hardened. 'What's it to you?'

Rose took a patient breath. 'Do you *still* not get it? Look around!' She gestured at the elk, and the shining road beneath their feet. 'This isn't a dream, Emer. Not this time. I need that stone. I told you. It's important.' Rose paused, unsure how much she should say. She stared at Emer, whose face shone blue in the bluish-silver light of the Road. The fear in her eyes looked too genuine to be an act; Emer never let anyone see anything except her strength, her bravado, her power, but this was something she couldn't hide. *She's been brought here for a reason, just like I was*, Rose realised. *I might need her too.* She paused, readying herself to continue. 'The stone's a weapon. I don't know yet how to use it or what I'm going to have to do, but I've got to have it back.'

Emer snorted, looking away. 'Yeah. Right.'

Rose swung herself off the elk's back, landing heavily amid the flowers. She took two fast paces towards Emer, who staggered a little, her eyes wide, taken by surprise at Rose's daring. 'Do you think you're dreaming now?' Rose asked. 'Do you think you're actually *capable* of imagining something like this? Well, you're not.' She paused, staring the taller girl down. 'I need to follow the Silver Road before its magic completely dies, and I've got to stop Balor. The Road is being destroyed and that means the magic that's kept Balor in prison for – well, for *ages* – is about to fail. And he might be on his way back. I have to stop it. Somehow.' She cleared her throat. 'Haven't quite worked that bit out yet.'

Emer blinked. 'Who's Balor?'

Rose sighed. 'Look. Do you have the stone?'

Emer nodded. 'It's in my pocket,' she said, her voice low.

'Then it might be better to explain it on the way.' Rose turned to the elk, getting ready to climb back on.

'There is *zero* chance I'm going –' Emer began.

Rose spun on her heel and strode towards Emer again, so quickly that Emer stumbled and tipped backwards into the silver flowers. She lay there, staring up at Rose, who stood over her with her hands curled into fists. 'There is literally no time for us to stand here *talking* about this stuff,' Rose said. 'If Balor wakes, then everyone and everything we love is *gone*. Kaput! Your folks, your fancy house, your *groundskeeper*, the whole lot of it.' Rose blinked hard as her family's faces swept across her mind. 'My brothers. My parents. Everyone. And time's running out. So, if you won't give me the stone, and if you won't come with me, then I'm going alone. And I'll find a way to stop Balor with or without you.' She paused, feeling herself shaking as she continued. 'I know I'm only a *charity case*, but this is all on me now. If you're not going to help, then get out of the way.' Rose whirled on the spot again and made her way to the elk, furiously wiping her cheeks as she went. The elk dipped its antler, and as Rose climbed on, she glanced around.

Emer was getting to her feet.

'Hey,' she called. 'Hey! Wait.'

Rose hopped to the ground. 'What?'

Emer clutched the neck of her dressing gown, taking a few steps in her direction. 'Don't – don't just *leave* me here, okay? I'll come.'

Rose gave a single nod and began to haul herself up the elk's antler again. When she reached the elk's back and looked down, Emer was gazing up at her with trepidation.

'Oh, come on,' Rose said, exasperated.

Emer's lip twisted but she reached for the closest jutting branch on the elk's antler, putting her slippers to work as she hauled herself up. Rose reached down to help.

'I'm fine!' Emer snapped, grabbing Rose's hand. 'It's just – I'm not really wearing the right *shoes* for climbing.'

Eventually, with much muttering and complaining, Emer reached the elk's neck. Rose helped her get settled behind her. 'Okay. So, hold on?' she said. 'This guy moves pretty fast.'

Tentatively, Emer reached around from behind Rose and grasped hold of her T-shirt. 'Right,' she said, and Rose pretended not to hear the wobble in her voice. 'I'm ready.'

The elk began to move again, slowly at first, and Rose felt Emer go rigid.

'It's okay,' she called over her shoulder. 'Honestly. He won't let us fall.'

'This is *unbelievable*,' Emer gasped. 'It literally cannot be happening!'

'It literally is,' Rose said.

'Where are we going?' Emer called.

Rose's mind's eye filled with the image she'd seen in Mamó's book, earlier that night. She remembered the powerful person in the drawing, the man with the light of battle in his eyes and the open-mouthed roar. Her uncle's favourite story – the mighty wolf-warrior. 'The Mac Tíre,' she whispered. He'd looked like a hero, hadn't he? Someone they could rely on to help them in the fight against an ancient, undead, fire-eyed god? Rose knew they needed to find Balor, but they couldn't stand alone against something as mighty as that. They needed help. 'The Lia Fáil!' she called, hoping the elk could hear her.

'We need to go to Tara!'

'*Tara?*' shrieked Emer. 'Like, the *Hill* of Tara? But that's hours away!'

'Not if you're travelling by elk,' Rose shouted in response.

'Oh my God,' Emer cried, pressing her face against Rose's back.

On and on the elk galloped, eating up the countryside in huge gulps. Rose looked up every once in a while, but she couldn't have said where they were. The Silver Road didn't follow many man-made roads – it seemed to follow its own track instead, sometimes even running through houses and gardens. More than once the elk had to make a mighty leap to clear someone's roof, landing with a thump that Rose was sure would wake everyone in the house – but nobody ever stirred. The moon hung high overhead, unmoving and still, steady as a lamp.

'We're actually doing this,' Rose whispered to the stars, looking up into the peace of the night sky. 'We're *actually* in a story, like the ones in Mamó's book.' She imagined, for a moment, the artist's impression of her, brave and strong on the back of the elk, and Emer in her bunny-rabbit slippers right behind her. *Rose the Brave, Rose the Clever, Rose the Fantastic –*

And then, out of the peaceful darkness and the silent sky, came a bolt of red lightning. As it flew, Rose could see it was a spear, thrown by an invisible enemy – and it was coming right for them.

The elk jerked its head to intercept it, and the spear clattered away against one of its antlers, making the massive animal stumble. It bellowed, long and loud – a sound of rage. Quickly, another spear followed the first, making the elk leap to one side as it dodged the blow.

'What's *happening*?' shouted Emer. Her grip on Rose's shirt tightened.

'I don't know!' Rose shouted back. 'Just – hold on!'

Spears rained down, one following another faster than Rose could believe. *Where are they coming from?* She looked around the elk's neck, trying to see. Up ahead, it looked like the light of the Silver Road was being overwhelmed by something red and black and yellow, something furious, like a fire out of control. From this fiery ball the spears were coming, impossibly fast, darts of red death.

'Someone has a good aim!' Emer shouted, burying her head

between Rose's shoulder blades, and something pinged to life in Rose's memory.

It was she who wounded the mighty Dagda with a spear-blow like lightning from the heavens . . .

'Cethlenn Crooked-Tooth,' she whispered, staring at the fire up ahead.

The elk bellowed again, almost like it was agreeing with Rose's assessment.

'Come on!' Rose shouted. 'We've got to make it! I know you can leap that fire. Please! We can't let her stop us.'

The giant beast screamed, a sound that was a mix of terror and excitement, and something about it made Rose's blood thrill. The elk began to pick up pace, lowering its mighty head as it ran straight for the fireball in its path. More spears came, but the elk batted them away.

'This is a *nightmare*!' yelled Emer from behind.

'I know!' Rose shouted back, her grin wild and wide.

And next thing they knew, the elk was airborne. It soared over the fire like a shooting star, kicking away spears with its impenetrable hooves, the contact making sparks fly.

Rose couldn't help but look down as they flew. In the centre of the fire stood a person – or, at the very least, a person-shaped thing. It stared up at the elk and the girls on its back with terrible hatred in its burning eyes, before smiling with a mouth full of terrifying, gigantic, crooked teeth. Then it reached up to rip a handful of hair out of its own head before throwing it at the elk; each strand of hair became a red-hot spear, and Rose ducked in against the elk's back, her heart thumping with terror and shock. As it landed, the elk gave a grunt of something that sounded like pain, but it didn't miss a step. Instantly it was off again, galloping with as much pace as before – and from behind them came a shriek of anger that shook the earth.

Rose clung to the elk, her mind a painful whirl. There had been something familiar about that terrible face amid the flames – but what? *It's like I recognised it – but that's impossible!* She shook the thought away and tried to focus.

'We're on the right path,' Rose said. 'If that's Cethlenn, and if she's trying to stop us, then we're doing the right thing.'

'Who is she?' Emer shouted.

'Cethlenn,' Rose called back. 'Cethlenn Crooked-Tooth. She's Balor's wife. And she wants to bring him back. He was dead, you see. Or, sort of dead. *Mostly* dead.'

There was a pause as Emer tried to digest this. '*What?*' she finally shouted.

'Balor! Of the Evil Eye! He's a god, power over fire and destruction and death and chaos, all that stuff. He was killed in a battle years ago – or, at least, that's what the stories say. Anyway, his wife – Cethlenn, the nice flamey lady with the spears, back there – is trying to . . . *wake* him, or bring him back from the dead, or whatever. And we've got to make sure it doesn't happen.'

'Okay, stop this deer,' Emer shouted. 'I want to get off.'

The elk's pace didn't slow. Rose shrugged. 'Sorry,' she said over her shoulder. 'It looks like you're in, whether you want it or not.'

'That's – *kidnapping*!' Emer shouted. 'My dad's going to –'

'Emer!' Rose shouted, turning to her. 'Shut up!'

The elk bellowed in agreement. Emer's mouth snapped closed as Rose faced forward once more. 'All this has something to do with that stone. Right?' she said eventually.

Rose nodded. 'It's a weapon,' she said. 'To kill Balor. Again.'

Emer screeched into Rose's ear. 'We're going to have to *kill* someone?'

'Well, – maybe! We might not have to *actually* do it ourselves.' She paused, trying to work things out in her head. 'We're going to try to wake up a hero to do it for us.'

'A *hero*?'

Rose looked around just enough to see the edge of Emer's face. 'The Mac Tíre. He's at the Hill of Tara.'

'So, we just walk up and ring his doorbell and say, "Hi! Fancy slaying a god for us this evening?"'

Rose pulled a face. 'Well, it might be a bit more complicated than that.'

Emer snorted. 'You don't say.' Rose felt her shifting position on the elk. After a moment, Emer turned back around. 'And, just so you know, that crooked-toothed woman seems to be after us,' she said into Rose's ear. 'In case it's important.'

15

'Can you go faster?' Rose called to the elk. The animal rolled its eye, the one nearest to Rose, fixing her with a glare. 'I know!' Rose shouted. 'But Cethlenn's behind us!'

The elk grunted, and Rose felt its muscles bunching hard beneath her as it did its best to build up even more speed – but the burst of effort didn't last long. The elk was beginning to tire.

'We must be nearly there,' Emer said. 'We're going a hundred miles an hour!'

'But we need to get there quicker,' Rose said. She freed one hand from the elk's fur and reached into her pocket. Nellie's sweets were still in there, and she dug around until she'd filled her palm. 'Here!' she shouted to the elk. 'Can you eat these?'

The elk turned its head, and she stretched her arm

223

out as far as it would go – but it wasn't far enough. Rose turned to Emer. 'Hold me!' she shouted before pushing herself slowly up until she was standing on the elk's shoulders. She pressed herself against its neck, clinging on to whatever fur she could grab as she leaned out and reached for the animal's head. She felt Emer's hands gripping her legs, her fingers digging in. Finally Rose felt the elk's tongue, huge and hot and rough, as it licked the cróigíní from her palm. 'Pull me back!' she shouted, and Emer did, grabbing her wherever she could get a handhold. Rose was barely tucked onto the elk again before it took off once more, with a burst of speed and power that put them well ahead of their pursuer.

They galloped over open countryside for many miles, clearing roads, motorways, powerlines and houses with a single leap, until finally on the horizon they could see a hill rising against the light of the moon. Right on top was a standing stone – Rose recognised it from the drawing in her mamó's book. The elk put on one more burst of speed as they drew near the wide river Boyne, its waters shining in the moonlight; with a leap, they cleared it, landing hard on the farside bank, and at last the elk began to slow, its breath coming in huge shuddering gasps. Soon it reached the first of several undulations in the earth, like waves beneath the soil. It stopped running, slowing to a trot and finally to a complete stop, its body shaking and its lungs rattling inside its chest.

'Thank you,' Rose whispered. The elk's ears flickered in friendly acknowledgement.

'Now what?' Emer said, gathering her dressing gown in her hands as she prepared to disembark. Rose went first. She turned and reached back to help Emer down as she did the same, grumbling all the while about the state of her slippers.

Rose's legs felt wobbly as she started to walk. She kept her eyes on the highest point of the hill in front of them with its single upright stone. 'The Lia Fáil,' she told Emer as they drew near. The effort of walking uphill was enough to make them both gasp. 'The Stone of Destiny. Something to do with the ancient kings.'

'Fabulous,' Emer snapped. 'But why are *we* here? Where does this –' she waved her hand dismissively – '*hero* person live?'

'Underneath it,' Rose said, hoping she was right.

'What?' Emer said, her face a twist of disgust. 'You mean, – like, a corpse? We're going to dig up a dead body, on a national monument, in the middle of the *night*?'

Rose stared at her. 'No! Of course not. Nothing like that.' She coughed, pulling the hammer out of her shorts and spinning it around in her hand before meeting Emer's eye. 'We're going to use this Shaping tool to open the earth and, you know, free him.'

Emer raised her hands and dropped them again, smacking them against her thighs. 'Yes, of course, I mean – *exactly*, right? What else would we possibly be doing with our Saturday night?' She rubbed her face hard with her hands. 'Come on,' she muttered. 'This is a dream. Wake *up*!'

Rose nodded towards the elk, quietly grazing a few feet away. 'Does that look like a dream?'

Emer opened her mouth to answer, only to find she had nothing to say.

'Now. Here goes nothing,' Rose muttered. She strode up to the Lia Fáil until she was close enough to touch it. The ground around it had been neatly paved with flat, rectangular stones, laid out in a sunburst pattern around the upright stone itself. The Lia Fáil, despite its impressive name, was barely up to her chest, thick and grey and weathered by the years it had spent on top of this hill. For the first time, Rose began to doubt. The Lia Fáil looked like a lump of something you could buy in a garden centre, or something you might find forgotten by the side of the road – a meaningless lump of rock. She swallowed hard, and then a grin lit her face as she thought about Nellie, Gracie, the cauldron, Catshee – even herself. 'Nothing lately has been as much or as little as it appears,' she whispered, holding up the Shaper's hammer. Its whorls glowed blue. She took that as a good sign.

She held out the hammer, gripping it with both hands. 'I call on the Mac Tíre,' Rose began in her clearest voice. 'I ask him to wake and – and help us to face an old enemy, Balor of the Evil Eye, and his wife, the witch Cethlenn. I ask this in the name of the Dagda, and of Nellie Sweeney, the Cauldron Keeper, and of Gracie Kinch, the Shaper.' She licked her lips. 'And I also ask for me, Rosaleen Darke.' She paused for a moment, thinking. 'Please,' she added finally. Her words faded into silence.

A minute passed and nothing happened. The night air continued to breathe around the Hill of Tara, and the Lia Fáil remained impassive.

'Brilliant,' Emer said from a few feet away.

Her scornful voice carried on the breeze. 'Really excellent hero-ing there.'

'I don't see you doing any better,' Rose snapped back.

'Maybe try *hitting* it?' Emer suggested scathingly. 'Isn't that what hammers are for?'

Rose looked back at the Lia Fáil. She closed her eyes and imagined Gracie, sitting in his cobbler's workshop back on Hargate Street. He'd often perch in the window, cross-legged, using his tools with a delicacy of touch, tipping the hammer so gently you'd barely see it move – but it would get the job done. Gracie didn't need to use force to get his hammer to work. Sometimes, instead, you just needed to know where to tap.

This hammer's not for destroying things, Rose realised, opening her eyes to look at the hammer again. *It's for making. It's for creating. It's for Shaping.* She took a breath and steadied her grip on the hammer's handle. Then, slowly, she reached out and tapped the Lia Fáil, very softly. Straight away she felt the humming. The vibration of something changing, deep within the earth.

'What's happening?' Emer said.

Rose stumbled back a few steps, looking around. Nothing looked different, but the humming vibrations had become a rumbling now, and the earth began to tremble – very slightly, but enough to make the girls unsteady on their feet. Rose yelped as she felt Emer's hands squeezing her arm. 'Let go!' she said, trying to pull herself free – and then, the Lia Fáil lit up from inside with a bright blue-white light that seemed to trickle down from its rounded top, starting right at the spot where Rose had tapped it with the Shaper's hammer. The light followed a pattern that looked a lot like the whorls on the hammer itself, swirling and organic, like some sort of magical glowing plant.

Rose and Emer stumbled backwards down the hill, their eyes on the glowing stone, until finally the Lia Fáil broke apart, its halves separating like a book being opened, and a spear of light burst from it into the night sky, straight and true. A boom of power pulsed from it, making Rose and Emer duck, but it did them no harm. Instead they turned to watch the countryside all around come to life – even more silver threads began to trace their way across the wide, flat landscape as far as they could see, joining up with the existing ones like tributary rivers meeting, growing stronger and brighter with every moment. Far away, along the horizon, a huge white-bright glow appeared, and Rose realised it was the Boyne – the mighty waterway filling with ancient magic, answering the call of the Seandraíocht in its own way.

'The Silver Road,' Rose said, blinking away tears of happiness as she stared. 'It's amazing!'

'Yeah, but where's this hero person?' Emer said, turning back to the Lia Fáil.

The mound of earth beneath the stone suddenly split, as though someone had struck it with a massive axe. The gap in the ground got deeper and darker, widening as it grew, until finally – and to their horror – the girls saw a pair of white-fingered hands begin to emerge from the soil, pushing and straining at the crack, forcing it to widen.

And then a gigantic man stepped from it, shaking the dirt off himself and looking around with eyes that were definitely more animal than human. He was at least two metres tall, with a wolf-pelt wrapped around his body. The wolf's head sat on top of his own head, its eyes bright and shining and its teeth framing the man's face like a crown. In one hand he held a thick-ended club, and in the other he had a shield with a swirling red pattern painted on the leather. Strapped to his back there was a huge spear. His gaze fell on the grazing elk and he grunted, with what Rose hoped was satisfaction and not anger.

Finally, he looked at Rose and Emer. For a long, long moment the three of them simply stood there. The man's gaze was steady as the rocks beneath their feet; Emer and Rose were wide-eyed with panic. Eventually he noticed the Shaper's hammer in Rose's hand and grunted again, the same noise as before.

'The . . . Mac Tíre?' Rose said, her voice barely more than a breath. 'Are you the Mac Tíre?'

From behind the girls came a horrifying shriek – like a choir of a thousand tormented voices mixed with the noise of screaming metal – and they spun round just in time to see the light of the Boyne suddenly flicker and go out.

'Cethlenn,' Rose whispered, no longer caring that Emer was holding her in a painfully tight grip. The girls clutched one another, and Rose pointed the Shaper's hammer at the oncoming witch. 'She must have crossed the river. She's caught up.'

Cethlenn was like a rolling fireball, growing

more massive with every breath. Her blood-chilling cry screeched out again, and the elk hurried to the girls' side, standing beside them protectively. Emer nudged Rose.

'Hey,' Emer whispered. 'Rose, look!'

Rose followed Emer's gaze. A bright red weal had risen on the elk's flank, like a burn.

'Oh no!' Rose cried, her face crumpling, remembering the spears Cethlenn had thrown as they'd flown over her earlier.

The elk looked down at her, and even though Rose could only really see one of its large, gentle eyes, she felt sure the animal was trying to reassure her. Even still, it felt as though a little light inside of Rose had gone out. Sure, they had the hammer – and yes, it had opened the earth and freed the Mac Tíre. But was it enough?

Cethlenn roared again, and from the fireball came another handful of flying red spears.

'Oh my God,' Emer gasped, as she and Rose huddled close to one another. Rose looked around, desperate for something to take shelter behind, and her eyes fell on the hole in the earth, ripped by the Mac Tíre as he'd pulled himself free.

'Come on!' She pulled Emer with her as she ran, keeping low, the elk covering their backs. The girls scrambled for the opened ground and threw themselves inside. The soil smelled rich and somehow metallic, which made Rose feel like throwing up. Beside her, Emer trembled, her teeth chattering, as they watched Cethlenn approach. Emer was muttering something to herself in a voice too low for Rose to hear the words.

'Hey,' Rose whispered. 'Emer! Are you okay?'

Emer made no reply, but Rose noticed her hand sliding into her dressing gown pocket, and a feeling of cold dread settled around her. The stone was in there – the stone that somehow seemed like it had a mind of its own. Before Rose could do anything about it, the elk bellowed, raising its mighty head to the sky, and both girls jerked in surprise. Some of the confusion and terror fell away from Emer's face, and her muttering finally stopped. She pulled her hand out of her pocket and dug it into the soil instead, meeting Rose's eye for the briefest glance.

'Sorry,' she whispered.

Rose nodded, giving the other girl a quick,

encouraging smile, and they looked back towards the battle.

The witch had drawn nearer, leaving a trail of blackened death where she passed, and every few minutes a fresh barrage of spears came flying. But this time, whenever a spear hit the ground it transformed into a warrior. *She's bringing an army*, Rose thought desperately.

Cethlenn's soldiers were tall and strong, each of them red-clad with yellow hair and burning eyes. Men and women both, armed with spears and swords, their voices part of Cethlenn's awful war cry, they ran. They flickered over the ground as fast as an approaching inferno.

Rose turned to the Mac Tíre, but his gaze was not on her. Instead, he watched Cethlenn's army with a strange light in his eyes – not fear but something else. He seemed to be waiting for the enemy to come – waiting until they were just close enough, and then . . .

At his waist he wore a horn. The Mac Tíre raised it to his mouth and blew, and across the plains and hills there rang a note that rattled Rose and Emer's chests, thrilling their blood and bones.

When the noise of the horn blast finally died away, all Rose could hear was her own panting breaths, and Emer's. They looked at one another fearfully, and then Emer's expression changed to one of confusion.

'Hey,' she whispered, reaching out to grab hold of Rose's arm. 'Do you feel that?'

Rose realised what she meant right at that second. The ground beneath them, and around them, was vibrating – and it was very quickly growing stronger. The girls met one another's eyes again, and Rose could see Emer's horror.

The elk whickered in distress, its eyes rolling as it began to move away. Rose scrambled out of the hole, dragging Emer with her. 'Come on!' she shouted. 'Something's coming!' Emer pulled herself free, and the girls began to run.

And in the very next moment, from the earth of Tara there burst a pack of mighty wolves, each one as big as a horse, their jaws wide and hungry, their eyes fixed on their prey. Emer screamed, dropping to the ground and curling into a ball. Rose scrambled backwards on all fours, her wide eyes trained on the hole in the earth where they'd taken shelter until a few seconds before, and which was now spewing incredible beasts like nothing she'd ever seen or even dreamed. But the wolves were paying the girls no heed. Their attention was entirely focused on the one who'd summoned them. The Mac Tíre shrugged into his wolf-pelt and transformed into a giant wolf before their eyes, his coat a burnished copper and his eyes a fearsome gold. Then, without a backward glance, he and his warriors attacked Cethlenn's army.

The wolves slammed into the ranks like a battering ram, scattering Cethlenn's warriors to either side. The warriors fought back with ferocious strength, but from the start it seemed that the wolves of the Mac Tíre's warband had the upper hand. They were simply too big, too vicious and too strong to be overwhelmed – but they did not fight without casualties. Rose and Emer covered their ears, scrunching down into tight balls beneath the elk's belly as they tried to block out the sounds of wolves screaming in pain, and the roar of voices in a courageous last stand. From the middle of the battle Rose heard the sound of the Mac Tíre's horn once again, and she opened her eyes, pushing herself up to see what was happening.

From a mound not far away came another flood

of warriors – these ones not of flesh and blood but instead made of light. They were responding to the call of the Mac Tíre, Rose was sure, coming to fight beside him because they heard the horn.

'Are those . . . *ghosts*?' Emer said as she watched the warriors of light attack the army of Cethlenn.

'Something like that, I guess,' Rose said. 'Spirits, maybe. Weren't people buried here?'

The battle raged for time beyond meaning. The moon stayed still in the sky, and the stars sparkled steadily. Nothing else in the world seemed to move or change. Rose watched Cethlenn rip handful upon handful of hair from her head, creating more and more doomed warriors, many of whom barely had time to draw breath before they fell beneath the jaws of a wolf. The Mac Tíre and his warriors were incredible – they fought without stopping, barely pausing for breath, determined and brave beyond all measure, and Rose began to feel the first tiny seedlings of hope. Maybe they did stand a chance here after all.

'There's something familiar about her,' Emer whispered from their makeshift hiding place. 'That witch, I mean. It's like I know her.'

Rose's eyes widened. 'I was thinking the same

thing,' she whispered back. The girls stared at the figure of Cethlenn in the thick of the battle, and a gust of wind blew her hair over her face, just for a moment. The witch wasted no time ripping the offending hank out of her head and flinging it to the ground, but in the brief second her face was half-veiled, Rose and Emer both gasped. Rose remembered where she'd seen that face before. On the TV, being led away from the High Court into a fancy car. *No wonder she always hid her eyes and hair and teeth.*

'It's *her*!' Emer said.

'Kathleen Ennis!' Rose confirmed. The girls stared at each other. 'It makes sense,' Rose continued. 'Kathleen and Cethlenn even sound a bit alike.'

'No, it *doesn't* make sense,' Emer said. 'Why would a witch who can, like, magic up an entire *army* need to pretend to be a human?'

Rose felt her brain unlocking. 'It's the job,' she said, staring at Emer. 'The one she's got your dad doing. And *my* dad. The excavation!'

'What?' Emer's face was twisted with confusion.

Rose looked back towards the witch. 'She needs *people* to help her dig,' she said. 'People to break the

238

Silver Road, to destroy its power, and an excuse for making a huge hole in the ground. Wherever your dad's site is, the one she's got him working on, that's where Balor is.' Rose felt a cold fear wash over her once again. 'And that means, no matter what happens here, Balor might still be on the move. It's great that we're holding our own against Cethlenn, but the bigger fight is going to be at the excavation site.'

Emer's mouth dropped open as she looked at Cethlenn again. 'My dad is going to *flip* when he finds out,' she whispered. Then, her expression twisted with pain, and she raised one hand to her head. 'Stop it,' she moaned softly.

'Is it the stone?' Rose asked, placing a gentle hand on her arm. 'It's hurting you, isn't it?'

'It's making me want to go over there,' Emer said through gritted teeth. 'It's filling my head up with – awful stuff. Bones and breaking and things.'

Rose nodded. 'It's a weapon, so it wants to be in the battle,' she said. 'No surprises there.'

'It made me sick,' Emer said. 'The stone. Not – not you, or the well or whatever. And when I was sick, I was Mum's priority for a few days. You know? She put things aside to look after me. And Dad would ring every few hours to check how I was.' Emer looked at Rose, her dark eyes filled with pain. 'I liked that,' she finished in a quiet voice.

Rose tried to smile. 'I get it,' she said hoarsely.

An earth-rending shriek made both girls look back towards the witch. The battle seemed to be winding down. Cethlenn's forces were slowing. Her handfuls of hair were getting thinner and thinner, and the witch herself was now almost bald. Already the hair had started to grow back on the far side of her head, but for now her army was crushed. With one last shriek of anger, Cethlenn began to retreat, her fireball rolling away across the countryside.

The Mac Tíre stood tall amid the carnage, back in his human form with the wolf-pelt wrapped around him like a cloak once more. He raised his voice and shouted, though Rose couldn't follow the words he used. Then he raised one arm and swept it through the air, in the direction of Cethlenn's retreat.

As his wolves and the spirit army rallied themselves to obey, the Mac Tíre leaped and changed in mid-air, transforming himself once more into the gigantic wolf he had been during the fight, his shield, club and spear strapped to his back. He ran after Cethlenn, vanishing into the darkness.

'He's calling them to follow him,' Emer said. 'Isn't he?'

All around them, wolves and shining fighters got to their feet and did just that. Beside the girls, the elk lowered an antler, as though urging them up. Rose scrambled onto its back, helping Emer on too, and as the elk began to move, Rose turned to look at her.

'And now we know where they're going,' she said.

16

The elk ran faster than ever, following the *yalloo*-ing of the wolves. All across the countryside, roads were quiet, houses remained dark, cows in their fields slept peacefully. Rose looked up at the moon. It was still exactly as it had been since the moment Rose had followed the Silver Road out of her house, hanging overhead like an unblinking eye, its position unchanged. Something about its gentle light gave Rose courage and hope.

'It hasn't moved,' she said. 'That must mean Gracie is okay.'

'Gracie is the old guy, right?' Emer asked. Rose had tried to fill her in on lots of things, and found she had to keep explaining some bits over and over again – like who Gracie and Nellie were, and why they were important. She'd tried to describe what

Catshee had looked like before he became an elk, but had given up on getting Emer to understand.

'He's not *just* an old guy,' Rose replied, trying to keep the irritation out of her voice. 'He's the *Shaper.* Like, super-powerful?'

'All right, all right,' Emer sighed. 'Sorry.'

Before Rose could say anything else, there was a sudden explosion of light from all around them. Rose closed her eyes against it, and she heard Emer cry out. The elk bellowed, its deep, sonorous voice sounding across the countryside – but as Rose tried to work out what was happening, she realised the Mac Tíre and his wolves were howling too – a huge sound of excitement and joy. The light faded a little, just enough for her to see what was causing it.

'The Silver Road,' she breathed, looking around in excitement. The strands of silver, spread like a fine filigree over the hills as far as they could see, were shining strongly now and pulsing with new life. 'Look!' she called to Emer, freeing one hand from the elk's neck and pointing.

Emer's eyes shone with the light from the Silver Road. She looked around, her mouth opening slightly as she tried to take it all in. 'I wish I had my phone,' she whispered. 'This would look *so* cool on my socials.'

Rose rolled her eyes, but she knew she was grinning too. On and on they galloped, the elk easily keeping pace with the wolves. Rose whispered encouragement to it as they went.

'Hey,' Emer said, after they'd been pounding their way across the country for what felt like hours. 'Hey, I think I know where we are! Look up there.'

Rose followed Emer's gaze and soon she saw what Emer had seen. Standing proud on top of a nearby hill was a huge metal sculpture of a mounted warrior on a horse. Rose had been up to it once or twice with her parents before the twins had been born. It stood looking out over the countryside near Boyle, and Rose had always felt something stirring in her heart every time she saw it – not just because it felt like home, but because it had a strange power of its own. The sculpture had been there for many years and sometimes, despite how much Rose loved it, she would admit it didn't always look its best; parts of it were rusted and there were usually mounds of rubbish left at the horse's feet.

But now the massive sculpture was glowing a

bright silver-blue. A branch of the Silver Road had unfurled all the way up the hillside where the horse and rider stood, filling the statue and the ground beneath it with bright magic. As Rose watched, the light curled its way back down the hill's other side, where it rejoined the glowing path beneath the hooves of the elk and the paws of the wolves.

'The Gaelic Chieftain.' She whispered the name her dad always gave the statue, smiling a little as she took it in. And then, as the elk galloped past it, Rose saw something that made her breath stop in her lungs.

With a metallic groaning that could be heard for miles around, the rider on the horse raised one mighty arm and, with the other, pulled his steed around. Then, moving as swiftly as a real horse and rider – albeit on a gigantic scale, the statue of the chieftain joined their dash across the country. The horse's hoofbeats thudded like miniature explosions, shaking the ground as it ran.

'Did you – . . . ? Did you . . . ? I mean that *can't* have happened,' Emer gasped from behind Rose.

'It did!' Rose laughed, a thrill of excitement bursting through her. She felt like roaring a war cry herself.

On they galloped, the landscape becoming hillier

and more uneven now, the moonlight shining brightly on the lakes and waterways as they passed them by. The elk never missed its footing, though Rose's heart ached as she listened to the huffing of its breath. 'Nearly there now,' she soothed, even though she really didn't know how much further they had to go.

'Your dad's site,' she shouted to Emer. 'Where is it exactly?'

Emer blinked, thinking. 'It's somewhere outside Enniskillen? It's huge – it goes for miles.'

'So if we've passed the Gaelic Chieftain way back, then we can't have much further to go,' Rose called in reply.

'What are we going to do when we get there?' Emer said. 'I mean, do you actually know?'

Rose didn't want to admit how little she knew about what to expect once they'd arrived at their destination. She didn't know what was facing them or how they were going to deal with any of it. 'I just know we have to stop Balor,' she called to Emer. 'We've got to find some way of putting him back into the ground, and the last time someone did that, they used the stone. It stopped him before, and we have to find a way to stop him again.' She glanced back at the other girl. 'And if I don't have the stone, I don't know what else to use.'

'Where did you even get it, anyway?' Emer called. 'The stone, I mean.'

'The Seandraíocht gave it to me,' Rose called back. 'The Old Magic.'

There was a thoughtful pause. 'But why *you*, though?' Emer said. 'What makes you special?'

Rose turned to her, as much as she could. 'Maybe nothing does,' she said, thinking of Mamó and her stories. 'I'm not any more special than you are, right? But that doesn't mean we're not important.'

A moment later, Rose felt Emer poke her in the side. She looked down to see Emer's hand, holding the stone. Rose's tummy lurched with something she couldn't quite name – fear, excitement, gratitude and more, all together. Emer's fingers were tight around the *tathlum*, almost like she was fighting with herself to let it go.

'If you want it, you'd better take it now,' Emer said, sounding like she was forcing the words out.

'Thanks,' Rose said, wriggling her fingers around the stone and pulling it free. Emer's hand relaxed as soon as the stone was removed, and she flexed her fingers once or twice as Rose stuffed the stone into the pocket of her shorts. She turned to look at Emer, but the other girl wouldn't meet her eye.

'I didn't want it any more, anyway,' Emer said. 'So, like, you're doing me a favour or whatever.'

'Well, thanks for nothing, then,' Rose said.

A genuine smile brightened Emer's face and Rose grinned as she turned back around, settling herself once more on the elk and trying to ignore the heat and weight of the stone in her pocket. It felt like a lump of meteorite, freshly fallen, or something that was about to explode at any moment.

The elk followed the chieftain and the wolves up the slope of a hill, their hooves and paws never leaving the Silver Road and, as they got higher, Rose looked to the left. From where they were she could see the sea – the Atlantic Ocean – a shimmering path laid down across it to the bright, coin-like moon overhead. The magic of the Silver Road unfurled towards it, trickling across the countryside like fingers stretching out, and then there was a burst of silver-blue light which made her sit up and pay attention. For a moment, she could have sworn there was a huge figure illuminated in the sky – a woman

248

wearing battle-gear – but in the next blink, she was gone. All Rose could see then was a bright blue-white glow coming from a round-topped hill, one with a smaller mound on top.

'Did you see that?' she called to Emer.

'Wasn't that Knocknarea?'

'Was it?' Rose had been there on a school trip once; her class had raced one another up its slopes to the cairn on top. Queen Maeve, the legendary warrior, was buried there, or so the stories said. 'The Hill of the Queen, right?'

'Right. Looks like she's awake, so let's hope she's in a good mood,' Emer said, staring at the hill, the glow reflected in her dark eyes.

For the next few miles there were no more triumphant shouts from the Mac Tíre and his wolves; they ran like hunters now, swift and silent, as they neared their prey. Rose's heart was thumping fiercely in her chest as she thought about the battle that might lie ahead. Would she know what to do? Would she be able to do it, in the heat of the moment? She wished, suddenly, that Gracie and Nellie would appear on either side of her, their kind faces looking familiar and comforting, their knowledge and power giving protection and strength to everyone around them – but there was no such luck. All that remained were the wolves, running on either side of the elk like a guard of honour, each of them bigger than a car and darker than a nightmare.

Then, from up ahead, there came the sound of the Mac Tíre's horn. It played two notes once, and then once more, the melody falling like a cry of pain. Before Rose could think about what was happening, she realised what was wrong. The light was fading in front of them. The bright silver-blue of the Seandraíocht, the power of the Silver Road, sputtered out into darkness up ahead. Her heart lurched at the thought of being without its protection. Huge tyre tracks gouged through the earth, cutting right across the flowers' path; pools of murky wastewater lay everywhere, their surfaces shining with oil. All around them there was churned-up mud and bits of discarded equipment – plastic fencing, pieces of piping, piles of iron rods going orange with rust. There was no way the magic of the Silver Road could exist here.

'Oh no,' Rose gasped, looking down. The flowers were scattered and dying around the elk's hooves, very few with any shining strength left in their petals.

The group began to draw to a halt, stopping at the frayed edges of the magic like they were afraid of tipping over the edge of a cliff. Rose stared at the Mac Tíre who was back in his human shape for now, his massive chest pumping in and out as he fought for breath. He raised his club in the air and hollered, the sinews and tendons in his neck and arms standing out like ropes. Some of his wolves looked uncertain, even afraid; a chorus of quiet whimpers began as they expressed their misgivings about continuing. Rose didn't think she could blame them. Beyond the light of the Silver Road, all was in darkness except for a dull orange glow on the hill a few miles away and the never-changing moon still suspended high above. Its light seemed fainter here, like it wished it didn't have to look down on what was happening on the earth far below.

'Why are we stopping?' Emer said, pointing right at the orange glow. 'Dad's site – look. It's just up there.'

'We did this,' Rose replied, her words tasting like ash in her mouth as she looked around at the broken Silver Road. 'Your dad and my dad and all the other workers here. This is our fault.'

'What's our fault?' Emer said, sounding genuinely confused.

Rose turned to her. 'Don't you see it? We've done so much damage, destroyed things that can never be replaced.'

'So what?' Emer retorted. 'It's just *business*, isn't it? It's not personal or whatever. You can't let feelings get in the way of progress. Right? That's what my dad always says.'

'But look,' Rose said, pointing at the flattened, dying flowers and at the stumps of newly felled trees nearby. 'How can you say this is progress? If the Silver Road hadn't been *dug up* none of this would have happened. The magic would have stayed strong, and Cethlenn wouldn't have had her chance to do whatever she's planning to do.'

Emer blinked, looking confused as she took in the sight. 'But my dad's worked so hard for this,' she said.

Rose swallowed. 'So has mine.'

There was silence for a few minutes as the girls tried to process everything they were seeing. 'I never really noticed it before,' Emer finally said, her voice wobbling. 'This – destruction? I mean, I see what you mean. It's not right, is it? There has to be a better way for my dad to do his thing without tearing everything else to shreds. He mightn't be the world's greatest *environmentalist*,' Emer snorted derisively, 'but he didn't mean any of the rest of this, you know?' Her voice was hoarse and she cleared her throat. 'I'm sure he didn't. He would have been doing a job. That's all.' She sniffed, rubbing quickly at her cheek. 'He didn't know anything about – magic or *gods* or . . . or . . .' Emer looked at the wolves all around her, breathing heavily in the night air, and the huge man clad in the wolf-skin at the head of the group, who stood warily. Somewhere in the darkness, its metal struts groaning as the horse shifted its weight, the chieftain waited.

'Look, it's a lot to take in,' Rose said. 'I know. And yeah, your dad probably didn't mean to do any of it.' She paused, thinking. 'It's probably something Cethlenn did to him – like, she put him under a spell or whatever. Or she forced him to dig exactly where she wanted him to.'

'She probably just paid him a load of money,' Emer said, giving a half-laugh. 'It wouldn't take much in the way of magic to get Dad to do what you wanted – so long as you have the cash.' She opened her eyes again and tried to smile, but it was washed through with sadness. 'Which probably explains why he doesn't do what I want, like, *ever*.'

'I think that's just a dad thing,' Rose replied, returning Emer's barely-there smile, but her grin fell away as the Mac Tíre's eyes met hers. They were golden and otherworldly. He stared at her and, after a long minute where it felt like her heart didn't beat at all, Rose finally understood. *I summoned him*, she thought. *So he's waiting for me to say it's okay – that this is the right way to go.* She took a deep breath, trying to calm her jangling nerves, and nodded. The Mac Tíre threw back his head and howled, acknowledging Rose's instructions, and gathering his pack.

With one shrug of his powerful shoulders, the Mac Tíre resumed his wolf-shape and began to run, leading his wolves forward into the darkness. They were running without the light of the Road now, so progress was slower. Rose was afraid the elk would lose its footing, or get hurt, as it tried to run without being able to see where it was putting its hooves.

'Take care!' she whispered to it, and its ears flicked in response.

It only felt like minutes before they were running up a low hill with a man-made barrier around its upper edge – a tall metal fence with barbed wire and spikes on top, with huge lamps set up every ten feet or so, casting the sickly orange light they'd seen from miles away. Large rectangular hoardings were attached to the fence, emblazoned with *Michael McGuire Plant Hire and Construction*, and the site itself was visible through the gaps between the hoardings. There was enough light for them to see their way now, and the pace increased – as did the volume of the wolves' growling. They weren't slowing as the barrier drew near. Instead they were speeding up, building enough power to crash right through it.

'Hey,' Emer said, stiffening behind Rose. 'Hey! Don't *damage* my dad's –'

Her words were cut off by the sound of buckling metal and smashing glass as a length of fencing collapsed beneath the weight of the wolf pack and the chieftain's horse.

'– property,' Emer finished weakly, settling back into her position behind Rose.

'Sorry!' Rose called to her. The elk picked its way over the fallen chain-link fence and leaped nimbly over the barbed wire, and then – they'd arrived. They were at the site where Emer's father, and Rose's, had been working to dig up the earth, to rip apart the protection of the Silver Road, and – if Rose's suspicions were correct – to raise the buried Balor from his pit. The wolf pack surged around them as the elk steadied itself, turning slowly as it tried to make sense of where it was.

All Rose could see, reaching as far as her vision lasted, was an unbelievably big hole in the earth. It went down for fifteen metres or more, the sloping sides of the hole darkening as they got deeper, and it appeared to be longer than the whole of Carriganawn. Roots poked out here and there like questing worms. At the bottom of the hole were machines, quiet now and still, the workers who drove them gone home for the night. There were tracks worn in the earth leading up and down from the dig site, pipes sticking out into nothingness, cabins and prefabs and portable toilets dotted all over, and around the top of the hole were broken trees and shattered rocks, destroyed by the relentless metal jaws of the digging machines.

We've got no protection here, and the Seandraíocht can't give us any help, Rose thought, despair rising in her chest. *We've got nothing.* The stone surged in her pocket, almost like it was reminding her it was there, but the sick feeling it left her with made Rose think that the *tathlum* was simply rejoicing, its destructive heart getting ready for the battle it knew was coming.

Eventually the elk followed the wolves, falling into step among them as they made their way around the hole, being careful to keep well away from it in case the edges crumbled beneath their great weight. The site seemed quiet. The lights all around the vast pit glowed the same acidic orange as Cethlenn's magic, which put everyone's nerves on edge – but there was no sign of her or her terrible warriors anywhere.

'I don't understand,' Rose said, turning this way and that from her perch on top of the elk. 'She's supposed to be here. This *has* to be it. Doesn't it?' She licked her lips, trying frantically to think. 'It's a gigantic disturbance in the earth, and it's destroyed the Silver Road,' she began. 'And it's clear they're digging *something* up – something that's been long buried, like Balor must have been. And Cethlenn was definitely going this way. Wasn't she?'

Emer shrugged. Her eyes were empty and exhausted. 'All I know is, if we're wrong, my dad's going to go ballistic when he sees that fence,' she muttered.

'We've got to be missing something,' Rose said, at just the same moment that a handful of spears – blood-red, fire-red, and thirsty for war – came sailing out of the darkness, aimed right at them.

17

The air was filled with the piteous sounds of howling as several of Cethlenn's spears found their mark. Rose was too shocked to speak, or even think, as she saw three or four of the Mac Tíre's wolf clan go tumbling head-over-tail down into the gigantic hole in the earth. The remainder whirled on the spot, facing the oncoming threat with their fangs bared, impatient for the command to attack. The Mac Tíre himself, tall and man-shaped at the head of his pack, stood and waited for Cethlenn to appear.

From over a mound of dirt, which had been piled high by the digging machines, the first wave of Cethlenn's witch-army came. They were blank-eyed and ferocious, their bodies painted red and yellow, and their hair like flames pouring down their backs. Most of them barely had time to brandish their spears before they fell, going down beneath a torrent of wolves and teeth. Another wave came, and they fell in the same way as the first.

'They're not real people,' Rose whispered to herself, squeezing her eyes tight against the sounds of carnage. 'They're not real people!'

'They *look* real!' Emer muttered as they huddled together on the back of the elk. 'With actual blood and everything.'

'Don't look!' Rose said, turning to Emer who was wide-eyed, staring at the battle.

'It's like a movie,' Emer whispered, her voice dreamy. Rose reached out to pull Emer's gaze away but before she had a chance to, the chieftain appeared. His metal horse raised a hoof and stamped among the warriors of Cethlenn. A flurry of spears greeted this, but they bounced harmlessly off the warrior's body and that of his steed.

The elk kept well back, staying as much as possible in the shadows around the battle. Emer and Rose watched in silence, feeling the elk's lungs labouring for breath beneath them, wondering with every moment which side was winning – and which was not. It seemed to switch and change with every moment. The warriors of Tara were invincible, but they weren't infinite. Cethlenn's army seemed never-ending, a ceaseless flow of people and weapons and single-minded courage, and soon they appeared to have the upper hand again.

'We won't be able to win unless we get rid of Cethlenn herself,' Rose said. 'She's creating all those warriors, and unless we stop her doing that we'll be here forever.'

'But how do we do that?' Emer asked. 'I mean, she's pretty powerful. Right?'

'Yes,' Rose said. 'But there's got to be a way.'

'How about we – Emer began, but whatever she was about to say was lost beneath a sudden burst of horrifying wailing. Next thing the girls knew, a roaring ball of flame came rolling over the ground behind them – and Cethlenn was at its heart. They could see her, eyes of dark orange and teeth like shards of jagged rock, hurrying towards them.

The elk bellowed for help and the girls screamed in fear, but it was too late. Cethlenn's fire was upon them. The elk reared, trying to avoid it, and one of its back legs caught on something in the earth – a root or a stray piece of metal – making it stumble and fall.

Emer and Rose grabbed one another as the elk fell to the ground, throwing them from its back. The elk held its head high, rolling its eyes as it searched for the girls, bellowing all the while.

Cethlenn reached into her hideous mouth and began to rip free her crooked teeth. She threw the teeth and they landed – *thunk-thunk-thunk* – in a tight circle around the fallen elk and the girls. The moment they were tossed into the air, each tooth became as tall and thick as a young tree, and they were too close together for anyone – let alone an elk – to squeeze between them. Rose spun, staring at the barrier around her. She ran to the nearest tooth, trying to push it aside or pull it loose, but it was covered with a burning acid-like gloop, and its sharp knife-like edges stung her skin. With a hiss of pain, she let go, wiping her palms on her T-shirt.

'Oh my God,' Emer gasped. 'Oh my *God*. What's happening?'

The ball of fire rolled even closer to the imprisoned girls. The elk kept bellowing and Rose dropped to her knees beside it. The elk's silver-blue glow seemed to be fading fast, overwhelmed by Cethlenn's fire, and Rose fought to keep the tears from her eyes.

'Catshee,' she whispered. 'Thank you.'

The elk took a huge breath and bellowed once again, the noise loud enough to make Rose cover her ears.

'Throw me the weapon,' came Cethlenn's voice from outside the wall of teeth. 'Throw me the *tathlum*, foolish child, and this can all be over. It should never have been yours to begin with. Sioc stole it from me. I guarded it for years uncounted, that none might use it against my mighty lord. I kept it safe all this time as I waited to regain my power, so that when I raised him from the dirt he would be beyond all harm and free to rule. And now I claim it back!' The witch's voice sounded like the crackling of flames, the roaring of a raging fire.

'It . . . it was you, then,' Rose said, trying to keep her voice steady. 'You were following Sioc that night. The night he gave it to me.'

'How *perceptive*,' the witch sneered. 'Yes, it was me. And when I crushed his body to powder, I did not find the weapon. So I knew he had hidden it behind the power –' she spat the word – 'of the Silver Road – a power that has been weakening for a thousand years, and which human *ingenuity* finally found a way to destroy completely. My patience has been rewarded.'

The witch's voice grew louder as the fireball rolled ever closer, and Cethlenn was right there, staring at Rose through the gap between two of her huge teeth. Rose was close enough to see that new teeth were already beginning to grow in Cethlenn's bleeding gums, and her hair was once more luscious and thick. 'How desperate Sioc must have been to choose *you*, of all humanity, to guard the *tathlum*, the weapon that once felled the greatest god who has ever walked this earth. How desperate – and how *stupid*.' Cethlenn reached in one skinny arm, pushing it through the gap, and grabbed Rose by the neck of her cardigan. 'As soon as you surrender it, Rosaleen Darke, all this pain and suffering shall end.' Cethlenn's eyes glinted maliciously. 'And then another era of pain shall begin – but that won't concern you. You shall not wake to see it.' She pulled Rose closer. 'I will have the weapon, child,' she growled.

Rose closed her eyes, her tears drying before they could make it halfway down her cheeks; Cethlenn radiated heat like a roaring inferno.

'Oi!' came an unexpected voice, and something hit

Cethlenn's arm with enough force to make the witch wince. 'Let her go, you horrible – . . . whatever you are! My dad's going to hear about this! You'd better not be expecting him to pay for all this mess!' Emer hit Cethlenn again, and Rose could see clearly enough to realise she'd taken off one of her bunny slippers and was using it to whack the witch's arm.

Cethlenn's ferocious eyes turned to Emer. She whispered a single word in some strange yet familiar-sounding language, and while Rose was trying to work out what it meant, Emer staggered backwards, clutching at her throat. She tried to speak, but all that came out was a dry retching sound.

'What have you done?' Rose shouted. She tried to turn to see Emer but Cethlenn had her in too strong a grip.

'The stone,' she hissed, drawing Rose closer still. The flames around her began to lick Rose's skin, leaving traces of pain wherever they touched.

'I'm not going to give it to you,' Rose managed to croak out. 'You'll have to burn me first.' She closed her eyes and waited for Cethlenn's wrath – but then a battle cry unlike anything else they'd heard tore through the air. It took everyone by surprise, including Cethlenn. She loosened her grip and Rose managed to pull away. She dropped to the ground and crawled towards Emer, who was still fighting for breath.

Light burst through between the gaps in the wall of teeth – but it wasn't the harsh orange-red firelight of Cethlenn and her magic. It was the bluish-silver of the elk, and of Gracie and Nellie, and of the chieftain. Rose looked up to see the face of a giant woman staring in, over the top of their prison. She seemed made of starlight yet solid, and her eyes widened when she saw the wounded elk.

'The woman from the hill,' Rose gasped, thinking back to the figure she'd seen silhouetted against the sky a few miles back, and how the Silver Road had seemed to sweep across the countryside to surround her burial place on Knocknarea. 'Queen Maeve!'

With a roar, the giant queen raised one arm and swept aside the teeth that had been keeping Rose, Emer and the elk imprisoned. A large gap formed in the enclosure wall and Rose watched as a band of women – all normal-sized but, like their gigantic leader, made of starlight and magic – descended upon Cethlenn. Cethlenn's own magic roared its response and her fire grew in intensity, drowning out the light of the warrior women. Screaming with rage, they fell back, and Cethlenn exploded out from among them, rolling down the hill towards the edge of the great pit. Her magic was so strong and her light so bright that she illuminated the massive hole as she went.

'She's going after Balor!' Rose shouted, clambering out through the fallen barrier of broken teeth. She reached in a hand to help Emer, who was retching and coughing but whose breath seemed to have returned. She held a hand to her throat as she struggled to get to her feet. The elk reared, pushing itself up, though it limped on a badly wrenched back leg as it made its way out after the girls.

Emer, Rose, the wounded elk and the women warriors made their way to the edge of the hole. Through the light and heat of Cethlenn's magic, they could make out a tangled mass of melted glass and steel – the remains of the digging equipment that had been left in the hole overnight – and standing in the midst of her fire-magic, Cethlenn. Her hands were raised as all around her the soil was lifting, as if it were being pushed from underneath. As the earth crumbled away, it became clear giant figures were pulling themselves free – giant figures with shocks of tangled hair, swirling tattoos painted over their skin, round shields with bosses of bronze and huge swords hanging from thick belts. They stood around their fire-witch, towering over her.

'Fomorians,' hissed a warrior nearby. Rose turned to look at her. The woman paid Rose no attention, turning away to spit on the soil. Her sisters repeated the gesture. Then they raised their shields and swords, beating them against one another, as they gave full voice to their war cry once again, a shout of ferocity and courage that made Rose's knees turn to water.

'But – they won't stand a chance!' Emer gasped, her voice rasping. 'Look at the size of those guys down there! One of their *swords* is as tall as each of these women.' She glanced up at their leader, who was scanning the battlefield. 'Besides the queen herself, of course.'

Rose stared up at the spectral figure of Queen Maeve, who was oblivious to the tiny girls below her. She raised her arm and lifted her sword, its tip so distant and faint that it disappeared into the darkness of the sky. Then she screamed to her army and, without a moment's hesitation, her warrior women poured themselves over the edge of the hole, down towards the fire, the Fomorian giants and the rising Balor.

Cethlenn's magic was working fast. Rose could see Balor's knee, the toe of his boot, the contours of a horrendously large face, and she knew they didn't have long before the entire body would be free from its earthen tomb.

She scrabbled in her pocket for the bag of cróigíní. There were three left, which she took as a good sign – exactly as many as she needed right in this moment. 'Here,' she said, handing one to Emer. She turned and fed one to the patient elk, whose eyes were damp and exhausted, though its light was beginning to return. And she took the final one herself, feeling the tendrils of its power – hope and courage and stamina and strength – curling their way through her.

Rose, Emer and the elk, the wolf clan, and the battered-looking chieftain stood side by side at the top of the excavation site. The Mac Tíre looked at the warriors of Queen Maeve, shrieking as they ran down the sides of the hole, and then he turned to Rose. She gave him a quick smile, an acknowledgement of what had to come next – and a farewell.

With a nod, he raised his arm and shouted a command to his wolves. In a wave of fur and teeth and claws, they rushed into battle.

Rose turned to the elk. Its eyes looked brighter, and its coat had a steady glow. 'Can you manage?' she whispered to it, stroking its soft nose. The elk flicked its ears once, and then lowered an antler.

'So, we're actually doing this, then?' Emer said, staring up at its shining head.

'Imagine how good it'll look on your socials,' Rose said with a wink, as she clambered onto the elk's back.

18

The army of the Dagda – for Rose could think of them in no other way – tore down into the pit, racing towards Cethlenn. Rose clung to the elk's neck, and Emer clung to her, as they followed the others down the slope, the elk working hard to keep its footing on the loose, stony soil. Eventually they reached flatter ground as the pit levelled out. Some of the Fomorian giants, newly released from the earth, were helping to dig up the body of Balor, but Cethlenn's magic was doing the hardest work. Slowly but inexorably, the massive figure of the fallen god began to emerge from the soil, the red tongues of Cethlenn's spell pushing aside the dirt and calling forth Balor from his slumber.

'That is *huge*,' Emer said into Rose's ear. Rose couldn't find the breath to say the words, but every inch of her agreed with Emer. Balor was huge beyond imagining, and he was beginning to move. Rose saw his knee drawing up, like a mountain being born.

Up ahead, the first sounds of battle could be heard – the warriors of Queen Maeve shrieking their battle cry, wolves snapping and growling, Fomorians roaring with rage, the clash of metal on bone – but before the Mac Tíre himself could get close enough to sink his teeth into Cethlenn's neck, the earth began to shake so badly that it threw everyone off their feet, including Cethlenn and her giants. Rose, Emer and the elk were far enough back that they just about kept their footing, but the elk drew itself to a halt.

The earth continued to shake, and Balor finally rose.

Soil and rocks and rubble cascaded down from his body, and the ground beneath him rumbled as he stepped back and forth, settling his balance. Rose stared up and up and *up* at the incredible head silhouetted against the round full moon. Rose's pocket buzzed with a ferocious, horrible energy as the stone seemed to burn with battle readiness, and on her other side she felt the coolness of the Shaper's hammer against her skin. Her weapons, at least, seemed eager to go. *But I still don't know what to do*, she thought, trying to quell her desperation.

'He's like a cyclops,' Emer said, her teeth chattering with terror as she stared up at Balor. She was right – Balor, as Rose had expected, only had one eye. Its lid was closed. Four metal rings were embedded in it, like grotesque eyelashes.

'We've got to stop him opening that eye,' Rose said, turning to Emer. The other girl was fixated on the rising giant, her own eyes wide. 'If he does, there's no hope for any of us.'

'What – What'll happen?' Emer asked in a quiet voice.

Rose licked her lips but her tongue was dry. 'He's the god of, like, fire and destruction,' she began. 'Chaos and death. I think, if he opens his eye, it means – . . . the whole world will burn.'

Emer blinked, still staring up. 'All this weather lately,' she said thoughtfully. 'That's his fault?'

Rose shrugged. 'His and Cethlenn's, I reckon. Though I don't think we can put that in our project for Mrs Mooney, somehow.'

Emer gave her a quick grin. 'So how do we stop

him opening his eye?' she said. 'It's not like we can glue it shut or whatever.'

Rose looked at the four rings pierced through Balor's eyelid and tried to remember the details of the story from her mother's book. 'I think it's actually too heavy for him to open on his own,' she began. 'That's what I read, anyway. See those rings? They're there so that someone else can help him lift his eyelid.'

Emer frowned. 'Not someone bigger than him, I hope,' she said.

Before Rose could answer, she saw the answer to the question they'd hardly been brave enough to ask. Four Fomorian warriors, giants who looked tiny in comparison to Balor, began to climb up his body, swinging from his tattered clothing and the hair on his body and then his beard, towards his head.

'Oh my God,' Rose gasped. 'They're too fast! We'll never –'

A flung sword struck one of the climbing Fomorians, hitting him squarely in the middle of the back. Without a word, he fell from Balor's body, but another giant immediately jumped up to take his place.

More swords and spears flew, some striking Balor

and others the climbing giants – but it never seemed like enough.

Queen Maeve, towering tall over her army of women, ran at Balor, her voice raised in a yell. She was barely as high as his waist, and Balor swept one great arm, knocking the queen to one side. Her yell died in her throat as she flew through the air, landing heavily in a crumpled heap not far from the wreckage of the digging equipment. Rose watched, horror-stricken, but the queen did not rise. Her women raised a battle cry as they besieged Balor, scrambling up his trunk-like legs. Balor lifted first one leg and then the other, shaking them off – but also dislodging the climbing Fomorians in the process.

'Rose! One of them has reached the eye!' Emer shouted, drawing Rose's attention to Balor's head. Emer was right – a burly Fomorian was standing on one of Balor's shoulders, hauling at the nearest metal ring. By himself, he wasn't equal to the task of lifting the eyelid, but he was doing a good job of trying. The eyelid lifted, very slightly, sending out a dart of power that hit the ground in front of Balor like a burst of fire from a flamethrower. Rose's heart quailed at the sound of yowling pain from the wolves who had been in its path. In the next moment the wolves launched themselves at the giant's legs, making Balor himself howl with pain and rage, and Cethlenn throw balls of flame that made their fur sizzle.

Rose and Emer looked from one site of battle to the other – Balor's feet, and his head. A second giant had joined the first on Balor's head, using a length of chain attached to another of the rings to haul up the eyelid. Within seconds, Rose knew there would be another, more sustained, blast of power from that deadly eye.

Rose closed her eyes and tried to think. *Please, Seandraíocht*, she begged, inside her head. *I have the weapon!* In her pocket, she felt the red stone jumping. She'd been able to feel its excitement, its sick energy, from the moment Emer had returned it. Somehow she knew that the stone could sense Balor and Cethlenn, and that it didn't want to be in her pocket, wrapped up in darkness. It didn't want to be kept in secrecy, unused and forgotten. It wanted to be flying through the air, wreaking havoc, breaking through flesh and bone, drawing blood, bringing death. It had fought to get away from her, and then it had tried to suck Emer into its embrace, and now that its chance was close, the stone was restless to be free. Her thoughts began to swirl. *Should I even have it at all? Do I have the right to keep such a weapon from its true purpose? Who am I, Rosaleen Darke, to stand in the way of power like this?*

Rose shook her head and tried to focus. She imagined a single silver-petalled flower, gently opening, and held it in her mind. *You chose me for a reason,* Rose thought, hoping the Seandraíocht could hear her. *You're the Old Magic – older than the trees! Older than the rocks, older than the stars ... older than the oldest bones buried in the ground. You've got to know what the right thing to do is. You've got to help me! Please. Help me to know what to do.*

But there was no answer. Rose opened her eyes, half-expecting to see a ghostly figure standing in front of her – maybe Nellie or Gracie, or even the Dagda himself. But there was nobody and nothing. All she could see was this terrible battlefield, some of it raging red with heat from Cethlenn's destructive magic, and more of it broken open and churned up from the excavation of Balor, a god asleep no longer, a terrifying figure who stood before them all, ready to destroy.

The second Fomorian warrior hauled hard on his chain, and the eyelid lifted. Another blast of horrible heat and flame exploded from Balor's eye, burning a blackened arc through the wolves and warriors at his feet. Rose felt her hope begin to die – she wanted to crumple into a heap on the ground, a pile of pieces of her former self that she no longer knew how to put together. She'd been holding herself together for so long, ever since the day her mother had come home from the hospital and told her that Mamó was gone . . . She hadn't been allowed to see her, not even one last time. Rose had shattered that day, but something about the Silver Road, something about the Seandraíocht and her time with Nellie and Gracie, had felt like it had begun to fix that terrible shattering, like glue mending a broken pot.

And now that had deserted her too.

'Rose!' Emer shouted, shaking her by the shoulders. 'Come on! There's got to be something we can do.'

Rose turned to her, blinking away her confusion. 'What? How are we – how am *I* – supposed to do anything to stop this? I don't even know why we're here! I don't *know* why we were called.' She paused, wiping the sweat and filth off her face with the back of one hand. 'I'm sorry for even bringing you into this, Emer. You're the *last* person I ever imagined being here with.'

Emer said nothing for a minute. 'I'm not sure if that's, like, an insult or not,' she finally began, 'but if it is, then I totally deserve it.' She stopped, looking at the ground. 'I was wrong. Okay? It was wrong to treat you the way I've treated you. I guess – I knew I could never be like you. Does that make sense?' She looked back at Rose. 'I mean, you're always just – *you*. Without apology or explanation or anything else. You do your own thing. And I really, actually, admire that? I mean, I wish I could do that.' Emer paused again, sucking on her top lip. 'You're the bravest person I know, Rose. You started in a new school, with no friends, and you're just . . . getting on with it, like a boss. And I can't say I ever imagined being on, like, a *primeval* battlefield with a fire-demon witch and a bunch of dead warriors and a werewolf army, riding on the back of a magical elk –' she laughed, and it sounded genuine – 'but if I *had* ever imagined it, then I *would* have imagined being here with you. Because you're fierce, Rose Darke. And fierce is what we need right now.'

She paused, looking away. 'So, I'm sorry I said all that stuff. About – you know. Your scholarship and things. You're not a charity case.' She blinked, looking back at Rose. 'Not that there's anything wrong with being one. A charity case, I mean. You earned your spot at the Grammar, unlike me.'

Rose didn't know what to say for a moment. She stared at Emer, and then cracked a grin. Emer returned it, looking relieved. 'Oh, no. Does this mean we're going to have to be friends or something?'

Emer shrugged. 'Yeah, absolutely. Regular BFFs.' They shared a shy smile, and then Rose straightened her shoulders, looking around.

'So, what are we going to do?'

Emer thought for a moment, scanning the battlefield. Her gaze swung between Cethlenn, still in the pit, wreathed in fire and magic, and the huge pile of earth that teetered over the slope just above her. Emer turned to Rose with a new look on her face. 'D'you reckon the elk could make it up that slope? Get us back up on top for a bit?'

'Did you hear that?' Rose asked the elk. It flicked its ears once, then twice. Rose turned to Emer. 'We'll take that as a "yes",' she said. 'What's the plan?'

'Tell you when we get there,' Emer said, her face set with determination.

But just as the elk made ready to turn away, the sound of a plaintive howl reached their ears. Rose's head whipped around, looking for a wounded wolf – but instead she saw the Mac Tíre himself coming in his wolf-shape, running towards them with fast, powerful strides. 'Wait,' she asked the elk. 'Please.'

The Mac Tíre drew up alongside the elk, breathing hard. He stank of blood and metal and singed flesh, and his muzzle was level with Rose and Emer, but despite all of this, they weren't afraid. He was battle-scarred and weary, a line of mangled red running through his fur, and his eyes – still amber-gold, whatever his shape – were heavy with something that looked like sorrow.

Rose reached out and touched him tentatively. 'I know,' she whispered. 'It's not looking good, is it?'

'Hey,' Emer said, her voice tight with something that sounded suspiciously like hope. 'Show him the stone-thing. The weapon, or whatever it is. Maybe he'll know what to do with it.'

Rose looked at her, blinking incredulously for a second or two, before pushing her fingers into her pocket. The fever-hot *tathlum* was there, vibrating, eager. Rose took it out, grimacing at its touch on her skin, and the Mac Tíre's eyes widened at the sight.

Then he took a step backwards, lifted his mighty head to the sky, and howled again – but there was a note of triumph in his voice this time. A note of power. He looked back at the girls, and Rose almost laughed at the new light in his eyes.

The huge wolf blinked and took a step forward, edging closer to the elk. For a moment Rose froze with indecision, until the Mac Tíre nuzzled her leg. *Come on*, he seemed to be saying. *We haven't got all night.*

'Is he – asking you to go with him?' Emer whispered.

'It sort of looks that way,' Rose said.

'Then do it,' Emer said.

Rose turned to her. 'But what about you?'

Emer gave a sideways smile. It didn't last long. 'I've got Rudolf,' she said, glancing at the elk. It gave a discontented *whuff*. 'I'll be okay.'

Rose snorted. '*Rudolf?*'

Emer looked embarrassed but pleased. 'It's just my little nickname for him.' She patted the elk's side. 'We understand each other, don't we, buddy?' The elk said nothing, and the girls smiled at one another. Then Emer reached out and pulled Rose into a tight hug. 'Just . . . do what you've got to do,' she whispered into Rose's ear. 'Do whatever you can, and I'll do whatever I can. And that has to be enough. Right?'

Rose nodded and Emer released her. 'Right,' she whispered back. 'Take care.'

'You too,' Emer said as Rose put the *tathlum* back into her pocket with great care. She slid off the elk and straight onto the back of the waiting wolf, careful to avoid his weapons, which were always firmly strapped to him no matter what shape he was in. He turned his head to look at her and bared his teeth. Rose swallowed hard, hoping it was the wolf equivalent of a smile.

Then, before she had a chance to look at Emer or the elk, the Mac Tíre was off, bounding across the floor of the pit, heading for the heart of the battle. Rose clung on, taking handfuls of his long, matted fur, hoping she wouldn't lose her grip before . . . Her thoughts sputtered out. *Before what?* She stared up at the approaching figure of Balor. His eye was still spitting gouts of burning plasma, reminding Rose of a sun flare; the Mac Tíre dodged these, and Rose tried to block out the sound of suffering wolves all around. Despite the heat and the pain and their injuries, they were still fighting – tooth and claw, with everything they had. The remnants of Queen Maeve's army fought too, the warrior women shouting their throaty battle cry, and they were joined by the men of Tara, who were looking thin and wispy and barely there, as though the magic that powered them was beginning to peter out. The chieftain swung his sword, his metal struts groaning and creaking as he moved. He was blackened and burned all down one side. Rose looked behind him – his steed had been reduced to a hunk of molten steel, overcome by the power of Cethlenn, and even though Rose knew it was only a sculpture and not a real horse, she felt a stab of sorrow.

They're all being so brave, she thought. *Fighting harder than ever, even though there's no hope.*

Rose's pocket gave another lurch, and she freed one hand from the wolf's pelt to grab at it before the stone inside could jump free. *Except*, she reminded herself, *there* is *hope*.

The Mac Tíre howled, long and loud, and Rose joined her voice to his as they raced ever closer.

19

Fire raged. Metal clashed against metal. Voices howled and roared and screamed. The whole world seemed to tumble around Rose as she tried to make sense of what was happening. Balor was right *there* – almost close enough to reach out and touch – but he was so big that her brain couldn't compute him. It was like standing beneath the Eiffel Tower, Rose thought; you can't understand how big it is, even as you're looking up at it. The sight of him made her dizzy and sick, and so she lowered her gaze.

Not far from Balor's foot stood Cethlenn. Her smoke and fire danced around her, and she wore her power like a veil. Her crooked teeth had grown back long enough to stick out of her mouth again, making her look like a sabre-toothed cat. The hair on one side of her head was gone, yanked out by the

285

root, but it was still long and thick and shining on the other.

Cethlenn shrieked, the noise like shredding metal, and waved her hands in mid-air as she gathered a fire spell. Within seconds she'd made a glowing red-hot sphere, a cannonball of flame, and Rose knew she would throw it at her – and that she would not miss. Beneath her, the Mac Tíre changed from his wolf-aspect to his man shape without missing a step, and Rose found herself shoved behind his back as the Mac Tíre deflected Cethlenn's fireball with his shield.

Rose stared up at the Mac Tíre. His eyes scanned the battlefield, and then his body tensed. He looked up – and Rose followed his gaze. A noise – a new noise – reached her ears. *That sounds like an engine*, Rose thought, the sound like a tiny droplet of something normal amid the haze of panic and chaos all around her. *A bulldozer engine?*

Squinting through the smoke, Rose saw the bucket of a bulldozer appearing on the slope right above Cethlenn's head. The machine was bright yellow, splattered with mud and grime from the building site. Its exhaust pipe belched black smoke as its engine roared again, and Rose caught a glimpse of the face in the cab window, a face which stared down into the fire of battle, a face which seemed to be looking for something.

'Emer!' Rose screamed. *She must have stolen the keys from the site office*, Rose realised, watching the other girl wrestle with a gear stick. *This must have been her plan! But what on earth's she trying to do?* Behind Emer's bulldozer the elk was bellowing loudly. 'Stay back from the edge!' Rose shouted.

The Mac Tíre watched too, frowning as he tried to understand. Then, above Cethlenn's head, a huge pile of earth began to move. Emer was pushing it from behind. Rose looked down the slope directly beneath the bulldozer's bucket. If Emer's plan worked, she would bury Cethlenn – and anyone near her – beneath tons of earth and rubble and rock. Rose knew simply burying Cethlenn wasn't enough to stop her, but it might buy them time to deal with Balor.

At her waist, the Shaper's hammer began to glow again, even more brightly than before. It caught Rose's eye and she yanked it free, feeling it buzz with energy in her hand. *I can Shape her*, Rose thought, blinking hard as she tried to clear her mind. *That's what this hammer does – I know that now. It doesn't destroy.*

It just changes things. So I can Shape her into something that can't use magic. Something that can't hurt us. She looked at the witch in desperation. *But what?*

The Mac Tíre placed his feet and deflected yet another of Cethlenn's fire spells, and this time the witch had had enough. With a roar, she began to run, right for the Mac Tíre and Rose – and Rose knew it was now or never. She had to do something or Cethlenn would be out of range of Emer's trap – and she herself would be a goner too, burned and destroyed beneath Cethlenn's rage.

Rose settled her grip on the hammer's oak handle, watching the glow of Balor's fire on its iron head. As before, it seemed to sit naturally in her palm, as though it was made to be held by her, and Rose stared down at it. Then she looked back at Cethlenn. *How can I touch her with it?* she thought in a panic. *If I'm going to use the hammer to stop her, I've got to get closer – but if I do, she'll kill me . . .*

Beside her, the Mac Tíre threw his spear at the approaching witch. Cethlenn dodged it easily, but it gave Rose an idea. She hefted the hammer in her hand and took a breath. *Come on, Seandraíocht,* she said inside her head. *Don't fail me now.*

And then, before she could think any more about it, Rose threw the hammer.

It sailed through the air, glowing even more brightly blue as it flew, leaving a comet-trail of light behind it. Cethlenn tried to dodge it, but the hammer flew too fast, and the smack it made as it landed echoed around the battlefield. The sound bounced off the walls of the pit like a sonic boom, making the earth crumble at the edges. Cethlenn was thrown several feet, landing hard on her back.

Rose blinked and stared at the fallen witch. The hammer had turned her to stone – grey like granite, with lines of red and yellow, copper-like, running through it. Her face was frozen in a howl of rage, her crooked teeth sticking out like the tusks of a hippopotamus, and her half-bare head bore the imprint of the hammer's blow.

Rose scanned the ground, but there was no sign of the hammer itself. She couldn't see its blue glow or its whorled pattern, and in the next breath the bulldozer overhead roared again as it pushed forward. A cascade of dirt and soil and rock tumbled down over the spot where Cethlenn had fallen, burying her deep – and the hammer along with her.

But the earth didn't stop moving when it had finished burying the witch. The tumble of dark soil kept coming, a suffocating wave, heading straight for Rose. For a second she stared at it, frozen solid with fear.

Then the Mac Tíre took a handful of Rose's cardigan and threw her onto his back. He ran from the oncoming flood of earth and rock, jumping clear of it. Instinctively Rose clung on to him, and the huge man leaped towards Balor's nearest leg, beginning to scale it with ease. He swung from Balor's clothes, quickly reaching the trailing strands of the giant's beard and using them like ropes, climbing up and up towards the angry god's face. The Fomorians began to hurl spears at him, and the Mac Tíre held up his shield to cover both himself and Rose, his pace slowing a little as he was reduced to climbing with one arm. Rose glanced down before burying her face in the Mac Tíre's back. His muscles strained and tensed as he tried to climb, and he grunted with effort as he worked to keep the shield steady. She knew he was beginning to struggle, and if he fell . . .

Rose took a deep breath and straightened her shoulders, staring up at the underside of the shield.

Then she braced her legs, holding herself steady on the Mac Tíre's back with one arm, and reached up with the other. The Mac Tíre glanced at her with a grateful look as he shucked his arm out of the shield's straps, leaving them free for Rose to hold. The shield was so heavy she almost dropped it, but she gritted her teeth and tightened her grip. The leather bit into her fingers and every spear-thump from overhead felt like a boulder being dropped on top of them, but Rose did not let go. The Mac Tíre picked up the pace, climbing faster and faster, far quicker and more agile than the Fomorians. Balor himself roared with anger, making a swipe for the Mac Tíre, but the wolf-man nimbly dodged the giant's grasping hand. Rose could barely breathe with terror, but she was sure she heard the Mac Tíre let out a sound that was halfway between a howl and a laugh of triumph.

They were approaching Balor's chin now. The cavern of his mouth roared above them as the giant looked down slightly, trying to see through his closed eyelid the enemy that was making its way up his body. One of the Fomorians trying to pull open Balor's eyelid lost his grip and fell from the top of the giant's head, yelling with rage, making a futile grab for Rose as he passed her, but there were two more ready at the eye. One stood on Balor's right shoulder, yanking at the ring nearest him; the other was on top of Balor's head, pulling at a chain attached to another of the rings. With a wordless shout of effort, the Fomorians began to pull, and Balor's eye started, very slowly, to open. Rose caught a glimpse of the inferno inside it, the endless all-consuming fire that was ready to be unleashed on an unsuspecting world – on an Ireland that was still asleep, held in Gracie's spell . . . Her head swam with the horror of it, and the heat and the terror of not knowing what to do next.

'*An tathlum!*' the Mac Tíre gasped, his voice rasping.

At the sound of his words, Rose snapped out of her own fear. *The stone.* It was still in her pocket, and Rose could feel it bashing itself against her leg with every moment that passed. Her brain raced and pulsed with thoughts and fears, but she tried to shove them all aside and focus on what she had to do. *Get the stone out.* Rose relinquished the shield and the Mac Tíre fitted his arm through the straps again as she took hold of his wolf-pelt. Then she reached into her shorts pocket. She felt the stone's heat, almost enough to make her pull her fingers back, but she refused to be beaten. She grimaced with fear and pain as she wrapped her hand around the stone and pulled it free from its dark prison. The stone's touch on her skin was blisteringly hot, like she was holding a live coal, and she pressed her teeth together as tightly as she could, hissing through the agony.

Rose closed her eyes and tried to remember the words in her mother's book. *Balor was killed at Moytura by ... by who?* She forced her thoughts to settle, and then the answer came to her, spearing through her memory. *Lugh. Lugh Lámhfada. And he killed him by putting out his eye, using the stone and a sling.* Rose opened her eyes again and stared down at her clenched hand. *I don't have a sling, but I can throw.*

The stone wriggled in her grip. Rose held on to the Mac Tíre's pelt, keeping herself secure as the Mac Tíre climbed ever higher. They were so close now to Balor's mouth that Rose could smell the stink of his breath, like raw meat left to go rotten. Rose screamed; the pain in her palm was so intense, it felt as though the stone was going to burn its way right through her hand, but still she didn't let go. The Mac

Tíre turned back to look at her, and something in his gaze told Rose she needed to be ready.

Then the Mac Tíre shrugged into his wolf-shape, and Rose found that she now had a handful of his copper-gold fur. The Mac Tíre opened his massive jaws and leaped forward, clamping them shut on Balor's face, sinking his teeth into the flesh of the giant's cheek and upper lip, and Rose looked up.

The opening eye was right above her now. The Fomorians were hauling for all they were worth, and the eye was almost halfway open. Searing whips of bright-hot fire were leaping from it.

The eye opened further still. Rose closed her own eyes but it didn't make much difference – Balor's furious power seeped through her eyelids, like she was staring directly at the sun.

And then Rose heard the sound of Emer's bulldozer, a hundred feet below, blaring out its horn. Again and again it sounded, the noise just loud enough to break through the terror of Balor's power. Rose knew it was Emer's way of saying, *Come on! You can do it – you can't stop now!*

She strengthened her grip on the wriggling, spinning, red-hot stone in her hand and she pulled back her arm. *Help me, Lugh!* she thought, hoping someone – anyone – would hear the desperate plea.

Then she opened her eyes, stared right into the maelstrom of terror and threw the *tathlum* as hard and as fast as she could, right into the heart of Balor's evil eye. For a split second she was sure she saw the stone's eye close over, but then it was gone from her sight.

The moment the stone passed into Balor's eye, his awful fire went out. Rose heard the breath escaping from his lips in a long, wet gasp, and then it was gone. The Fomorians on his head howled, dropping his eyelid, which slammed shut with a heavy, wet slap. Rose pressed herself tightly against the Mac Tíre's back as one of the thick chains fell down past them, a little too close for comfort. The wolf still had his jaws clamped tight on Balor's face and Rose knew she had to hold on to him. She pressed her eyes tight shut, her retinas burning with the afterglow of Balor's eye, and clung to his fur.

Finally, and very slowly, like a great tree being felled, Balor began to topple to the ground. He fell straight back, his arms loose and flopping on either side, and Rose held her breath, too afraid to cry out, as she felt herself pitch forward. The Mac Tíre held on long enough for Balor's body to hit the ground, but as soon as it did, the wolf released his grip and leaped free. All Rose could feel was the jerking and bunching of the Mac Tíre's muscles as he ran. Her eyes were still tightly shut. Her nose was filled with the sweat and blood and animal reek of the Mac Tíre, and her ears rang with the shouts of triumph from the army of the Dagda.

Finally the Mac Tíre slowed and came to a stop. Rose felt frozen in place, her muscles and joints locked tight. Her fists ached, holding their handfuls of fur, and she was overcome with an exhaustion so complete that she would happily have slept right there on the back of the Mac Tíre himself.

'Rose?' came a voice. It was like the first gleam of sunlight on a dark morning. 'Rose, are you all right?' There was a pause. 'Well. No. I know you're not all right. I mean, how could anyone be all right? But – you know what I mean.'

Slowly, Rose opened her eyes. Through the bleary haze she could see the outline of Emer's head against her father's floodlights. The Mac Tíre had brought her to the top of the pit, beside a part of the fence that was still upright. Something about that made Rose want to laugh. She sat up slowly, her body creaking like the timbers of an old ship, and tried to look around. She was still dazzled, and her eyes weren't focusing properly, but she was sure she could see the glow of the elk not too far away – and right beside it, the face of Emer McGuire.

'What did I miss?' Rose asked, and Emer gave an amused laugh.

'Take a look,' she said, indicating the battlefield below with a jerk of her head. The remaining warriors were putting down the last of the Fomorians, with the help of the Mac Tíre's wolves. Without Cethlenn's magic, the earth was reclaiming Balor's body and those of the fallen Fomorians; as they watched, the giant began to sink beneath the soil. The earth wrapped itself over him and then, to Rose and Emer's delight, the flowers of the Silver Road sprang up from the ruined ground. Within a blink there were so many flowers that the light rose into the sky like a pillar.

Rose looked at the Mac Tíre. He bared his teeth in an unmistakeable grin, and then he transformed into his man-shape, one arm around Rose so that she wouldn't fall. Gently, he put her on the ground before dropping to one knee in front of her. The Mac Tíre held out his arm for Rose to grasp, before doing the same to Emer. Then, with a nod of farewell to the girls and the elk, he leaped into the air and shrugged himself back into his wolf-form. He ran down the slope into the pit, howling to his pack as he went. They followed their leader up and out, vanishing into the darkness. The men of Tara were next, their feet following the path of the Silver Road. As they passed Rose and Emer they paused and looked up, waving swords and shields in tribute.

The women warriors carried the fallen Queen Maeve shoulder high as they marched away from the battle, screaming an ululation of triumph and mourning as they walked, following a different branch of the Silver Road to their resting place under the mountain.

Finally the three of them were left alone. The battlefield – now a building site once more – stretched out beneath them, empty and in ruins.

'What's your dad going to say when he sees –' Rose began.

'Oh my God, will you shut up about my dad?' Emer retorted before Rose had even had a chance to finish speaking. 'Who cares what he thinks?' Emer looked sidelong at Rose, a sparkle of mischief in her eyes. 'Plus, he has insurance. Though I'd like to see him explain *this*.'

Rose gazed up at the moon. It was still shining, bright and round as ever, but clouds had begun to skim across its surface. A gentle wind blew, and something told Rose that Gracie's spell was at an end. Time was passing once more, and it was growing late.

She turned to the elk, hugging the end of its snout. It smelled of blood and smoke and dirt. The weal on its flank seemed to have dried up, no longer bright red, and it could only gingerly put its weight on its wrenched back leg, but even so it whuffed out a hot breath and looked at Emer with a calm, unclouded eye. 'Are you okay?' Rose whispered to it, and the elk flicked its ears.

'I guess that's a "yes",' Emer said. 'Or an "I'll have to do, because how else are we going to get home?", at least.'

The elk snorted, almost like it was laughing, and Rose and Emer gave one another a delighted look. Then the massive animal kneeled, bringing its shoulders down as low as it could, while tipping its antlers to one side.

'After you,' Emer said, gesturing at Rose, who began to climb onto the elk's back once more.

'Too kind,' Rose replied as she got herself settled. Once both girls were safely aboard, the elk got to its feet again with a groan, and Rose patted it gently.

'Come on, so,' she said as the elk turned away from the site. 'I guess it's time for us all to go home.'

20

Bzz-bzz, went something near Rose's ear. *Bzz-bzz*, it went again.

She blinked her eyes open, trying to figure out where she was. A face floated into view. With another blink or two, the face settled into a familiar shape. *Mamó.* Rose's eyes were raw, and she tried to focus her brain. *Mamó's picture. On my locker. I'm at home.*

She fumbled out one hand to find her phone, pressing the unlock key – and there were unread messages waiting for her. Rose pulled the phone towards her, holding her breath, as she opened them.

Hey, read the first. It was from Sophia. *Sorry for no texts. My uncle was really sick. He's okay now. Want to meet up?*

Rose clicked into the next message. *You coming to the park later?* It was from Rory.

She grinned, locking the phone and pushing it back onto her locker, promising herself she would reply to her friends once she'd solved a more pressing problem. There was a delicious smell in the air – bacon frying in the kitchen – and that needed investigation first. Rose pushed herself up onto her elbows, shoving her hair out of her face, and took a look around. There was her bookcase, stuffed to the brim; there was her teddy-bear lamp, one paw raised in a wave. She turned the other way. Her chair, with a cushion propped on it. Her runners, filthy on the floor. An old band T-shirt, ripped and dirty, and her cardigan, and her shorts with their empty pockets . . .

Rose let herself flop back onto her pillow again. Her mind raced. Had last night *really* happened? She ached from head to foot, and she was *filthy* – but that wasn't proof of anything much. She looked down at her hand, the palm that had held the stone, and flexed her fingers gently. Her skin was slightly reddened, but it wasn't burned, or blistered – it looked totally normal. *But I did it*, she thought. *I know I did.*

She cast her mind back to what had happened after the battle was over. She and Emer hadn't spoken much as the elk had brought them home to Carriganawn,

302

following the fading glow of the Silver Road. They'd stopped at Emer's house first, her alarmed gates mysteriously opening as soon as they'd drawn close, and Emer had climbed up the elk's antler to her balcony, safely deposited – albeit minus one bunny-eared slipper. Emer had waved once before vanishing into her bedroom and pulling the curtains shut.

Then, silently, the elk had carried Rose home too, and she'd climbed down its antler. Her front-door key was still in the pocket of her shorts, and she'd quietly opened the door, but not before giving the elk a kiss on the nose. She'd hugged its face, rubbing her own cheeks gently against its soft fur, until finally it was time to part.

Rose had watched the elk disappear down her road into the night. After a few steps the animal had been wreathed in bright silver-blue light, and when the light had cleared, Rose felt fairly certain the elk had shrunk, resuming the shape of a short, bad-tempered not-cat with ferny ears and a fanlike tail – but perhaps that part had been her imagination.

Rose turned her head again, gazing at the photo of her mamó. She smiled at it, and her mamó smiled back.

'Thanks, Mamó,' Rose whispered. If it hadn't

been for the book and the connections Mamó had forged between Rose and the old stories, Rose didn't know how she would've worked out what the Silver Road needed her to do – and if it hadn't been for the power of the Silver Road filling her up, helping to fix the cracks inside Rose's heart at the same time as she helped the Road to knit itself back together, she knew she wouldn't have stood a chance against Cethlenn and Balor. She still missed Mamó, and she always would, but she knew now: *things can always be mended*. Even hearts.

Quietly Rose heaved herself out of bed and scurried to the bathroom. She hopped into the shower, hoping there was enough hot water in the tank, and scrubbed herself clean. Finally she was ready to face her family, the remnants of the battlefield washed safely down the drain.

'Well, now. Here she is,' Mrs Darke said as Rose entered the kitchen. Her brothers were in their playpen. Colm crowed happily as his sister came into view, and Rose smiled back at him. 'Did you have a good sleep, pet?' her mother continued, turning the bacon she was frying. 'You look like a different person this morning. I knew the rest would do you good.'

Rose smiled. Her stomach roared at the smell of the food. 'Yes, Mam.' She ran a hand through her still-wet hair. *I am a different person*, she thought, though not in the way her mother meant.

'Now. Get settled at the table,' Mrs Darke said. 'I'll bring you over tea in a minute. Dad's just gone to the shops for a drop of orange juice and some other bits and pieces.'

Rose looked over at her mother in surprise. 'Dad? Isn't he working today?'

'Well,' Mrs Darke said, transferring some rashers from the pan to a warm plate beneath the grill, 'about that. It seems there was some sort of a break-in at the site last night. Machines vandalised, fencing broken, that sort of thing. A lot of damage done, it seems. And as for herself?' Mrs Darke tutted, laying some fresh rashers in the pan. 'That Ennis woman, the one who was bankrolling it all? She's disappeared. Vanished! Nobody has the foggiest clue where she's skedaddled off to. So Michael McGuire is left now with a right headache to sort out.' Mrs Darke looked over at Rose. 'But that's not our problem.' She winked.

Rose grinned. She glanced out the kitchen window.

The day was bright and dry, but the sky had clouded over. 'It's not so hot today,' she said.

'And thank goodness for that,' Mrs Darke replied with feeling.

There was the sound of a key turning in the front door and the rustling of shopping bags being carried into the house. 'Everyone awake?' Mr Darke called, aiming his voice up the stairs.

'I'm in here!' Rose shouted back with a laugh. Mr Darke bustled into the kitchen, his hands clutching two full bags. He paused to drop a kiss onto the crown of Rose's head before lumbering towards his wife and kissing her on the cheek.

'Town is full of talk,' he said as he hauled the bags up onto the counter.

'Oh?' said Mrs Darke inquiringly as she took the last lot of bacon off the pan.

'Earthquakes up Enniskillen direction, some were saying. Not too far from the site, mind you, so it might have something to do with what happened to Michael McGuire's property. People waking to find crockery fallen off shelves, cracks in their gardens, that sort of thing, though nobody seems to have heard a peep. There's some sort of kerfuffle about animal tracks too, like there was a hunt that tore through the countryside. Only it's not the season for it and nobody organised one – and nobody saw or heard anything.' Mr Darke frowned, unpacking some eggs and placing them on the counter. Mrs Darke picked them up and cracked a couple into the still-hot pan.

'That all sounds very odd,' she agreed, poking gently at the edges of the frying eggs with her triple-scrubbed wooden spoon, now good as new.

'It does indeed. And what with the change in the weather . . .' Mr Darke gave a theatrical shiver. 'It's enough to make a body nervous.' He winked over at Rose, who smiled back at him. 'Someone is looking bright-eyed and bushy-tailed this morning,' he said, gazing fondly at his daughter.

'I slept well, Dad,' Rose said. *Eventually*, she added to herself.

'So I see.' Mr Darke took his seat at the table right beside Rose. 'I think we all did. It felt like the night was longer than usual – d'you know what I mean? As impossible as it might sound.' Her dad glanced at her. 'What's your plan for the day, then?'

'I might go and visit Nellie and Gracie,' she said with a one-shouldered shrug. 'See how they're doing.'

'You're very good to remember those elderly people, Rose,' Mrs Darke said, filling up plates with fried bacon and egg. Rose's stomach ached with anticipation. 'I'm sure they love having visits.'

'But maybe don't forget your friends,' her dad reminded her, sitting back as Mrs Darke carried his plate to the table. 'Sophia and Rory, and whoever else. It's good for you to have people your own age to hang around with too.'

'I'm meeting them in the park later, actually,' Rose replied happily.

'Good girl,' Mrs Darke said, putting Rose's plate in front of her.

Rose looked up at both her parents, one at a time. 'But I have to visit Gracie and Nellie for another reason too.' She swallowed back a mouthful of guilt, putting her cutlery down before she'd even had a bite of breakfast. 'I – I lost something belonging to Gracie. Something he'd let me borrow.' She paused, trying to gauge her parents' reactions. 'It was one of his old cobbler's tools, you know – a little hammer? But it's gone now. And I want to apologise.'

Mr Darke nodded. 'Tell Mr Kinch we'll replace the hammer for him,' he said, putting a forkful of food into his mouth and chewing it for a moment. 'Whatever it is, we'll find the money,' he continued, his words muffled. He swallowed. 'Though I hope it wasn't an antique.'

'Don't talk with your mouth full,' Rose said, and she caught her mother's eye. They shared a grin as Mr Darke whuffed out a laugh.

Rose's pocket buzzed and she raced to pull her phone out before her parents could complain about her having it at the breakfast table. She glanced at the screen, frowning at the caller name she saw there.

'Emer never *rings* me,' she muttered.

'You don't have to answer it,' her mother pointed out, taking a large bite of her bacon sandwich.

Rose glanced at her mother and shrugged as she swiped to answer. 'Hello?' she said, getting up from the table as she spoke.

'So. Um. Morning?' Emer said.

'Seems to be,' Rose replied, wandering slowly down the hallway. Her eyes lingered on a family photograph and she stroked its surface gently. 'What's up?'

'So, like, my slippers are ruined,' Emer began. 'Or, rather, my *slipper*, as the other one has inexplicably vanished. And my pyjamas are filthy. I don't even want to think about my dressing gown. I had to shove it right down at the bottom of the laundry basket in case Mum saw it. She'd puke! And then ground me *forever*.' She cleared her throat. 'What exactly *happened* last night?'

'We saved the world,' Rose said. 'I think.'

There was a thoughtful pause. 'Yeah,' Emer said. 'That's what I was thinking too.'

Rose heard someone raising their voice on Emer's end of the phone and the muffled sound of Emer covering the speaker with her hand. Then, a moment later, she was back. 'Rose?'

'Still here.'

'That was . . . my mum. She was reminding me to apologise to you.'

Rose blinked in surprise. 'For what?'

Emer cleared her throat. Rose heard the voice of Emer's mother, closer now, as though she'd come to stand beside her daughter. 'Say it, Emer Ifetundun,' Mrs McGuire said, her tone sharp and irritated, and Rose winced in sympathy at the use of Emer's middle name. That was *never* a good sign.

'All right!' Emer hissed at her mother. 'God. Look,

310

Rose, I'm sorry for what happened down at the well. Okay? Rachel showed her mum the video she took on her phone, and then *her* mum showed *my* mum, and – anyway. I'm in a bit of trouble.'

Rose recalled, like it was a dream, how Rachel, the girl with the red hair, had been filming that day. 'She recorded you going into the water?'

Emer's silence was guilty. Her voice, when she spoke again, was low. 'It was like it wasn't me. Y'know? I don't remember it. Not properly. But it *was* me, clear as anything. And I really am sorry. I shouldn't have said what I said.' She paused again. 'Especially not about your dad and his job. That's all sorted. He doesn't need to worry.'

Rose took in a big breath. 'Okay,' she said. 'I mean, it's all right.'

'Seriously?' Emer's voice was bright with surprise.

Rose darted a look back towards the kitchen. Her family were absorbed in eating breakfast, her dad making *choo-choo* noises in an attempt to get Brian to eat his cereal. Nobody was listening, but she spoke quietly anyway. 'It was the stone, I think. The *tathlum*. It wasn't really you, saying those things.' Rose paused. *It wasn't all you, at least,* she thought, smiling to herself. 'It was changing you, y'know? Making you do things you wouldn't normally do. Let's forget about it.' She cleared her throat to change the subject. 'Speaking of dads. How's yours?'

'His mobile's about to melt down,' Emer said, and Rose could hear the laughter in her voice. 'He's on to the insurers, to Kathleen Ennis's people, to the government – he got a new contract from them to clear up a strange mess at the Hill of Tara, actually, however *that* happened –' she paused, and Rose smiled at the phone – 'so everyone's going to be busy for a while. He's also going to dispatch a team to start cleaning up the site and filling it all in again. You know. Burying whatever's under the earth *really* well. And he's committed to replanting all the trees that were cut down, and he's getting in some fancy horticulturalist to work with him on *rewilding* the place or something – almost like he's trying to hide any evidence that he's ever set foot on the site.' Emer paused again, very carefully. 'He was *very* ticked off about the fence, and his fancy lighting though,' she finished, and Rose could tell she was trying not to laugh.

'That's a shame,' Rose said, smiling widely. 'Hey.

I'm going to visit Gracie and Nellie soon. Want to meet me there?'

There was some muffled discussion on Emer's end of the line as she had a quick whispered conversation with her mother. 'Mum says I can,' Emer said. 'I'll be an hour or so though. She's got some work to do first.'

'Okay. See you there. Oh – and bring your science book. We can get started on our project while we're there.'

'Sure thing,' Emer said. 'Um. What's it called again?'

Rose sighed patiently, though she was grinning too. 'Building Towards Sustainable Eco-Construction,' she said. The idea had come to her on the journey home the previous night, and somehow it seemed just right.

There was a pause. 'Okay, so we're definitely putting me in charge of coming up with snappier titles,' Emer said, and hung up.

Rose wandered back into the kitchen. Her parents' worried eyes met hers.

'It's all fine,' Rose said. 'Emer and me have buried the hatchet.' *Among other things*, she thought, stifling a smile as she sat to finish her food.

Mr and Mrs Darke shared a look. 'Right, so,' Mr Darke said.

'Miracles do happen,' Mrs Darke remarked, before taking a mouthful of tea.

Rose pulled on her runners and got ready to leave as soon as the breakfast dishes were done. She slid the porch door closed and stepped out into the day, breathing it in. Flowers scented the breeze, and somewhere close by a bee buzzed. Rose turned to look at the narrow flowerbed outside her house, and her eye was caught by the neat imprint of a large hoof, right in the middle of it. It seemed to be lined with silver, which gleamed for a moment before vanishing.

She turned and made her way down the street. Her neighbours were sitting in their front gardens, chatting companionably over the fences. Mr Okongwu was singing, his living-room window flung open to the day. Someone at the end of the road was painting their front wall, and they gave Rose a friendly wave as she jogged past. In no time at all, she was at Hargate Street, her eyes full of Nellie's silver-blooming hanging baskets.

Rose pushed open the sweet-shop door and made her way inside.

'Come on through, pet!' called Nellie from the

kitchen. Rose stepped down into the bright room. The teapot was steaming, Catshee was curled up in front of the range, Gracie was sitting cross-legged beside the open garden door, and Nellie was settling a cake onto a plate in the middle of the table. Rose didn't know which of them to run to first.

Nellie settled the conundrum by hurrying towards Rose, her arms out for a hug. Moments later, Gracie joined the embrace. 'You did us proud, a stór,' Nellie said, her voice choked with emotion. 'We couldn't have dreamed you'd do better.'

'It was the cróigíní really,' Rose said, feeling her cheeks go pink. She pushed herself out of the embrace, just far enough to see Nellie and Gracie's faces.

Nellie laughed, kindly. 'Oh, now. Those old things? They only help you to feel – and trust in – the courage you've already got, my girl. You owe nothing to them.' She stroked Rose's hair. 'It was all you.'

Rose blinked, remembering how it had felt to hold the Mac Tíre's shield over his head and hers. 'Really?'

'Really, Rose. You have my word.'

Rose looked at Gracie. 'But I lost your hammer,' she said.

Gracie waved one skinny arm in the air. 'Ah, yerra,

315

not to worry,' he said, unconcerned. 'That yoke has a habit of turning up where it's least expected.' He gave Rose a gummy grin. 'No doubt I'll be digging in my rose bushes in a week or so and it'll pop up out of the dirt, all innocent-looking, letting on that it's been there for a thousand years, quietly causing trouble to neither man nor beast. It never stays lost for long.'

'How often does it get lost?' Rose asked.

'More often than you'd think,' Gracie replied with a wink.

'Now. Sit down, do, and have some tea. And that cake won't eat itself,' Nellie said, fussing her into a chair. She brandished her cake-cutting knife with as much skill as any warrior with her sword, and quickly made short work of carving out a slice as big as Rose's head.

'Is the Silver Road okay?' Rose asked, looking at the cake on her plate. 'I mean, is it – healed or whatever?'

Gracie chuckled. 'Healed? It's better than ever. And all thanks to you – its newest guardian.' He gazed steadily at her. 'If you'd like the title, that is.' He looked up, over Rose's shoulder. 'And you too, young miss,' he continued. Rose turned; Emer was standing in the doorway, looking down into Nellie's kitchen as though it were the most magical thing she'd ever seen.

'Guardians of the Silver Road?' Emer said, glancing at Rose. 'I reckon we could go for that. Right?'

'Right,' Rose said, pulling out a chair for her.

'Now,' Nellie said, pouring Emer a cup of tea. 'Let's hear more about you.'

Rose swallowed her mouthful of cake. 'If it's okay,' she said, 'could I go out and have a word with the cauldron?'

'With the what?' Emer said, her mouth full.

'Go on ahead,' Nellie said, waving her towards the garden door. 'I'll get our guest up to date on how things work around here.' Gracie twinkled at her as she passed him by, and she paused long enough to give him a kiss on his soft old cheek.

Rose sank her feet into Nellie's lawn, and then made her way to the steps leading to the Dagda's cauldron. She reached the edge and looked down into the water. It was still and quiet and calm, reflecting her and the sky behind her. 'So,' she said. 'You gave me what I asked you for. Do you remember?'

The water rippled, very slightly.

'When I asked you to let Emer McGuire leave me

317

in peace, this isn't exactly how I imagined you'd go about it,' Rose continued. A gust of laughter burst from the kitchen door and Rose turned back to see Gracie doing a stiff-legged jig on the tiled floor, with Nellie and Emer clapping along. Catshee came streaking across the grass and up the steps, and Rose dropped to her knees, letting the not-cat land in a purring, rolling heap on her lap. She stroked his ears, watching them flatten out and then spring back to their usual shape, and Catshee licked her palm, very gently. She turned back to the cauldron, her eye caught by a carving on the side – the face of a man with a long beard and a smiling, genial face. Rose looked the carving in the eye as she continued. 'But, I guess, thank you? And, please, – don't ever grant me anything else I need or want ever again. Okay?'

The wind soughed around the inside of the huge cauldron, and Rose could have sworn it sounded like a laugh, long and loud and clear.

Characters

Irish mythology is as rich and ancient as any other major world mythology, though perhaps not as well known. It is filled with heroes, warriors, bards, gods and goddesses, giants and monsters and more, and some of them have found their way into *The Silver Road*. Read on for more information on the characters I've used, and the ones I've invented completely, in the creation of my story.

Balor (*Bal-urr*) Old Irish god of chaos and destruction, allegedly killed with the *tathlum* at the Battle of Moytura. Some legends see him as being a type of sun-god. He had one huge eye which, when opened, unleashed fire and terror. Some tales say Balor had seven eyelids, each of which had to be lifted for his eye to open; others say he had rings attached to his eyelid which were lifted by a chain-and-pulley system. Either way: aargh!

Cethlenn (*Keh-lin*) **Balor**'s wife, and a powerful witch.

Cúchulainn (*Coo-cull-inn*) The greatest Irish hero, a

demi-god. Cúchulainn literally means 'the hound of Cullen'. He was known as Setanta until he accidentally killed a hound which belonged to a man called Culainn while playing hurling one day, and to atone for his mistake, he swore he would live the rest of his life as 'the hound of Cullen', and so became known as Cúchulainn.

Dagda (*Dog-da*) The king of the **Tuatha Dé Danann**; the god of plenty, agriculture, hospitality and wisdom.

Fomorians (*Foe-more-eeans*) A legendary race of beings who once lived in Ireland, who were seen as hostile or destructive. **Balor** was once their leader.

Lugh Lámhfada (*Loo Lawv-odda*) Literally 'Lugh of the Long Arm'. Lugh was a god of the **Tuatha Dé Danann** famed for his skill with a spear, his courage and his wisdom.

Mac Tíre (*Mock Teer-ah*) Literally 'Son of the Land' or 'Son of the Country'; used in modern Irish to mean 'wolf'. The Mac Tíre is a character of my own invention.

Maeve (*Mayve*) The anglicised version of the Irish name Medb, or Maedhbh, the warrior queen who started a war over a bull!

Oighir (*Eye-urr*) Literally 'ice'; in *The Silver Road,*
    Oighir is the name of the king of the ice giants.
    I invented the ice giants for this story.

Sioc (*Shuck*) Literally 'ice', 'frost'; in *The Silver Road,*
    Sioc is the name of the last ice giant.

Tuatha Dé Danann (*Too-ha Day Dan-inn*)
    A legendary race of deities who once ruled Ireland.
    The **Fomorians** were their enemies. Legends say
    they eventually dispersed, becoming the Aes Sídhe
    (*Ace Shee*), or the fairies of folklore.

The Four Treasures of the Tuatha Dé Danann

At least three texts written in an old form of Irish known
as Middle Irish talk about the legends of the Tuatha Dé
Danann and the treasures connected to them, but the
sources tend to differ about what exactly the treasures
consisted of. It's generally taken that the treasures are:

The Lia Fáil (*Lee-ah Foil*), or the Stone of Destiny,
    which was brought by the Tuatha Dé Danann from
    the island city of Falias. The Lia Fáil was said to
    cry out whenever the true king of Ireland was

crowned, and its cry could be heard all across the land. A stone still stands at the Hill of Tara, which some believe to be the real Lia Fáil.

The Spear of Lugh, which was brought by the Tuatha Dé Danann from the island city of Gorias. The spear of Lugh was said to never fail to hit its mark.

Claoímh Solais (*Cly-iv Sull-ish*) or the Sword of Light, which belonged to Núada Silverarm, and which was brought from the island city of Findias. Similarly to the spear, the Claoímh Solais would withstand any attack against it.

The Cauldron of the Dagda, also called the Coire Ainsic (*currah an-sich*) in Middle Irish, which came from the island city of Murias, was always my favourite of the treasures. It was said to fulfil the needs of any company who came upon it.

Unfortunately, as Nellie says, 'Millennia have passed. Things get lost. So it is.' Besides the Stone of Destiny, nobody really knows where the treasures have ended up – so keep your eyes peeled for them . . .

Places

In *The Silver Road*, I have combined real locations in Ireland with ones conjured in my imagination. Here is some information about the places, real and imagined, that can be found in the book:

Bóthar na hAirgead (*Bo-hurr nah Har-gid*) The Road of Silver. In modern Irish, 'airgead' means 'money' instead of 'silver', because silver was used as money in ancient Ireland. But the word carries both meanings, and in my book it is used to mean 'silver'. 'Hargate' is an anglicisation – when a word is taken from Irish and written down in a way that makes sense to English speakers, while retaining the sound of the original Irish word. Many place names in Ireland are made this way.

Carriganawn (*Car-ig-un-awn*) Literally 'The rock of the river'; a fictionalised town which might be found, if it weren't a made-up place, somewhere near the real town of Carrick-on-Shannon, in County Roscommon.

Knocknarea (*Nock-nah-ray*) A mountain in County Sligo, with a cairn on top which is the burial place (according to legend, at least) of the warrior queen, Maeve. The name of the mountain can be translated as 'Mountain of the Stripes', 'Mountain of the Kings', or 'Mount of the Executions', but I prefer the translation in this book: the Hill of the Queen.

Moytura (*Moy-toor-ah*) There were two battles of Moytura, but one happened in Cong, County Mayo and the second at Lough Arrow in County Sligo near the place where the Gaelic Chieftain statue now stands. The first was between the Tuatha Dé Danann and the Fir Bolg, a monstrous race of supernatural beings, and the second was between the Tuatha Dé Danann and the Fomorians, at which Balor was slain by his grandson, Lugh, with the powerful weapon known as the *tathlum*.

Toraigh (*Toe-ray*) Tory Island, off the coast of Donegal, is the traditional birthplace of Balor, and its soil is a vital part of this story . . .

Tor Mór (*Turr-more*) This literally means 'the great rock tower', and it's the highest point on Tory Island, which is Ireland's most remote inhabited island. Legend has it that Balor built a tower here from which to keep an eye on his enemies.

Phrases

Irish (or 'Gaeilge') is a very old language, which has existed in some form in Ireland since about 2000 BCE. It is distinct from Gaelic, one of Scotland's national languages, though it's related to both it and to Welsh, Cornish, Breton and other Celtic languages. It was the principal language of Ireland until around 1800, co-existing with Latin and English (after the twelfth century) before almost being eradicated completely during the nineteenth century. It was revived during the early twentieth century and is now spoken as a native language in many parts of Ireland. It is one of Ireland's official languages, taught in schools and used at all levels of Irish life, and a vital part of the rich culture of modern Ireland.

An tSeandraíocht   The Old Magic
(*On Chan-dree-ucht*)
Ar ais, arís   Back, again
(*Arr-ash, arr-eesh*)

Cad é an fadhb?
(*Cod ay on fibe*)

What's the problem?

Cailín
(*Col-een* or *Cal-een*)

The Irish word for 'girl'

Cara mo chroí
(*Carr-a muh chree*)

Friend of my heart

Craythur (*Cray-thurr*)

A pronunciation of 'creature', used to communicate affectionate concern for the person being addressed, or sometimes gentle mockery – though Nellie's use of it is definitely affectionate

Cróga (*Crow-gah*)

Brave; courageous

Cróigíní
(*Crow-ghee-knee*)

Courage drops, made by Nellie Sweeney

Gasún (*Goss-oon*)

(Slang, informal) Little boy

Geas (*Gy-ass*)

An obligation; a contract; a vow

Guards

A way of referring to the Gardaí Síochána (*Garr-dee Shee-uh-ch-awna*), the Irish police force. Their Irish name literally

	means 'Guardians of the Peace'. (The 'ch' in 'Síochána' is like 'ch' in 'loch').
Mar dhea (*Marr yah*)	An interjection which means something like 'yeah, right!', which is used to cast gentle doubt on whatever the speaker has just said
Mise Raifteirí	See note, below*
Mo chroí (*Muh chree*) (ch like 'loch')	My heart (in the sense of 'my dear one')
Mo stór (*Muh store*)	My darling
Seandraíocht (*Shan-dree-ucht*) (uch like 'loch')	Old Magic
Stad (*Stodd*)	Stop
Stóirín (*Store-een*)	Little darling
Tá brón orm (*Taw brone urr-um*)	I'm sorry
Tá sí ina dúiseacht (*Taw shee innah doo-shocked*)	She is awake/she has awoken

Tar ar ais orm (*Tarr err ash urrum*)	Come back to me again
Yerra (*As it's written*)	An anglicisation of 'Dhera', which is used to signify a lack of care or worry for the subject under discussion. 'Not to worry' would be a good translation!
Yoke (*As it's written*)	General Irish term for a thing of any description!

* Mise Raifteirí an file, lán dóchas is grá,
le súile gan solas, le ciúnas gan chrá.

These are the opening lines of a famous Irish poem, assumed for a long time to have been written *by* the person it's written about! The poem is about a famed Irish poet, Antoine Ó Raifteirí (Anthony Raftery) who lived from 1779 to 1835, but it was actually written by another poet, Seán Ó Ceallaigh (John Kelly) in New York, some time in the 1880s.

Raifteirí became blind after contracting smallpox as a child, and travelled the country as a 'bard' or wandering poet, bringing his harp with him to accompany his performances. He is considered to be the last of the wandering bards of Ireland.

The opening lines of the poem, recited by Gracie in *The Silver Road,* literally mean, 'I am Raftery the poet, filled with comfort and love, my eyes without light, my silence without suffering.' The poem was commonly learned at school in Ireland a generation or two ago, and my own dad still likes to recite it – I was thinking of him when I wrote Gracie's performance! The lines also appeared on the old Irish five-pound note, before Ireland adopted the euro in 2002.

Acknowledgements

Is í an leabhar seo scéal ón chroí agamsa . . .
This book is a story from my heart.

Like every book I've been lucky enough to write, this one owes a lot to some very special people. My first thanks, in this instance, must go to the Arts Council of Ireland, An Chomhairle Ealaíon, whose generous financial support in the form of a Literature Bursary during 2021 was of immense help to me in writing *The Silver Road*. The award was of value not just financially, but also as an endorsement of what I was trying to achieve through writing this story, and I am hugely grateful.

As always, my family – mo chlann – deserve special thanks. My husband Fergal, my daughter Clodagh, my parents Tom and Doreen (to whom this book is dedicated, with all my heart), my brother Graham and his lovely partner Lisa, my parents-in-law Michael and Gretta, and my wonderful extended family whose support has been invaluable all these years – cheers, lads. Carron Row Abú!

Thank you to my agent Polly Nolan of PaperCuts Literary Agency and Consultancy, who believed in this story right from the start, when it was nothing more than a few thousand sample words and an outline. Thanks, Polly, for being this story's cheerleader.

Thank you to Ruth Bennett, my editor at Piccadilly Press, whose enthusiasm for this story was evident as soon as it went on submission. Thank you for 'getting it', Ruth, and for helping me to make it as good as I'm capable of. I hope you're as proud of the finished product as I am. Is eagarthóir den scoth thú.

To all the team at Piccadilly Press who helped to make this book shine – my proofreader Anna Bowles, my copy-editor Melissa Hyder, and the wonderful art team of Dominica Clements and Manuel Šumberac who designed and created its incredible cover – my gratitude is endless. To the entire Bonnier UK and Piccadilly Press team, a huge thanks for welcoming me to the family! I'm especially grateful to Rob Power, Amber Ivatt and Isobel Taylor, who helped so much in getting the book 'out there' and seen, which counts for so much.

To Shannon Byrne-Winter and Kieran Fanning, who read drafts of *The Silver Road* in its early stages, and whose feedback and enthusiastic support was so valuable – thank you both. And thanks, Kieran, for your invaluable help with my Lia Fáil question. (Anyone interested in the myths and legends of Ireland could do worse than check out Kieran's book, *Irish Fairy Tales, Myths and Legends* (Scholastic, 2020) – it's almost as good as Mamó's book!)

To my friend and fellow author, Susan Cahill, whose hare-brained and brilliant idea it was to start our podcast – thanks for giving my crackling, overwhelming, all-consuming love for books and stories such a rewarding home. I really love co-hosting Storyshaped with you and I hope we'll be nattering about stories, and the shapes they make, for years to come.

To Eddie Lenihan, poet and storyteller of renown, whose voice is the one I hear in my head when I think of the name of Balor – thank you for introducing me, and so many other children, to the brilliance of our old tales. And to the late Pat O'Shea, whose monumental novel *The Hounds of the Mórrígan* shaped my childhood, and my life. *The Silver Road* would not exist without it.

The town of Gorey, where I grew up, and the landscape of the north-west of Ireland, which I have come to love in adulthood, are at the heart of this book. Gracie and Nellie, in my story, owe much to two real-life people, a gréasaí and a sweet-shop owner, whose shops faced one another across a small side-street in my home town and whose smiles and stories were a huge part of my childhood. The statue of the Gaelic Chieftain on his hill outside Boyle will always grab my imagination – I'm so glad I got to put him in a story, just as I promised the first time I saw him! Thanks to the sculptor, Maurice Harron. And thanks to the staff and conservators of the Natural History Museum in Dublin, popularly known as 'the Dead Zoo', where I first saw the skeleton of a great Irish elk on a visit during my childhood – the majesty of the sight has never left me.

This story is about Ireland, her old magic and her new, her stories and legends, and the people who make the country what it is, whether born there or not – so I'm grateful for every bit of my Irishness, and for my country's rich history and folklore, which is full of inspiration. Thanks to everyone who makes Ireland the country it is today, and who call the island 'home'.

And, as always, my last word of thanks is to you, the reader, who has accompanied Rose and Emer and Catshee on their quest. It wouldn't have been the same without you. Go raibh maith agat – thank you.

About the Author

Sinéad O'Hart is a children's author, a children's literature podcaster (she co-hosts *Storyshaped,* available on all podcasting platforms), and a parent, all of which keeps her busy (but not too busy to read). She's the author of *The Eye of the North, The Star-Spun Web, Skyborn, The Time Tider* and *The Silver Road,* and sometimes she can't quite believe she's lucky enough to do what she loves most (putting fictional people into frankly dangerous situations) as a job!

PRESS

We hope you loved your Piccadilly Press book!

For all the latest bookish news, freebies and exclusive
content, sign up to the Piccadilly Press newsletter –
scan the QR code or visit lnk.to/PiccadillyNewsletter

Follow us on social media:

bonnierbooks.co.uk/PiccadillyPress